DARK SHAMAN

A Robert Sable Mystery

Book 3

By Sean E. Thomas

To Ralph

a great friend

SE Thomas

Printed in Victoria, Canada

Published by White Amber Press in conjunction with Trafford publishing.

National Library of Canada Cataloguing in Publication Data

Dark shaman / Sean E. Thomas
ISBN 1-55395-787-3
      I. Title.
PS3620.H667D37 2003   813'.6   C2003-900968-8

TRAFFORD

This book was published *on-demand* in cooperation with Trafford Publishing.
On-demand publishing is a unique process and service of making a book available for retail sale to the public taking advantage of on-demand manufacturing and Internet marketing. **On-demand publishing** includes promotions, retail sales, manufacturing, order fulfilment, accounting and collecting royalties on behalf of the author.

Suite 6E, 2333 Government St., Victoria, B.C. V8T 4P4, CANADA
Phone   250-383-6864   Toll-free   1-888-232-4444 (Canada & US)
Fax   250-383-6804   E-mail   sales@trafford.com
Web site   www.trafford.com   TRAFFORD PUBLISHING IS A DIVISION OF TRAFFORD
HOLDINGS LTD.
Trafford Catalogue #03-0150   www.trafford.com/robots/03-0150.html

10   9   8   7   6   5   4   3   2

For my wonderful wife, Doris, son, Robert, and good friends Dorothy, Jan (Kaa-Saan-Da-Ooo; Nahx-oo-steh) and her father Walter (Taaw-Chun) who inspired and helped me in this endeavor.

DARK SHAMAN

Other Books by Sean E. Thomas

Dark Project

Dark Soul

Dark Shaman

Dark Gold

Future Books

Dark Conspiracy

Dark Stalker

CHAPTER 1
The Present

A dozen, dog-eared, manila folders lay scattered across Sergeant Robert Sable's battered oaken desk. He'd inherited the missing children's case just a few days earlier along with his new assignment to the Token detachment. Sable had handled some pretty horrific cases in his ten years with the Alaska State Troopers, but no other case had so repulsed and intrigued him. His first hour in the office, he had posted enlarged photographs of ten lost children, Athabascan, Tlingit and white, on a large bulletin board with diagrams and lists of facts. Under each picture was the child's name and the date of his or her disappearance. Time had run out for two of the children--their bodies had been found with their hearts cut out. Sable only hoped the others were still alive. Sergeant Nicholas Kelly, who had been investigating the case, had also vanished without a trace. His empty car had been found several miles back in the bush, far from the nearest road. Within a week of the sergeant's disappearance, Sable was transferred from Juneau specifically to handle the Kelly case. Before Sable had arrived, Matthew Grady, another trooper, working on the case, had been murdered, his body found next to one of the slain children. Several troopers from different parts of the state were being assigned to the investigation, but their arrival was still a month away.

The children's photos pulled at his heart, especially the photograph he held in his hands. Bobby Mills, a 12-year-old boy in a typical student pose, smiled back at him. The boy was the same age as his son—that is, if his son had lived. He laid the folder down, bit his lip and forced back a tear as his gaze drifted to the silver-frame at the corner of his desk holding the photograph of his deceased wife and son. He studied their faces and started to pick up the frame but stopped as a knock on the door brought him back to the present.

Corporal Jason Lum ducked under the doorjamb and leaned his huge frame against a nearby wall, his green eyes peering out from under shaggy, blond hair. "Do you think we'll find any of them alive?" His voice carried the waver of uncertainty.

"After all this time, I doubt it." Sable glanced out the window, deep in thought. Pushing his raven hair from his eyes, he returned his gaze to the folder. Frowning, he studied the missing person's reports from the villages of Tetlin, Kanashig, Tanak and Token. The reports seemed inexplicable. At first, one child had vanished each month. Now it was one every week. At each scene, the forensics teams found very little--just a few footprints and some animal tracks. Last summer, when the first four children vanished, Kelly thought the children had either run away or been killed by a wild animal. Then, as the list grew, rapists and serial killers had been considered—serial killers always started slow, then escalated.

And Token, just 15 miles from Tok, was an easy place for a killer to hide. The town was situated in the center of the state—pristine wilderness. It was why people moved here. In Token, murders, rapes, muggings, domestic violence and child abuse were nonexistent. It was a small town surrounded by dense forests of birch, alder, and fir, rugged mountains with large, spiraling glaciers, roaring waterfalls, raging creeks and deep cold rivers. Finding a killer among this diverse population was next to impossible. The people, like the region, were self-reliant, considering themselves rugged frontiersmen and women. They came to this country, seeking solitude—a way to leave society and their troubles behind. During the summer months the population increased a thousand-fold as tourists descended on the area to take in the unspoiled beauty and splendor of the area. In the late summer and fall, sportsmen arrived to escape the drudgery of everyday life to find the serenity of nature.

"I've never seen so many cases," Lum said.

"Did Kelly check the state website and our list of the sex offenders living in the area?"

"Sure did, but there weren't any."

"Check again. I'll bet that some of the perverts haven't registered. How about Fairbanks, Delta Junction, or Glennallen?" He had to consider that the predator's territory could range a couple hundred miles or more.

"You've got to remember a recent state Supreme Court ruling required us to drop about 65 percent of the damn scumbags from the list. You know, from before the molester registration law went into effect. But, I'll . . ." Lum paused, "let my fingers do a little walking across the keyboard."

Sable nodded but hardly glanced up from the folder.

"After Kelly vanished, I even checked current releases from the correctional facilities. No luck so far."

"It could also be that there's a new psychopath in the area." Sable set the report on his desk and stretched. "Do a national search and see if we could possibly have a transplant from another state."

"The man leaves no clues."

"Or woman. Let's review the facts. What's the same about each case?" Sable hoped to pick Lum's brain in order to view the case from a new perspective.

"They were Indian as well as white children taken after school. In a few of the cases there were mukluk or moccasin tracks found in the vicinity; in others, only dog or wolf tracks, leading one to believe that the killer is an Indian."

"Or someone who wants us to think that."

"None of the children struggled. So they knew their kidnapper."

"Not necessarily. They could have been drugged," Sable said as he grabbed a sketchpad and then drew a circle on a blank sheet of paper and mulled over the problem. The first disappearance had been in the early fall. As the toll increased, his predecessor had sent out his best men to question hundreds of potential witnesses and follow numerous leads, but they came back with nothing.

"They all were taken during daylight with no witnesses." Lum stood, walked to a chair opposite of Sable's desk and sat.

"Wrong, Kelly and Grady probably saw something, but one's dead and the other's missing."

"I hate to say it, but Grady has to be dead."

Sable nodded.

"Ronald Phillips' disappearance was the strangest--with his tracks stopping in freshly fallen snow and the surrounding snow not being disturbed." Lum shuddered. "Kind of spooky."

"The killer must have brushed out his tracks. Maybe even used a leaf blower."

"But the investigator said the snow hadn't been disturbed."

The phone pulsed and Sable snatched it up. "Sable."

"This is Benson. We found the body of a missing child—it's . . . it's Jenny Dawson." Benson's voice sounded reluctant.

"Was she raped?"

For a moment silence met his question, then Benson began, "No, sir. Not so as I can tell, but . . . her heart was cut out."

"Where are you?" Sable asked.

The sergeant told him and added, "I've sealed off the crime scene."

"I'm on my way," Sable said and hung up the phone, feeling his anger rise. As he stood, his uniform drooped on him. Sable was leanly built, but sometimes his uniforms hung on him as if he'd bought them from a used or second-hand clothing store. And of course lately, he hadn't been eating right—and some days not eating at all.

"Bad news?" Lum asked.

Sable sketched out the problem and Lum whistled. "Looks like we have one sick mother out there."

"Where's agent Carpenter?" Though he didn't like the FBI, Carpenter didn't fit the mold. She was easy going, not the normal Washington bureaucrat. And she didn't dress like them either.

"Out following up on a few leads."

"Tell Zerck to hold down the fort while we're gone and I'll see you in the Suburban."

"It's covered," Lum said and headed to the secretary's office.

Sable's anger overflowed and he slammed his fist into the wall as he stepped through the doorway. He had to catch this killer. The grieving families deserved answers. The problem was where to find the time to keep the investigation on track and handle the rest of the workload.

Sable knew a lot—too much about grieving for family members. Sable had been living the good life with a wife and son to be proud of. Promotions were coming easily. Just after winding up a case against mob boss David Meyers, he had been promoted to sergeant for his excellent work and investigative technique. He was making a name for himself within the troopers. In fact, he was the first Tlingit to make the grade so quickly. Sable had compiled hard evidence to put Meyers in the state correctional facility for life, but as Meyers marched away in handcuffs, the man had vowed his revenge. Sable hadn't taken the threat seriously. He wished now that he had. An assassin hired by Meyers killed his family in a murder for hire meant for Sable. However, justice had been done. Meyers had been killed on the way to the courtroom.

Sable tried to push the thoughts from his mind as he slipped into the Suburban. "Ready?" His voice sounded hollow.

"As you are," Lum quipped, strapping on his seatbelt.

Sable turned left onto the Alaska Highway and headed east toward the Canadian Border. They rode in silence, dreading what was to come. For miles, the roadside was covered with grass and brush seeking to decimate the burned hulks of trees. After passing over the muddy, green waters of the Tanana River, Sable scanned the trees climbing up the hillsides. He found a narrow hunting road and turned off. The Suburban rocked violently from side to side as he navigated between ridges and ruts, heading constantly uphill. At the crest, he saw Benson's sedan and wondered how the man had gotten this far into the forest.

"Well, here goes." Sable parked behind the blue undercover trooper sedan and then stepped out. His knees weakened as a dark cloud in the shape of a lean, powerful and dangerous Indian dressed in buckskins blocked his vision. The man wasn't Athabascan or Tlingit—Sable sensed this evil was from some forgotten era. He found himself reaching out to the vehicle for some type of purchase. When his vision cleared, he felt confused; his premonitions had been dormant since the Meyers' case. As he took a deep breath to regain his composure, he found the stench of death pervasive.

Lum stepped briskly from the vehicle. "What's the best way into the scene?"

"First, let's slip into overwhites and sterile shoes," Sable said. They couldn't afford the unintentional contamination or trampling of the crime scene. This could prove very damaging to the investigation. Care had to be taken to ensure that the forensic team could easily do their trace analysis, blood spatter interpretation, and DNA comparison. Special effort had to be made not to disturb things while assessing the situation.

Sable and Lum walked over to a large cardboard box, which held a clipboard with sign-in roster. To dull the stench, Sable also put a thick gob of Vicks on his upper lip while scanning the crime scene. Around a large clearing, brush and grass gradually turned into alder and birch and then growing into a thickly packed, never-ending forest. Yellow police tape cordoned off the center of the scene where Benson kneeled over the body.

"This is spooky. Don't you feel it?" Lum asked.

Sable shrugged, his ESP tingling as if he had grabbed onto wire from a main power line. In the recent past, deep currents of evil has passed through the area.

Following Benson's footprints, Sable stepped over the tape. Scanning the area for the killer's footprints, he found only the child's tracks paralleling his sergeant's boot prints. Despite his many years on the force, Sable was still shocked by the savagery of the scene. He stopped and felt a chill run up his spine. Slipping on the latex gloves, he sensed a low current of evil in the background that seemed to grow, as he got closer to the child. Though he told himself that it was his imagination, something else told him it was not. "It's just another crime scene--nothing else," he tried to tell himself.

"This looks like the child's been through a slaughter house. It . . . she . . ." Lum's words drifted off as they neared Benson. Sable watched the man's eyes widen in recognition and then in horror. A gagging sound came from Lum's throat. His face had gone deathly white, maybe from the odor or maybe from the gruesome scene.

God, he hated this—even Sable could never get used to crime scenes, especially those involving children. With each step that brought him closer to Benson, his dread heightened. Sable looked away, looked back at the corpse, shivered and then looked away again. He forced his gaze back to the girl's body. Though she had been missing for months, he could tell the murder had taken place in the last few days.

"Why are we just finding Jenny, when she's been missing for almost six months?" Sable asked rhetorically. "Do you think the date of her death has some type of significance? Zodiak wanabe, maybe?"

Benson shrugged.

Sable gasped at the stench of rotting flesh that seemed to surround him. Sable stood over the body, his stomach churning and his mouth dry. This morning was worse than most. Though he'd seen bodies severely mutilated in the past, he'd never seen a child done this way. Animals had scavenged the body, the entrails scattered across the field and partially eaten.

When he turned to look at Lum, the man's face paled, he stepped aside, retched and vomited. "Who could have done this, gutting a young girl from pubis to her throat?"

"How long have you been a trooper?"

"Only a year." Lum staggered slightly as he tried to hold himself erect. "All I've done are traffic stops and handling a few domestic disturbances."

"Don't worry, you're doing fine."

"Do you ever get used to it?"

Sable shook his head and leaned forward. "What do you have so far?"

"The same as the other missing person's reports—nothing except that we now have a body," Benson said.

Jenny's nude body lay spread-eagled in a large pool of dried blood, her eyes staring vacantly at the sky. Luckily for them, animals had not yet eaten all the body. It took all Sable's nerve to evaluate the child: her rib cage had been chopped with some type of large blade or ax, spread open, and her heart removed. Though Benson swatted at several large horseflies scavenging the flesh, they remained persistent while more circled the air above, occasionally diving in and out and attacking indiscriminately.

"What we have here, best guess, is a male killer. The removal of the heart alone is a sick statement." Sable reached out with his hand and ran it over the remnants of the sternum.

"We know the killer is also careful from the way he discards the bodies in the wilderness," Benson said.

"We've got a murderer, a real sick one." Lum's voice was barely a whisper.

"When you have this type of ritual killing, you know that this is only the beginning." Sable fought to control the rage in his voice.

Benson nodded.

Across Jenny's forehead, someone had written a number of cryptic symbols with a type of black ink. He remembered that Mary Lou Cranston, the first victim, had similar markings. An odd tingle raced down Sable's spine, and he shivered. Each crime scene was different, requiring different approaches to processing. And this one was definitely different. But that didn't detract from the basics. The basic protocol required careful examination, then photographing, sketching, and processing the scene.

"Find any footprints?" Sable asked.

"Some type of soft shoe with no tread or stepped heel-- mukluk or moccasin. I've got the plaster setting up."

"Same as before?"

"Could be."

"Did you follow them?"

"Yes, for about a hundred feet, until they disappeared. Found lots of wolf or dog tracks though. Of course, I'm not much of a tracker, but the killer should have left some sign." Benson wrote in his notebook. "The craziest thing was wolf tracks."

"Why's that?"

"The ground was soft and wet; but the shoe tracks just ended, but the wolf tracks continued on."

"Maybe he ran and jumped," Lum offered.

"I thought of that, but then the last set of impressions should have been deeper. I also searched a pattern 200 hundred feet beyond the tracks. I've never seen anything like it. There was just no trace." Benson voice had a shaky quality.

An acid taste rolled over Sable's tongue as he contemplated his next task—examining the body. He squatted and tried to sense the personality of the killer, letting the darkness of that essence radiate through him. Was it an orgasmic release from the hunt of the prey or something darker? He could feel the dark pulling at him, wanting to merge, but he drew away. Just like when his wife was murdered. When he had gone after Meyers, his soul had carried a bottomless rage that had almost pulled him into the depths of hell. He'd believed that, just as in the Bible, blood debts had to be paid in blood. Even after all the years, he felt like a puzzle with a number of pieces missing from the box.

Sable hunkered down over the body again while he examined the open cavity. The repeated blows by what appeared to have been an ax had cut the cartilage jaggedly. The scent of fetid flesh clogged the air he breathed in spite of his precautions and he turned away momentarily. His eyes misted over--she was too young to die this way. The bitterness of bile coated his tongue and he tried to swish the taste away while he stretched and worked on the kinks in his muscles.

He forced himself to lift one of her hands and study it. The arm barley moved due to rigor mortis. He knew that people who killed in such an organized fashion wouldn't stop until they were caught. "Looks like blood and skin. Make sure that her hands are bagged before the ME takes the body."

"If we ever find this asshole--we've got him cold."
Benson's voice was hard, cold and cutting.

"Any fresh tire tracks?" Sable asked.

"Only mine. I walked nearly a mile up and down the road
in both directions."

Lum whispered quietly in the background. "This mother
has to be one sick puppy!"

"Got the camera ready?"

"Yes. I'm right on it." Lum unsnapped the cover of the
Nikon, lifted it, and focused. He didn't snap the shutter for several
seconds.

Sable pulled his notebook and pen from his shirt pocket,
rolled the pen over his knuckles and clicked it. "Did you question
the children who found her?"

"I tried, but they were so badly shaken I'll try again this
evening."

"Once the Fairbanks medical examiner arrives, she might
find something more before she ships the body to Anchorage for
the full boat." As Sable gently rolled the stiff body partially to the
side, he found two large eagle feathers and a bone-handled
hunting knife drenched in blood with highly visible fingerprints.
The murderer had finally made a mistake--leaving crucial
evidence.

"The killer screwed up." Benson's voice sounded like
sandpaper grating on wood.

"Here." As Lum helped support the body, he handed Sable
a plastic bag.

"Thanks." Gingerly, Sable picked up the feathers and
turned them over in his hand. Written in a delicate hand and great
precision on the shaft of the quills were strange pictorial glyphs,
closely resembling hieroglyphics.

"What do you make of them?" Benson asked.

"Your guess is as good as mine," Sable said. "Maybe we'll
need an archeologist for this one." He dropped the feathers into

the bag, sealed it and handed it to Benson who in turn numbered the evidence and opened another bag.

Sable picked up the knife by the blade and turned it over in his hand. The initials "JJ" were carved in the handle. "Gotcha!"

Benson looked over his shoulder. "The only JJ in the area is Jim James. I'd bet a month's wages on that."

"Isn't he the one who was reported missing last August within days of the first child's disappearance?" Lum asked.

"I'd say slightly before." Benson stood, stretched and rolled his neck to remove the kinks.

"Don't jump to conclusions—this is just too picture perfect." Sable studied the knife carefully as not to disturb the bloody fingerprints lining the handle and blade. "Let's see what the medical examiner and the crime lab have to say. It could be that the killer took care of James, too. See if we have a file on James, and if not, check AFIS. Take this and let it dry before putting it in the bag." Sable carefully handed the knife to Benson. If the prints were in AFIS, the Automated Fingerprint Identification System, they would get a hit.

"Maybe the ME can find traces of the killer's skin, blood or hair and gin up a DNA profile." Benson looked as if Sable had handed him a cursed object.

"Have you notified Jenny's parents?" Sable stood and in his mind's eye tried to reach out, use his clairvoyance, to make contact with the killer but nothing happened. He silently cursed himself because his gift only worked sporadically.

"No sir." Benson's voice trembled.

"Do you want me to handle it?" Lum asked.

"I'll take care of it." Sable let out a sigh and tried to keep his voice even. "Stay here and help Benson. See if you can find more evidence," Sable said, stripping off his gloves and handing them to Lum.

As Sable got behind the steering wheel, he clutched and kneaded it. The hardest task any trooper had to do was to notify the parents. Backing out onto the clearing, he turned the Suburban around and headed down the road. Not even the jarring from the road bothered him and his swirling thoughts. He tried to link the puzzle pieces together. How could he face the parents and tell them how Jenny died? What hope could he give them for catching the killer?

CHAPTER 2

Sable turned onto the Alaska Highway; ahead lay the Canadian border and Kanashig. He never really understood the English translation of the town's name--on the verge of darkness. He'd visit Jon George before seeing Jenny's parents. Maybe his long-time friend, who was also a village elder, could go with him to see the parents.

About a half an hour later, he pulled into the Kanashig council parking lot, stopped the vehicle and gazed at the lodge. For a moment, he couldn't move. Though the building gave a warm, comforting feeling, at the same time it reflected his sadness back. Made of hand-hewn logs bronzed by varnish and stain, the lodge had an alpine roof spreading far out over the entranceway, supported by large, log pillars. At each side of the entrance were kū-tī-ga (*totem poles*). A hierarchy of colorful carved figures of jēlch (*raven*), chūts (*bear*), gūtsch (*wolf*), chichtsch (*frog*) and tschāk (*eagle*) told of the tribe's lineage. The deck was surrounded by a finely crafted railing and above, two large windows gave the impression of sorrowful eyes looking outward from the building. Shaking his head, Sable stepped from the vehicle. Before he could move, Jon George came through the door and walked over to the Suburban.

"Xhoots'een, it's good to see you, old friend," Jon said. His white hair fell over the youthful brow of a man in his twenties, though he should have been in his eighties. Across a finely chiseled face, he flashed a warm, friendly smile. "Uásse-i-tú-eti?" Sable translated the greeting in his mind (*How is your heart?*).

"Ka-denchro-denik, chetsinach tuu chrat." Sable offered his hand, remembering the greeting--My heart is strong. Jon had used Sable's chosen Tlingit name Xhoots'een, the man who talks to animals.

"It's good to see you."

"Klēd-jēlch (*White Raven*), it's good to see you, too.
"Jon, you know Jon." Jon clutched Sable's hand.
I still can't get used to how young you look. Tléi ee
wdasháan (*You don't show any signs of age*)."
"Let's not talk of these things now. To what do I owe the
pleasure of your company?"
Sable still couldn't believe the change in his friend. Two
years ago, when Sable had been assigned to the Delta Junction
trooper detachment, Jon had been a spry 80 years old. Exposed to
an Army experimental virus, his aging process had reversed.
Now, Jon looked younger than Sable. Jon had always been well
built and now his white hair and youthful appearance, set off by
his dark, tanned, copper skin, were a marvel. And, of course, Jon
was traditional in the Indian lifestyle in every respect. Today
however, he wore a white shirt and black slacks.
Jon just smiled, nodded, and became serious. "You look
sad. What's wrong? I've never seen you short of words," he said,
worry crossing his face.
"We've found the Dawson girl." Sable stumbled over the
words.
"Dead, I presume? All human beings must die. But it's a
tragedy at such a young age."
Sable nodded. "I need you to come with me and help tell
the parents."
"How did it happen?"
"Her heart was cut from her chest," Sable said.
Jon stepped backwards. "Auktelchnĩk (*Nobody bothers him
about his feathers*)!"
"Did you say Auktelchnĩk?"
"Yes. Just some ancient legends my parents told me.
Nothing that would apply today." Jon looped his fingers around
his belt and rocked on his heels while in thought.
"You don't have to worry about ancient evil coming back.
This killer's real."
"There is always some truth in any legend or myth."

"But not in this case. Have you heard anything about Jim James?"

"No. Do you suspect him?"

"You'll have to keep what I tell you in confidence."

"You know me. My lips are sealed."

"Just a while ago, I found what I believe could be James' knife at the crime scene."

"But you're not sure." Jon stroked his chin.

"First, I need to see the Dawsons. Then, later, I'd like to talk to James' family and to anyone who knew Jim." Sable wiped the sweat from his hand onto his pants legs.

"No problem. His uncle, Dan-e-wåk, whom I know well, raised him. Now, let's go to Dawsons'. It's close so we'll walk."

"A walk'll do me good. Haven't had a chance to exercise much in the last month," Sable said as he rushed to keep up with Jon.

They remained silent for the journey, not wanting to dwell on the horror of the situation. As Jon opened the white, picket gate, apprehension clutched at Sable's throat. The distance they were crossing to the house seemed insurmountable. This house, like the others on the street, was all white except that its paint had a weather-beaten quality with large blisters and chips peeling away while a faded, blue trim outlined the doors, windows and roof. Sable stepped up to the door alongside Jon and rang the doorbell. Seconds passed and he heard the scurrying of children inside the living room. Finally, the door opened slowly. An Indian woman stood with a small baby cradled in her arms as she examined them quizzically. Even having practiced the meeting, he still wasn't prepared—god, he hated this. For a moment, Sable stood silent trying to form the words.

A smile broke on Jinette Dawson's face. "They've found my daughter. Is she all right?"

Sable shook his head. "I'm sorry . . ."

"Oh God no--not my baby!" Her shoulders slumped and she fell against the jamb, her body shaking violently as she broke into sobs.

Jon and Sable helped Jinette to a chair and stayed with her until she was more composed. Jon found a neighbor and friend to come over and console her.

Knowing he'd be unable to garner anything new that would help the case, Sable took a business card from his pocket and handed it to her. "I can be reached through this number 24 hours a day." He watched her study the card, her face ashen and hands trembling.

CHAPTER 3

Dan-e-wåk's *(Silver Eyes)* home was nestled at the back of
the village in birch and alder trees. The house had a soft, earthen-
brown tone faded by the elements. Sable's and Jon's footsteps
crunched on the gravel walkway to the house, but before they
could knock on the door, it opened and Dan-e-wåk stepped out.
     "I've been expecting you." Dan-e-wåk--Sable never knew
his Christian name--motioned for them to enter. "How's your
uncle, Chlawūch-tschāk *(Gray Eagle)*?"
     "Fine. He's coming to visit me next month," Sable said. He
searched the man's face for something familiar as he offered his
hand--it was spooky for the last time he'd seen Dan-e-wåk the man
has been in his sixties. Today, he appeared to be in his twenties.
If Dan-e-wåk hadn't been taller and thinner, Sable could have
sworn he and Jon were brothers.
     "You probably don't know it, but I've known your uncle for
about 20 years."
     "I'll let him know that you asked about him," Sable said as
he stepped into the dim room and let his eyes become accustomed
to the dimness. Sable scanned the interior of the living room.
Although the furniture was worn and from another era, the room
was spotless. One of the walls held lances, a dagger with bear's
head, bows, arrows, and ceremonial masks of wolf and bear.
     "Would you like some coffee or anything to drink?"
     "No, thanks."
     "Then, how can I help you?" Dan-e-wåk motioned to his
large, well-worn sofa.
     "You know why we're here, Dan-e-wåk." Jon took a seat at
one corner of it, resting his arms on his knees while Sable took the
opposite end.
     "I was being courteous. Sometimes it's hard for visitors to
understand second sight." Dan-e-wåk pulled up a wooden chair

made from what appeared to be birch, turned it around, stepped over it, and sat, resting his arms on its back.

"I came to talk to you about . . ."

"What do you want to know about Tūtsch-gūtsch *(Black Wolf)*?"

Dan-e-wåk had used Jim James' chosen name. Athabascan, Haida and Tlingit and other Alaskan Natives sometimes select a name on entrance to adulthood. "Has he tried to contact you since his disappearance last fall?"

"No, but I've tried to contact him with little or no success. It's like . . . an evil presence masks my link with Tūtsch-gūtsch. It is the first time I've been thwarted in talking to him."

"Are you sure he's not dead?" Sable asked. If his uncle, Chlawūch-tschāk, hadn't been a shaman too, he might have disregarded the trend of the conversation. Telepathy was no mystery to Sable.

"No, I can still feel his presence, but not enough to track him."

"Could he be capable of kidnapping and murder?" Sable hunched forward, his hands on his knees.

"I raised Tūtsch-gūtsch from a small boy and I know he doesn't have an evil bone in his body."

"People change." Sable studied Dan-e-wåk for a moment.

"Not Tūtsch-gūtsch. Now I've told you everything I know—but you know yourself how you can solve the case." Dan-e-wåk said. "The tsāk-ssēt ya-t'ook *(the amulet chooses)*."

Sable ignored the reference to the tsāk-ssēt. His uncle had said the very same thing long ago. "Could I see Jim--I mean Tūtsch-gūtsch's room?"

"Sure, but you will find nothing." Dan-e-wåk pointed toward the hallway. "At the end and to the right."

Sable saw Jon arch an eyebrow, indicating that he was potentially eating from the forbidden fruit—searching the young man's possessions without permission. Much would depend on how the judge interpreted any evidence found.

As Sable entered the bedroom, he found it quite large, but with minimal furniture. Tūtsch-gūtsch had a bed, dresser, a bookcase filled with books and a desk. Under his bed, several pairs of shoes and boots were perfectly lined up. Along one of the walls hung large portraits of Chief Joseph, Sitting Bull, Crazy Horse, Geronimo and Cochise. Another held a red dschénu (*ceremonial dance blanket*) bordered with white fringe. In the center of each was a large, symbolic portrait of a tūtsch-gūtsch's head.

Sable went directly to the dresser and looked back questioningly at Dan-e-wåk. "May I look?"

Dan-e-wåk shrugged. "If it'll help, but you'll find nothing."

And that's exactly what Sable did find--nothing. All Tūtsch-gūtsch's clothing was folded and put away neatly. The desk yielded even less. A thorough search of the closet yielded the same. Sable went back to the dresser, pulled a number of hair strands from a comb, and placed them in a plastic bag.

Dan-e-wåk shook his head. "Tūtsch-gūtsch's DNA will not match that of the killers."

"Juk'ē *(good)*, then this will clear him." Sable stuffed the bag into his pocket. "Could we have another current photograph of him?"

"Sure, you can have the one on the dresser—the one of us together."

After the visit, they headed to the council lodge while Sable pondered Dan-e-wåk's comment. He must have been telling him to use the tsāk-ssēt.

"Have you heard from Janet lately?"

"No." Sable hadn't heard a word from Janet Blaine for several months. He'd met her while recovering from the loss of his wife and son. Until then, his life had been on autopilot, bent on revenge to kill David Meyers for killing his family. When they met, he had been working with the Department of Fish and Game at Elk Bay trying to catch poachers. One morning a large, white boat carrying a load of drugs exploded in the bay and among the wreckage, he'd found a lone woman survivor suffering from hypothermia and amnesia. At first, he had thought the amnesia was an act, but then during her recovery, David Meyers had sailed into the harbor expecting to rendezvous with the drug dealers and kill Sable in one coup-de-gras. However, when Meyers found the drug runner's boat in pieces and he assumed Sable had the drugs. Meyers sent his men after the pair and Sable had to flee. As Janet regained her memory during their pursuit, they fell in love. Once they were safe, Janet decided to go back to Seattle to settle her affairs. She'd promised to return, but that was the last he had heard from her except for a "Dear Sable" letter.

"You look sad," Jon said. "Janet?"

Jon's voice was in the background and Sable remembered the letter as if he'd read it yesterday. Janet had said in the letter that his job was too dangerous. After what they'd been through together, Sable wasn't surprised she was spooked. But he wondered if she was just trying to let him down easy.

"It's the case," Sable hedged.

They walked through the rows of houses in silence.

"I have a surprise for you. I hope it will brighten your day in spite of the circumstances. I'd like you to come over Friday night and meet an archeology professor," Jon said.

"This professor wouldn't be a she and you wouldn't be trying to set me up again?"

"Dr. Elizabeth Ridell is a woman, but set you up—no."

"Several a months ago, after Janet left me, you tried to set me up was with one of your granddaughters."

"If you think that, you've hurt me," Jon said, putting his hand over his heart and taking on a forlorn attitude. "To the quick."

"Of course there were a couple others after her," Sable said as they turned the corner to a side street. The houses seemed to close in as the street narrowed.

"It's just that I have a special treat. I know you have a fondness for archeology and Ridell's from the University of Alaska."

"Why would an archeologist come to Kanashig?"

"Jim James, I mean Tūtsch-gūtsch, found a cavern full of petroglyphs and ancient artifacts just a few miles upriver about a month before he disappeared." Jon reached the Suburban first and opened the door for Sable—a door that he could have sworn he'd locked.

"Thanks. I think I'd like to visit the dig." Sable slipped into the front seat and rolled down the electric window so as not to block the conversation. "But on something this important, why are you bringing in the university? I thought your people were suspicious when dealing with archeologists. Especially after having them and the health department crawling all over the village a couple years ago."

"Oh, since then, we've taken extensive measures. Our lawyers drew up contracts to protect the cavern, its artifacts and any other remains." Jon offered his hand to say good-bye. "See you Friday night."

"Sure, what time?"

"5:30."

"Ditch the suit clothes. You look better in your hunting clothes."

Jon shrugged.

CHAPTER 4

Sable pulled up in front of the detachment, turned off the engine, and studied the building, trying not to think about the children. The structure was three stories, long, rectangular, and built with concrete cinder blocks painted beige. Its windows were reinforced with a metal mesh and covered with grills that had been painted gray, giving the building the look of a security facility. To detract from the austere look, Sergeant Nicholas Kelly and the staff had landscaped the lawn with flowers and silver-spruce trees. Soon, he would have to add his touch, but now there were more pressing matters.

As Sable entered the detachment, Agent Annelle Carpenter of the FBI tapped his shoulder. "I have something you need to see." Following her down the corridor to her office, Sable raised his hands to shield his eyes from the fluorescent lights and let them focus. The concrete-block walls were painted a traditional government chalk-white to increase illumination. Sometimes he felt like he needed to wear sunglasses just to navigate the halls.

After the abductions, Carpenter had been assigned to a joint FBI task force dedicated to finding the children. Now other task force members had been placed on higher priority cases across the country since the terrorist attacks. As they stepped into her office, Sable took full measure. It was decorated with traditional Native American paintings, Athabascan war lances and other artifacts. Sable studied his new partner for a moment. She kept her raven-black hair tied into a ponytail and her dark-brown eyes seemed to pierce the soul. When she turned, her smile made her classic Athabascan face somehow softer.

"Here, I taped this for you." She went to the TV, inserted the tape into the player, hit the button, and stood back. A grocery store owner commented on seeing a couple of the missing children two days ago. As Sable studied the tape, Carpenter pointed to a man in the background.

"There's the reason I called you. He's the scumbag I arrested for child molestation a number of years ago."

"Is he registered?"

"No, that's the problem," Carpenter said. "William Oliver beat the rap only because the kid changed his story during the trial."

She reached over, ejected the tape and handed it to Sable.

"Is there anything you can tell me about Oliver?"

"Yeah, he thinks he's a hard ass. He asked for his lawyer and then kept his mouth shut until the man arrived. But when I put him in the cell, he almost cracked up. Said that he'd confess to anything if I let him out."

"Well, did he?"

"Confess? Yeah, he did and I almost lost my job over it. The asshole was claustrophobic."

"Can I keep the tape?"

Carpenter nodded.

"Since you know the bastard, why don't we pay him a visit this afternoon."

Back in his office, Sable sat behind his desk and pondered the report he had to write up. It seemed he was never caught up. He looked at his desk where files, paperwork, and books were strewn about. His place was in the field where the bad guys were, not in the office processing paperwork. His problem was that in the Alaskan Bush, the Troopers did it all from speeding tickets to murder investigations. And there weren't enough troopers to cover all the crimes. He reached for the phone and dialed the intercom of Corporal Lum. "Do you have a printout of that pervert list yet?"

"The sex offenders' list? Yeah, and I have three great candidates and one you might know, Mukpik Kaomarek."

Sable cursed to himself at the mention of the name.

After consolidating his notes and report in the computer and backing them up on disk, Sable headed to lunch at Token's

Branding Iron Diner. As he entered, he could've sworn the restaurant hadn't changed since he and his father had visited 10 years earlier. It still had the rustic, log-cabin atmosphere with tables and chairs made of birch that were stained as dark as the walls. He seated himself and began checking the menu.

He motioned to the waitress and watched her saunter over. In the background of the restaurant, dishes clattered and pans slammed against metal, and he could almost swear that he heard the grill sizzling. This afternoon, he was hungrier than usual. It had to be all the hours he'd been working lately that caused his body to crave carbohydrates. In fact, he felt more like eating breakfast than lunch. Before the waitress moved on, Sable ordered a French toast, scrambled eggs, bacon and orange juice.

After pouring fireweed syrup, the specialty of the Branding Iron, over his plate, Sable attacked his mid afternoon breakfast with a vengeance, slicing the toast into bite size pieces, stabbing them, and plopping each piece carefully in his mouth. Sable tried not to think about the case, but seconds seemed like minutes and each minute away from the case meant the killer was gaining distance from the crime scene. It was the first twenty-four hours that were the most crucial to the investigation, but with no leads, he was at a dead end. He had to make his own leads.

After he finished his breakfast-lunch, Carpenter found him and they headed off to their first suspect on Lum's list, Nicholas Avery. Sable wanted to clear the rest of the list before they went after Oliver.

As they drove up the long and windy, rutted dirt road, Avery's house came into view. It was severely weathered, with peeling white paint and large patches of bare, gray wood. The house sat in the center of a yard strewn with old worn tires, rusted metal drums, junk cars in various stage of decay and piles of faded rotting lumber. The window shutters, trimmed in blue, hung by one hinge. This was definitely not what he expected would be the house of a Harvard graduate. When Sable stopped and turned off the Suburban, he saw the fleeting image of someone who glanced out the window and disappeared.

"Do you think he's going to run?" Carpenter asked as she loosened her .38 in its holster.

"Let's have a look see." Sable put on his hat.

As they walked up an overgrown, concrete-block walkway, they passed a snarling Labrador that threw itself against its chain trying to get at them. To Sable the chain looked very thin. He moved to one side of the door, Carpenter took the other, and then he knocked. "FBI and Alaska State Troopers, we want ask you some questions."

"Just a minute, I'm coming." Nicholas Avery, the man who opened the door, didn't look like his mug shot or fit his physical description. Though he was tall and broad shouldered, with light-red hair, his face was a mass of scars and he had a prosthesis for his left arm, with a hook in place of a hand.

Sable and Carpenter introduced themselves and told him that they were investigating the "Ripper Murders" as the news media had dubbed them.

"Yeah, so what the hell do you want from me?"

"You haven't registered as a child molester as required by law and . . ."

"Your records are crap. I don't have to register." Avery held a sheaf of legal documents in the air. "This shows that my case was overturned, that I'm not guilty."

"Still, we want to ask . . ."

"You see this." He tapped his prosthesis. "You see these." He pointed to the scars on his face. "What woman or child would come near me?"

"Still . . .," Carpenter began.

"You damn, overzealous troopers are the reason I'm this way."

"FBI." Carpenter corrected him.

"Yeah, you're all the same. Ready to charge someone before they get all the facts. Well, you assholes finally caught the bad guy. But only after the parent's lynch mob did this to me and I spent two years in prison for something I didn't do."

"Sorry, but if . . ."

"Here's my lawyer's business card." Avery pushed the card in Sable's face. "You can talk to him. Now, go screw yourselves." He stepped back into the house and slammed the door.

As they walked back to the Suburban, Sable offered his version of a sheepish smile. "I think that that went rather well, don't you?"

Carpenter arched her eyebrows and shrugged.

Sable headed 50 miles west toward Delta Junction where he had worked at the trooper detachment only a few years before. Carpenter pressed him about the Army's attack on Kanashig while he'd worked there. Sable feared that if he told her any more, he could put his friends in danger. A virus had escaped one of the military's black research projects at Fort Greely and accidentally infected the village. Even after it was found that the virus had beneficial side effects, the Department of Defense couldn't afford the adverse publicity. So the commanding general of the project sent in an elite shadow force to wipe out the village. Like many of the villages in the state, Kanashig had a National Guard unit. But this unit was prepared for the attack and turned the tables. Now, even though the Army and DOD lost, they kept a wary eye on the village. And if they knew his friends were still alive, they wouldn't last twenty-four hours.

As Sable pulled off the road he saw Mathew Farley's address painted crudely on a wooden mailbox. Its door hung by only one hinge. Sable pulled the Suburban into the dirt driveway, turned off the engine, and studied the house. As they got closer to the house, a one-story ranch, it was evident that it hadn't been painted for years. Farley's yard was a shambles with waist high weeds and grass.

"I think we need a weed whacker not only for the grass but the perp." Sable headed across the yard, slogging his way through the mess.

"Hope you brought your radio in case we get lost before we find his house." Carpenter followed in his footsteps.

Before they could knock, Farley met them at the door as though he had been waiting. "Come in. As though I had a choice." He had shaggy brown hair with a hint of gray in his sideburns.

In spite of the disarray outside, his house seemed clean and well kept. His furniture was 70's style and in good condition, considering the age. The arrangement of the front room was simple: a couch, easy chair, coffee table, and television. He plopped himself in the lounger and motioned toward the couch. "What are you here for, as if I didn't know?"

"This concerns the missing and murdered children; you're at the top of the list as one of the suspects." Sable pulled a notepad and pen from his shirt pocket, rolled the pen in and around his knuckles, clicked it and began writing.

"I know nothing about them, so you can leave," Farley barked and then scowled.

"We know that you like little kiddies. So you know something or were involved." Carpenter's voice became sharp and challenging as she hunched forward from the couch. Sable watched her carefully, noting to himself that he might have to restrain her from doing what he'd like to do himself.

"I have an alibi for every kid."

"Yeah, sure. And the Eskimos run their reindeer herds down to the Mojave each winter."

"Yeah sure." Farley raised his pant leg and tapped a tracking bracelet on his leg. "This says I got an iron-cad alibi— you can check with the courts. I can't leave a 50 foot radius around my house."

Restraining herself, Carpenter went over to Farley and checked the tracker. "It hasn't been tampered with."

"Well, you know who else is a pervert in the local area. Gives us their names."

"I haven't got the slightest idea and if I did, I wouldn't tell you." Farley smiled and stretched back in his chair.

"If you won't help us," Sable said. "We'll ensure you go back to jail." He took a deep breath. "Carpenter, unlock the tracker."

For a moment, Carpenter seemed confused, but caught his suggestion and grasped the device in her hand. "Sure, no problem."

"Now wait a damn minute." Farley tried to stand but Carpenter pushed him back into the chair.

"This should be easy." Carpenter drew something that looked like a pick kit from her pocket.

"Okay, okay. One's Cole Eastman and the other's Bill Oliver."

"Tell me how you know them." Sable stood and continued with his flurry of note taking.

"We use to trade kiddy porn on the computer until the Feds took mine away."

"Do they still do it?" Carpenter gave a good yank on the bracelet.

"Can't say. I haven't talked to them in a year." Farley's lips turned into a fine line and Sable knew they wouldn't get anything further from him.

As they drove back toward Token, Carpenter said. "Oliver's name keeps coming up. If he's still in the game, I hope we nail the bastard."

Sable called into the detachment and got Benson. "Well, what did the medical examiner say about this one?"

"The preliminary examination says that it's the same killer."

Under her breath, Carpenter said, "Well, duh. As if you couldn't tell from the crime scene."

Sable decided it was time for a visit to the office of the dead—the state medical examiner in Anchorage. "Let's check Oliver out and we'll hit Eastman tomorrow after I get back from the ME's office."

Some minutes later, they found Oliver in his motorcycle shop behind his log cabin. When he met them at the door, he sneered challengingly. "What the hell do you want?" He was medium height, his body honed into fine muscles that bulged from his oily tee-shirt. The rest of his body was stuffed in blue jeans that left little to the imagination. The jeans had several, irregular large holes that were reminiscent of the 90's style.

"We're here to ask you questions about the missing children." Sable didn't introduce himself or his partner since the uniforms and nametags were self-evident.

"What children?" Oliver had the husky voice of a four-pack-a-day smoker.

Sable told him.

"I don't know anything about any of them." Oliver took a drag off his cigarette. "And if I did I wouldn't help you."

Sable felt his anger rising. "Let me put it this way, either you cooperate of we'll make your life a living hell. We'll turn your business inside out. One way or another you'll talk with us. Don't be surprised if customers stop coming to your shop."

"Hey, that's harassment and violates my rights."

"I don't see anyone violating his rights, do you?" Carpenter moved to the side and tensed up, signaling Sable that she was ready for any type of confrontation.

"Go pound sand. Talk to my lawyer. You have his name in your files." In a display of defiance, Oliver ground the cigarette in the palm of his hand, flicked it into the dirt and went back into his shop.

Sable slipped on a latex glove, picked up the cigarette, and stuffed it into an evidence bag and marked it. "Hey, luck's with us. In this age of technology we still have a few dumb ones. When we get back, I'll give it to the lab. They can send it out to have the DNA checked with the samples found at the crime scene."

"Good show."

"Let's call it a day."

CHAPTER 5

Sable decided he needed a beer before heading home. In hopes of finding Mukpik Kaomarek, he decided to stop at the more notorious bar in town, the Copper Nugget. Sable was out of uniform and he was new enough in Token he wouldn't draw much attention to himself. There was no possible way to miss the Nugget. It was a dingy one-story log cabin located about a mile from Token. The gravel crunched under the Suburban's tires as he entered the nearly empty parking lot and brought the vehicle to a halt. A couple of beaters held together by what he surmised was rust, were parked on each side of the door.

As he entered the bar, he waited for a moment to let his eyes adjust to the dark. The investigation was not going well. At the bar, Kaomarek was nursing what Sable supposed was a "genuine draft beer." Sable sat in the corner of the bar so he could watch to see when Kaomarek left. By positioning himself between the kitchen and toilet, his quarry would not use them as an exit without his knowledge.

Sable beckoned the waitress and ordered a hamburger and Coors and went back to studying Kaomarek. His broad shoulders stretched the cotton fabric of his shirt as he hunched over the bar. The man watched the dishwater blonde sway her hips as she walked back from the restroom and up to the bar. Sable guessed she was in her mid-twenties and just the type of prey that Kaomarek loved. She wore a white blouse, a loose blue skirt that swayed over her shapely hips and legs and had what appeared to be a new set of Nikes.

As she passed Sable, she nodded and winked, her hair bouncing up and down. She sidled up to the bar far away from Kaomarek and asked for a beer.

Kaomarek took a quick and nervous look around the tavern. When he was satisfied no one was looking, he looked at the woman. "Sweet thing, why don't you come down and join me."

"Sorry, I'm waiting for a friend."

Kaomarek went silent for a while running his hand roughly over the beer bottle.

The waitress brought Sable his order. He bit a piece of the hamburger and began chewing while intermittently sipping the Coors. He noted Kaomarek's increasing agitation.

Kaomarek slipped off the barstool and moved down next to the blond where he said something that Sable couldn't hear.

"Get away from me, you creep." The woman yelled.

Kaomarek's thundering voice drifted across the bar as he grabbed her roughly by the arm. "You'll dance with me, bitch, or else."

"Get your damn hands off me."

Sable could see that Kaomarek was seething with anger. He put down his hamburger, stood and dabbed his face with a napkin. Things were definitely about to get rough. Pushing his chair aside, he strode across the bar. "Kaomarek, leave the lady alone."

Kaomarek turned toward Sable, clenched his fists, and brought them up signifying he was ready for a fight. "Back off, the bitch is mine."

"I'm not anyone's . . . woman."

"We'll see about . . ." Kaomarek raised his hand intending to strike the blonde.

"Stop, if you go any further, you are under arrest." Sable pulled his badge and held it high in the air for all to see.

"You think that tin star will stop me from stomping your ass into the ground." Kaomarek closed the distance with Sable. "You got another thing coming."

"Just calm down and think about what you're doing. You hit me and you'll get five to ten in the best security prison Alaska can provide."

Kaomarek laughed and threw the punch. Sable
sidestepped, grabbed the man's arm, rolled his hip under
Kaomarek and threw him to the floor. As Kaomarek's head
bounced off the floor, Sable landed with his knee in the man's
back. He pulled each arm back separately, snapping on a set of
handcuffs. With a large plastic tie, Sable bound Kaomarek's feet.
Sable leaned over and whispered in the man's ear, "Don't pull that
crap on me again or you'll regret it."

"Thanks," the woman said as she came up behind Sable.

Sable looked up and smiled grimly. "All in a day's
work."

"I don't know what I would have done without you." Her
eyes locked with his. She straightened her blouse and skirt, then
brushed her hair back with one hand.

Sable stood and shrugged. "If you plan to come here
again, bring a body builder with you."

"Can I join you after you come back from hauling this dirt
bag away?"

"Why not now? I'm going back to my dinner."

"You mean to leave him like that."

"Sure, why not." Sable nudged Kaomarek with a foot and
the man grunted. "He's not going anywhere and he'd better not
say anything without his attorney." Sable leaned toward the man.
"He has the right to remain silent and he better do so."

She followed him back to his table and Sable introduced
himself. She leaned toward him, smiled and offered her hand.
"I'm Linda Reed."

"Hello, Linda Reed." Sable couldn't hold back a sheepish
grin.

Sable found out that Linda was a graduate student in
mathematics at the University of Alaska Fairbanks and was on her
way to visit relatives in Whitehorse. She also liked the things he
did: hunting, fishing, camping, and he guessed a few other things
too. He gave her an edited version of his life.

As she rose to leave, she slipped him a piece of paper. "I was just passing through, but I'd like to see you again."

"Same here." Sable slipped the piece of paper in his pocket. Why the hell not—hadn't he been lonely long enough? He wrote down his address and phone number on the back of his business card and handed it to her. Then he walked her to the door, where she kissed him on the cheek. He watched her leave in one of the rusted beaters, called the detachment and arranged for his men to take care of Kaomarek, and then returned to his table.

After Sable left the Copper Nugget, he headed home. He lived alone, so there was no one to disturb when he walked in at 10:30. Sable's grief for his dead wife, Amy, always colored each relationship, preventing him for getting close to anyone. His home echoed his relationships—empty. Though his house was a two-bedroom ranch, most of the rooms were devoid of furniture. His front room had only an easy chair, couch, coffee table and a television gathering dust in a corner. Scattered across the table were numerous unread magazines and unopened pieces of mail, some covering a telephone answering machine. He stopped next to the table, swept some of the clutter away from the recorder, and then pushed the blinking message button. Only the buzzing of the phone's dial tone could be heard on the tape, indicating that either someone had gotten the wrong number or wanted to talk to a real voice. He pushed the next button. "You have no further messages. Answer off," the machine said in a distinctly digital voice.

Sable went to his kitchen and checked the refrigerator. It was mostly bare with the exception of a pizza box. Still hungry, he grabbed a slice of suspect pizza that he couldn't remember when he'd bought, then took a gulp of Diet Coke. After he smelled it, he took a bite of the pizza, then chased it down with his Coke. Later, Sable stood under the shower, allowing the water to beat against his neck and shoulders and draw away the tension of the case. Minutes later he stumbled into the bedroom. Strange dreams taunted him most of the night. Flames danced, wavered, and shadows grew and receded as a dark figure with a mask of a wolf face danced around a fire. Near the fire, a woman with short brown hair struggled, her hands and feet bound behind. When he woke, Sable felt the draw of his tsāk-ssēt *(shaman's amulet)* from his dresser, but ignored it. He knew that using it might lead to the killer or something worse. Not only was it the something worse that he feared, the amulet took a considerable toll, draining him physically and psychologically, but sometimes yielded nothing at all.

CHAPTER 6

Early the next morning, Sable flew a friend's Beechcraft to Anchorage. He landed at Merrill Field and took a cab to the ME's office. As Sable pushed the stainless steel doors open, he stepped into a brightly lit, stainless steel morgue. The distinctive odor of death made him gag. Along the far wall were twelve freezers and down the center of the room were several stainless steel tables. Above each table was a microphone and weight scale. Near one end of the room, the corpse of a young woman lay on an autopsy cart. An intermastoidal incision had been made in the skullcap, the scalp had been pulled forward, and the front quadrant of the skull and brain had been removed. A "Y" incision extended across the chest from shoulder to shoulder and then continued down from the thorax to the pubis. Wally Davenport, who liked to be called "Coroner," talked into a microphone while weighing the liver in the small scale hanging above the table. A steady stream of frigid air came from the ceiling vents making the Office of the Dead feel comparable to a winter tour of Barrow.

"Hey it's freezing in here. Why don't you turn up the heat?" He couldn't help thinking of Jenny's mom and dad who were at that moment on their way to the morgue to identify her body. He dreaded the meeting.

"You say that every time you see me," Davenport said. "Besides they never give me enough money to pay the heating bill. I guess they just don't want me to stink up the place."

Sable had the fingers of his hands looped in his belt. He hoped that Davenport would give a ray of hope to a dark case that was getting darker each day.

"What can I do for you today?"

"I came to get the copies of the Dawson case and the others we've found." Sable edged up behind Davenport, looking over his shoulder and nodded toward the woman. "What'd she die of?"

"Brain hemorrhage."

"Tough way to go—so young."

"This one went badly. Took her several days to die. Her friends found her just hours after her death."

Sable frowned. "Definitely it's a rough way to die—to die alone. But it's nothing compared to the way these children went."

"I'd like to castrate the son of a bitch when you get a hold of him. Bring him by after you get him and I'll do the job for free." Davenport limped around the gurney using it as a brace. He'd recovered quickly after Panama--several wounds to his chest, the loss of his right leg and a bullet lodged next to his spine. The Army Reserves gave him a medical discharge and the doctors thought he'd never walk again. But he had surprised everyone by recovering when the prognosis said he wouldn't.

"You got it."

Davenport tapped his plastic leg. "This keeps me from all the fun."

"Tell you what. If I can, I'll let you in on the kill," Sable said.

"Just give me the privilege of dissecting the asshole."

"Did he strangle Jenny Dawson, then harvest her heart?"

"No. There's still a lot of blood in the internal organs and body. She was eviscerated at the time of death. In other words, she was alive when the monster gutted her. If Jenny had still had her heart, its pumping would have caused more blood loss."

"Can you keep the markings on her forehead from the press?"

"No problem."

A trooper entered and said. "The Dawsons are here."

Davenport hobbled, using his cane, to meet them. Dave and Jinette Dawson were barely able to walk to the freezer. They still clung to each other, Dawson having difficulty supporting his wife though he was moderately tall and seemed somewhat fit. He helped his wife along with a supporting arm around her waist. Even from a distance, Sable could see that Jinette's eyes, a blue-gray shade, were bloodshot from crying. The examiner pulled open the door, slid out the table and pulled off the sheet covering Jenny's face. The mother's legs folded under her, and the husband tried to catch her but had to follow her down. She opened her mouth, but nothing came out. All the father could do was nod. Finally with a croak and sob, he said. "It's our Jenny." He braced himself on the table and looked at Sable with sorrowful eyes. "Will you keep me abreast of what you're doing to catch her killer?"

"I'll tell you whatever I can, but you know the way things are. There are things I can't tell you about the case." Sable tried to meet James Dawson's eyes squarely without flinching.

After the Dawsons left, Sable asked Davenport for copies of the files. The only thing that Davenport could tell him was that none of the children had been sexually assaulted and the samples of skin and blood found under the fingernails were still being analyzed.

CHAPTER 7

As Sable landed the Beechcraft in Token, his cell phone rang. After he finished taxiing and parking the plane, he called the number back. "What have you got for me?"

"We've . . . " Carpenter paused and took a breath. "We've got another one."

"Shit. Won't this maniac ever stop? Tell me where I can find you." Sable was already jogging toward the Suburban and had a hard time keeping the phone to his ear.

She gave him directions to the crime scene.

Within twenty minutes, Sable pulled in behind Carpenter's vehicle. He had no problem finding the crime scene, though this time it was deep in the forest.

Benson stood, held up his hand and waggled his fingers at Sable.

Trying not to disturb the crime scene, Sable carefully made his way down a brushy slope leading to the Tanana River. From his vantage, he could see that the body lay posed in a small clearing, the only clearing for several hundred yards. Someone wanted the body to be found. As he neared the child, he saw that one of the footprints—a mukluk or moccasin imprint--near the body was deep and distinct. Nowadays, almost no Indian wore mukluks or moccasins except for traditional celebrations. From the depth and size of the impression, the print had to be a man's.

In and around the body, the grass and brush had been crushed as the killer had circled his victim. He doubted that the footprints were indicative of an Indian for he knew from his other cases footprints could lie. The killer could be trying to throw suspicion onto an Indian. Even the size of a shoe didn't always provide accurate facts. A large person couldn't wear smaller shoes, but the opposite wasn't necessarily true.

When he saw the gutted boy close up, even after seeing Jenny and the other morgue photographs, the brutality and savagery of the situation made his hands tremble. Was it from horror, disgust or rage? He wasn't sure which, but he took a deep breath to steady himself. The child was dressed in jeans, a blue and green-striped T-shirt, and Nike purple and white jogging shoes. Sable walked to the boy's head, pulled a pair of surgical gloves from his pocket and snapped them on. The child reminded him of his dead son: the same age when his life had been snuffed out.

The feeling he was missing something nagged at him. Carpenter and Benson nodded as though they found it impossible to say anything. He nodded back, then hunkered down over the boy. Every crime scene has a flaw and it was up to him to find it-- something the criminal didn't intend to leave behind.

Carpenter flexed her knees and squatted down. Her face was white as a newly painted room as she studied the body at close range.

Maybe there were two murderers working in unison; but he couldn't be sure. Across the child's forehead were the symbols similar to those on the other children. Though similar in nature, maybe the symbols were different markings for some type of code or satanic ceremony. For several minutes he remained unmoving, lost in reflection as he studied every nuance of the scene. Suddenly, he tensed. His head jerked up, then cocked to one side. It was as though he was hearing distant drumming. "Do you hear that?"

The troopers shook their heads.

Momentarily he was confused. It could have been thunder. Sable looked up at the sky. Overhead, a jet left a fine line of white mist in its wake, reminding Sable how out of place the entire situation seemed to be—the Alaskan bush, a millennium's distance from the modern world and technology. "Do we have an ID yet?"

"I believe it's Timothy Slaymaker. He went missing last night," Benson said, his voice hoarse and stilted.

Sable raised his eyebrows at the name. "The killings are happening with more frequency, accelerating. The need is becoming all consuming—his appetite ravenous." While at Alaska Methodist University, Sable had taken several psychology courses, not only wanting to know why people kill, but why some enjoyed doing it. What insane fury was driving this serial killer? The lust, the enjoyment, the adrenaline rush, repeating the experience--it began with some basic cause. And he thought he knew something about the killer too. The way the bodies were posed, the psycho wanted his work known and understood.

"How many more children will be slaughtered?" Benson asked, knowing the others knew he did not expect an answer.

"Who could do something like this, especially to a child?" Carpenter asked.

"Maybe the first time was an accident, maybe an experiment. But now he's driven, needs the adrenaline rush or sexual thrill to fulfill his sick fantasy. He's addicted. This psycho bastard has a real taste for blood, craving it much like a junkie's desire for crack cocaine."

"But what if he stops? We'll never find him."

"He won't. It's in his blood like a wolf running down its kill." He sighed, then gently rolled the splayed body on its side. Underneath Timothy were another set of feathers with the same glyphs he had seen before. Sable picked up the feathers and turned them over in his hand. The writing was the same, delicate and scribed with great precision. "Any signs the man killed the child someplace else and dumped him here?"

Benson shook his head.

"There's something else that's bothering me." Carpenter looked over Sable's shoulder, pointing to the symbols. "Just what does it mean?"

Benson ran his hand through his hair. "The crime lab's got some whiz kid checking all language databases. No hits yet."

"I need a Polaroid of Timothy so I can show it to his parents." As Sable stood, a weakness ran throughout his body. "The face only."

"Already done." Benson said and handed him the photograph, which Sable stuffed in his shirt pocket.

Sable flipped his notebook closed and let his gaze follow a game trail up a small hill. "I want you to start the report and draw a map of the whole area—just the approximate distances—include the terrain. Also, check out the game trail and see if you find any tracks. If you do, take a search team and see if you can find any clues. This time let's bring in the dogs and see if we can track down this asshole."

Benson began writing furiously.

"Sabe, the families of the murder victims, along with the village elders of Kanashig, are meeting tonight to discuss measures they can take to protect their children. I think we need to attend to stop them from going vigilante," Carpenter said.

Sable sighed. "Though I don't blame them, I agree. We need to stop this before they kill one of our suspects."

On the ridge, the Fairbanks medical examiner's hearse pulled around the troopers' cruisers and backed up to the crime scene tape. After the ME, Wendy Loy, left the vehicle, she stepped over the tape and followed the path down to the body, her assistant following close behind. Loy usually did the preliminary investigation then forwarded the body to Anchorage.

"Shit, not another one. There's no need for me to be here. I can tell you right now that he's dead." She ran her hand through her thick, sandy-blond hair, but it had frizzed from what possibly could have been a morning shower she'd been called from. It was beyond fixing.

Sable glowered. "Funny."

She slipped on a pair of latex gloves, hunched down, and began probing the chest. "Yup, just like all the others. He has no heart."

Sable looked around at the assemblage. "I want to make it clear to everyone here. I don't want anything said about the hearts being missing."

"Bag and tag him. I want his hands bagged so the tissue fragments aren't disturbed." And be especially careful of the face. We might get partials we can use."

"Are you going to ship this one back to Anchorage like the others?"

"Of course. I don't have the staff to handle all the customers you're sending me."

CHAPTER 8

Marsha Slaymaker's house was a well-kept duplex with aluminum siding on a spacious lot with several birch trees in the front yard. Marsha met them at the door, where Sable and Carpenter introduced themselves, showed her a photograph and told her about her nephew.

"No! He can't be dead. I thought he'd run off because of the bad grades on his report card." Martha seemed confused. A couple of tears flowed out and onto her cheeks and slowly ran down her face, but she wasn't sobbing. Haltingly, she invited them in. She walked to a beige couch, but her stride was forced. She was a dark-skinned, grandmotherly type who wore a flowered dress, a gold chain and cameo pendant plus several gold bracelets. In spite of her age, she held her shoulders square and her eyes were a clear and faded blue. She collapsed onto the sofa.

Sable pulled out photographs of some of the suspects and showed them to the woman. "Do you recognize any of these men?

She studied each photograph with an intensity he had rarely seen, as though she were trying to will some type of recognition. Her lips quivered and she stammered, "No."

"Have you seen any strangers near your home lately?"

She thought for several moments. And Sable could almost sense that she was considering that one of her friends, possibly a neighbor, could be the murderer. She shook her head, her voice barely audible. "No."

Sable could see he was getting nowhere. It was too soon for her to think clearly about her nephew's death.

"Could we please see Timothy's room?" Carpenter's voice was smooth, soothing and had a melodic quality he hadn't heard before.

Marsha barely lifted her hand and motioned toward the back of the house.

Carpenter gently placed her hand on Marsha's shoulder. "We'll find it."

Timothy's room was typical of a normal ten-year old. His bed wasn't made. Underneath it, Sable found shoes, a stamp collection and a large box containing a rock collection. Sable opened the dresser drawers. Each was stuffed with clothes in various stages of disarray. Behind him, he heard Carpenter rummaging through the closet. He looked over his shoulder to see if she was making better progress—she wasn't: shoes, clothes, and trash covered the floor.

"I'm going to need a gallon of disinfectant to clean up after this." Carpenter stood and arched her back while using her hands to add to the stretch. "Damn, nothing," she huffed.

"Same here," Sable said. "We should have time to just catch Cole Eastman before we visit Kanashig."

Within minutes Sable and Carpenter were standing before a moderately sized, unpainted, ranch-styled home. Sable knocked and cleared his throat. "Troopers. Cole Eastman, open up."

"Yeah? What the hell do you want?" Eastman opened and came through the door looking hungover. He wasn't a handsome man. His close-cropped, copper hair was flecked with gray. His nose was a little too long, thick and squashed as though he'd been a boxer in hundreds of fights. And his eyes gave off a predatory hunger, like an animal on the hunt. He wore a faded gabardine shirt and jeans.

"Have you been following the news?" Sable asked. This was a very dangerous man who needed watching.

"I try to keep up with things. So why are you here?" Eastman leaned against the door.

Sable took a moment, then spoke firmly. "Were you home last night?"

"Yes."

"Anyone with you?" Carpenter asked.

"The answer's 'no.'"

"Where were you on . . .?" Sable spouted off the most recent dates of the missing and murdered children.

Eastman pondered the questions for several moments. "How should I know? I don't keep a diary, but if those were the dates the kids were lost, I was at home."

"Convenient."

"I don't care what you think."

"We can talk here or we can talk at the detachment."

"You don't have any right to roust me."

"See, that's where you're wrong." Sable moved to the side and glanced over Eastman's shoulder. "Your parole officer told us we could. So move aside, I've decided we're going to search your home."

Eastman blocked him. Carpenter rammed her palm into Eastman's shoulder, setting him off balance and then did a leg sweep, throwing him to the ground. Carpenter immobilized the man while Sable grabbed the gabardine shirt at the collar and jerked him upright. Then Carpenter took one arm and Sable the other. They snapped on the cuffs.

"You guys will never learn. Don't mess with the law," Sable said as they shoved Eastman through the door and pushed him into the closest chair. "I'll talk to this desperado while you check out the house."

Several minutes later Carpenter was back and Sable had been unsuccessful at questioning Eastman. Sable could see the anger flare behind her eyes. She cleared her throat before speaking. "I found folders of pornographic material on your computer and in your file cabinet. They were very graphic pictures of sodomy between boys and men and women. Do you want to explain them?"

"There's nothing illegal about having pornography."

"It is, if it's child pornography." Sable smiled sardonically.

"You can't go into my computer without a warrant."

"Again, that's where you're wrong. As I mentioned before, your parole officer gave us carte blanche. Besides we have articulable suspicion. Your friend you trade kiddy porn with copped you out."

"Damn Farley." He sat silently for a moment. "I want my lawyer."

"This time, I don't think he's going to help. This is a federal crime and you're going away for a very, very long time."

After detachment personnel had arrested Eastman and read him his rights, Sable and Carpenter headed toward Kanashig.

"Do you think we got our sicko?" Carpenter asked, looking out the window at the passing scenery.

Sable glanced at his partner. Her hands were tightly clasped in her lap. "I sure as heck hope so. When we get the DNA tests in, we'll know for sure. But I have a feeling that it's not him."

Sable's cell phone rang. He popped it open. "Speak to me."

"It's Benson. We've got a readout from the computer on the symbols."

"Well, hit me with it."

"I'm going on the theory that this is a satanic crime. The message the murderer scrawled across Jennifer and Timothy's foreheads indicates he was invoking some type of deity. There's something there, but I'm not sure what it is."

"Then why call me? We need to know the secret of the message. The words will lead us to the killer."

"Our computer expert said some of the letters had a similarity to ancient Egyptian and others to Tlingit."

"What'd the crime lab say was used for ink?"

"You won't believe this."

"Okay. What?"

"It's all natural components—soot, clay, and berry juices."

"Has he translated the symbols?" Sable was getting exasperated.

"No, but he figures that our serial killer may be a shaman."

"In other words, we're back to Jim James. Thanks." Sable folded the phone.

"You know you shouldn't drive and talk on one of those things." Carpenter said.

Sable shrugged, then filled her in on the discussion.

"Ooh, a shaman. With the full moon tonight let's hope the crazies don't come out."

"You know in mid-summer we may have a moon, but we have no night." Sable looked up at the sky, saw the sun and moon, shook his head, and bit his lip. "With the moon out day and night maybe we're dealing with a werewolf instead."

Carpenter raised an eyebrow at the joke.

Sable pulled up in front of the Kanashig Tribal Council Lodge. As he and Carpenter left the Suburban, they heard a loud rumble of voices rise and fall from it. As Sable started toward the entrance, he scrutinized the kū-tī-ga (*totem poles*) that stood on each side of the double doors. The hierarchy of colorful, carved figures this time made him shiver, but he wasn't sure why.

Once inside, Sable surveyed the room. Rumbling of the villager's voices seemed to set up a low vibration in the room. Next to several of the chairs were rifles.

In front of the room, at the dais, Sable recognized Chief Harry Greybettle who went by his Indian name Kukākínok (*Flying Squirrel*). He was tall, thin, had a long, narrow face, and his white hair flowed over his shoulders. He slammed his carved power staff down several times, trying to stop to the tumult. "Yanayadel (*guardians*) come to order."

The chief moved to the podium and picked up his gavel and waited while surveying the council chamber. It seemed the whole village was here at the meeting. Tribal artifacts were hung neatly around the room--masks in the image of bear, eagle and wolf from ritual and sacred ceremonies. Artifacts from eras gone by such as hand-carved bows, arrows, knives, daggers with bears' heads, lances, axes, armor, painted ceremonial oars were placed on the walls, giving a sense of tribal history and heritage. On the walls behind the dais and council table were dschénu blankets, one red and one green, each bordered with white fringe depicting symbolic portraits of bear and eagle.

Sable and Carpenter moved quickly to take seats in the rear. As they sat, a couple of the villagers acknowledged Sable. "Xhoots'een."

Though he didn't remember their names, Sable returned their greeting by nodding. Sable knew that he and his partner needed to listen patiently to the villagers venting their hostility before commenting. If they took a proactive approach, they could wind up being the targets without solving anything.

The council discussion was completely in Tlingit. As Sable tried to follow the conversations, he quietly translated the Tlingit for Carpenter.

Kukākínok summarized the reason for the meeting, though everyone knew. "We must come up with a sound method for safeguarding our children since the Alaska State Troopers can't. Let's try to keep our discussions brief and to the point." When Kukākínok looked at him, his clear blue eyes cut to Sable's soul. He felt the sting of the man's comment and knew that there was little he could do but try to find the killer before he killed again.

Dan-e-wåk, the village ícht'a *(shaman)*, raised his hand at the same time as several others. Sable saw the annoyance of Kukākínok, though the chief tried to maintain a poker face.

"Kāg *(Lynx)*, come up to the dais and say what is troubling your heart."

"I'll speak from here." Kāg lifted his rifle and waved it in the air. "This the only voice we need to speak for us. We should set up a community patrol to escort our children to and from school." In the background, there were murmurs of agreement.

Sable grumbled to himself. That was all he and the troopers needed--a group of vigilantes running around shooting every suspicious person in sight.

Two others got up, put their rifles across their chests and said a beat apart. "I agree with Kāg. How else can we protect our children?" The chief acknowledged another.

A village member in the far corner stood. "There are other measures we can take. We don't need weapons. We can purchase a school bus so our children won't have to walk to school. Or, we can use members of the PTA to shuttle our children. We, as parents, can even walk with other children. Again I say that there is no need for such extreme methods."

Sable breathed a sigh of relief—at least one rational voice in the crowd. For a while a number of options were reviewed, always coming back to using lethal force. Then the chief finally pointed to Dan-e-wåk who had his hand up for the entire time. "Please try to keep your comments short."

Dan-e-wåk stood and straightened his pants. "Kanashig is yán-dei yaa *kanashgit--on the verge of darkness.* Our children are not being killed by a serial killer as the troopers would have us believe." He paused for effect. "Auktelchnīk has returned and is seeking vengeance for sending him to Tūtsch-schiā-nách *(black valley).* We, the Yanayadel, have always been the guardians against the evil of Auktelchnīk. We must take action to send him back."

Though he was a Tlingit from Taku in southeast Alaska and of the Raven clan, Sable was familiar with many of the myths, legends and traditions of the interior Indians. He just couldn't remember the story behind Auktelchnīk. Yet, he knew that Tūtsch-schiā-nách was limbo caught between the light and dark, a purgatory of sorts. The other day, Jon had mentioned Auktelchnīk and that there was a myth associated with him.

"Auktelchnīk's a myth. Every child knows the story," Kukākínok said.

"If you don't believe my words believe my message--Auktelchnīk's returned. Centuries ago our village was built here to protect against him."

"Dan-e-wåk, be reasonable. You can't believe that."
Kukākínok paused, and then raised his hand as if he were going to
select another person.

Sable shook his head in disbelief. Though he was a
college man and immune to many of the myths, Sable knew there
were many strange things that he couldn't explain. An ancient
shaman coming back to life, however, was beyond rationality. So
as a matter of interest only, when he saw Jon on Friday, he'd ask
him about the story. Maybe someone was trying to imitate
Auktelchnīk—a copycat of sorts.

"I was right about the Army attacking us a few years ago:
why am I wrong now? We have to find the staff of ages—the
caduceus. Only then can we defeat Auktelchnīk," Dan-e-wåk
said.

For several seconds there was an eerie silence in the
lodge, then Kukākínok said with a restrained voice. "Michael
Worker."

Worker jogged up to the dais and stepped behind the
podium. "We have our own police force right in the village and
we should use them. I'm referring to the Army National Guard.
They've helped us in the past and now we need them again.
Whether the governor activates the unit or not, we should use
them. I would like to hear from Maroak."

Dressed in camouflage fatigues that hung loosely on his
tall, thin frame, Captain Smith Maroak sprang from his chair and
walked to the dais.

Sable noted to himself that Maroak was the commander of
the 57th Heavy Armored Attack Company. Kanashig was lucky
enough to have an Alaska Army National Guard unit, as did some
Tlingit, Athabascan, Yup'ik, and Inuit villages throughout the
state. If they couldn't protect the children, no one could.

Maroak folded his arms. "I agree. I'll talk to the State
headquarters and ask for activation, financed or not."

"And what if you're denied?" Kāg called from the
audience.

"Then we'll activate ourselves as we have in the past."
Sable raised his hand and waved. "You all know my
uncle, Chlawūch-tschāk--Richard Gray Eagle, the ícht'a of Taku.
I would like to say something." Sable said in English as he looked
over at Carpenter for support.

"You're a better speaker than I am," Carpenter whispered.
"Go for it."

"There is no need for an introduction," Kukākínok
responded in Tlingit. "You've helped, I mean, saved our village
many times before. The chair recognizes Xhoots'een."
Kukākínok motioned Sable to come forward to the podium.

Sable grasped both edges of the lectern, cleared his voice,
and chose his words carefully. "I'm glad to see that Kanashig has
taken a progressive move to help the state troopers, but Maroak
and Worker are right. The Guard can provide security for your
children and families until we find the killer."

James Dawson yelled in Tlingit. "I want whoever kill my
daughter in jail."

"We all want that," Sable said, his fingernails digging into
the wood.

"What are you doing about it?"

"The troopers already have one suspect in custody and we
are very seriously looking at others."

"Then why aren't the others in jail too," Kāg shouted.

"We have to have evidence to make an arrest."

"While our children are being kidnapped and murdered?"
James Dawson shook his fist.

"We can't put someone in jail without just cause or
tipping our hand," Sable said and then to himself, *"or stepping all
over their civil rights."*

"I think we've already come to a solution," Kukākínok said,
looking over the assembly. "Raise your hand if you believe we
should use the National Guard to protect our children." All of the
villagers raised their hands, including the head table. "All
opposed, same," he said. Not a single hand was raised. "Motion
carried unanimously."

Kukākínok turned to Maroak. "We place the lives of our children in your hands."

Maroak responded with a nod.

"The Alaska State Troopers will help you any way they can," Sable said. "Please, if you see anything suspicious, call us immediately."

"By the time we see anything suspicious, another child may be gone," Dawson said.

"I'll try to station troopers to watch each of the schools during the day. But first, I'll have to talk to Juneau." Sable knew it was a delaying tactic. He wasn't sure if the governor would back his hand. However, being an election year, he might.

"What's the trooper to square mile ratio—one to every 50 square miles? Where are you going to get them?" Kāg asked.

"I'm sure the governor will try to find a way even if it means activating all the Guard units in the vicinity." Sable stifled an urge to wipe the sweat from his brow. "Tomorrow, the troopers will canvas all the schools again. So we'll need your assistance."

"The National Guard is ready. We don't need the troopers," Maroak said.

As they left, Sable made a mental note to call Juneau. Then he summarized the results of the meeting for Carpenter.

CHAPTER 9

Sable reached the detachment a little after 6 a.m. with a slight headache from not eating. Hoping to massage the pain away, he slowly ran his hands over his thick unruly hair, once raven but now checked with fine lines of gray. At the front desk, he waved at the secretary, Linda Talbot, but she stopped him.

"I've already had several calls from the press this morning. They want to talk to you about the ripper murders." She had straight black hair and rimless glasses that covered big green eyes that were presently inspecting him.

"I wish they'd stop calling them the ripper murders?"

"What should I tell them?" She handed him the morning Token Review.

"That I'm out on a case." His hands shook with anger when he read the headline that screamed SERIAL KILLER STALKS THE ALASKAN BUSH. His gaze stopped at the first sentence: "An ancient Shaman worse than Jack the Ripper is stalking Alaskan Bush children."

He folded the paper and stuffed it under his arm then headed toward his office.

"Gee, thanks," she called after him. "You owe me a buck for the paper."

In the breakroom, Sable passed the donuts and went to the Mr. Coffee knockoff where he poured the dregs of the coffee from the night shift. He tried to put himself into the mind of the killer, wondering what the killer's next heinous act would be. As Sable recalled from his physics and chemistry classes, this endeavor would be about as successful as finding an electron spinning around an atom's nucleus. He shook his head and took a swig of the bitter coffee, trying to remember whether it was better than military coffee or not, then headed to the office where he slumped back in his office chair. The rigid, tired muscles in his shoulders wouldn't let go. Sable flipped through the messages that the secretary had piled on his desk. He made a list of the calls he had to make in order of importance for later in the morning.

"Hey, when are you going to get things under control?" Sable recognized a voice from years past. "There aren't enough of us to go around, okay?"

Sable looked up to see his old partner, Sergeant Walter Masters, duck through the doorway. At six-foot four and 260 pounds, Masters was Scandinavian with dishwater blond hair.

"You still need a haircut." Masters gave a mock salute.

"And the shag you've grown is enough to scare a full grown grizzly."

"You look like shit." Masters slipped into an office chair next to the desk.

"So what else is new?" Sable tried to hide his irritation, stood, reached across the desk and shook Masters' outstretched hand. Sable knew how he looked. He looked as if he hadn't slept, there were dark circles under his eyes, and his face was gaunt from missing meals half of the time. There was something else going on inside, making it hard to sleep. And he knew what and who that was--Amy.

"I just stopped by to say howdy. I'm on my way to a new assignment in Fairbanks."

"So you're back in the good graces of the powers that be?"

"Yeah. I busted a drug ring bringing in coke from Canada."

"Looks like you got a promotion. Sergeant First Class— wow, should I bow and pay homage or something?" Sable hunched forward, picked up his pen and slipped it into a cup with several others. A few years ago, he had worked with Masters investigating the strange disappearance of six scientists from Fort Greely. In the process, they discovered a secret Army project where a number of scientists had gathered under the leadership of a ruthless general, Charles Dean, to create the ultimate soldier.

During a catastrophe, an experimental virus had escaped from the project. Thinking the virus was deadly, Dean tracked one of the scientists exposed to that virus to Kanashig. To contain the virus and protect his secrets, Dean decided to destroy the village and all its inhabitants. Sable, along with Masters and the Alaska Army National Guard, not only saved the village but tracked the general into Canada, where the man died in a firefight.

"Damn straight. Maybe even light some candles and burn some incense in my honor." Masters nodded. "How's the case going?"

"Not good. No leads." Sable shrugged, then gave Masters an overview of the case.

"I don't envy you on this one. This case could put your career in the crapper—permanently." Masters tilted the chair back onto two legs.

"You don't have to tell me. I know that," Sable said. The same intuitive feel for crime made him a good trooper. He knew how to ferret out the smallest clue and turn it into a solid lead. On one level, he functioned calmly and on another, his mind was a whirl of linking clues. But this time the clues were not linking.

"Well if you need help, give me a call. We sure made one hell of a team. I figure if we put our heads together, we could solve this in 48 hours." Masters slipped a card with his new address and phone number across the desk. Sable glanced at it briefly then nodded. The rest of the conversation was spent on Masters' hunting and fishing escapades.

"Don't forget to give me a call." Masters half saluted, then left the office, closing the door behind him.

Sable wished he could be in the field with the rest of the teams interviewing the teachers at the grade schools and churches. The interview search area covered a circle of about a hundred miles from where the children had been found. However, he had to finish up the duty roster and assignments for the week. He found it hard to conduct the daily situation report or SITREP with the staff, so he tried to accomplish it by sending out e-mails. He was an investigator, and he knew he never could become a desk jockey. He couldn't wait for the new detachment commander to arrive.

The phone rang on Sable's desk and he snatched it up. It was Lum. "What do you have?"

"I have a lead. At Kanashig Middle School, a teacher identified William Oliver. Said he'd been hanging around the school recently."

Sable thanked him and called the state prosecutor in Fairbanks to arrange for search warrants to be flown to Token. In the meantime, Sable requisitioned a surveillance van and crew. He called Lum.

"What did the AFIS run show?"

"The computer came up with a couple of hits. They were close, but not that close."

"Damn. Are these guys in the area?"

"Sorry. One guy's doing time in an Arizona prison and the other's living in Florida."

"Do we have any new pedophiles in the area from out of state?"

"I've coordinated with several other states and found that we have three very nasty new visitors, but they're not listed."

"Why aren't they in the state database?"

"Because their crimes were well before the law went into effect."

"Do any live in Token or the vicinity?"

"Yeah, his name is Caleb Nicodemus, but he's out of town until next week." Lum gave Sable the man's address.

"Thanks, good work." As Sable hung up, he cursed.

Early the next morning, Carpenter parked the van about a block from Oliver's home. "How can you wait? I'm ready to bust in, grab the asshole by the balls and string him up." She looked at Sable, her dark brown eyes angry.

Sable shrugged. "You have to have patience to ensure that this time Oliver doesn't slip the noose. Every 't' has to be crossed and 'i' dotted."

"What's that?" Carpenter pointed to the tree line behind Oliver's house.

Sable looked over his shoulder, hunched over and went back to the monitors. "Can you give a replay on that?"

As they replayed the tape, a small figure ran low and between trees and bushes and disappeared behind the house. "Damn, Carpenter, you've got good eyes," Lum said.

"Run it again, but this time slower," Sable said.

Carpenter moved in behind Sable and looked over his shoulder, her breath brushing his ear. He tried to concentrate and pointed to the upper portion of the screen. "Can you enlarge this segment?"

Lum enlarged the area and hit several keystrokes. Though the figure became clearer there still was no further definition of the person's face.

"Can you get the picture clearer?"

Lum shook his head. "Not with what we have here. I'll have to take it back to the detachment."

"What do you think?" When Sable turned, his face was within inches of Carpenter's. "It looks like a young girl to me."

"You're stretching it, Sabe. Though I would like to crash in there right now, as you said before, this needs to be tied up with ribbons and bows."

"I didn't put it quite that way."

There was a knock on the back door and Benson entered. He raised the warrant in the air so that everyone could see. "We got it. Let's go."

The troopers slipped on their vests, grabbed their M16s and headed for the house. Lum and Benson took the back of the house and Sable and Carpenter the front. Sable slipped next to the door jamb. Sable spoke into his headset. "Ready?"

Lum and Benson rogered a beat apart.

Sable looked at Carpenter.

She nodded.

"Open up! Troopers!" Sable yelled. He didn't wait for a response. He hit the door with a well-placed front kick that splintered door. Sable went right and Carpenter left.

Standing at the far side of the room was Oliver naked with a young girl, also naked and kneeling before him with his hardened penis in her hand. Sable guessed she was about fifteen. She appeared to be terrified for Oliver had a knife at her throat. He was tall, slender, forty-ish and rapidly losing his hair.

"Drop the knife. Now!" Sable leveled his gun at the man. Oliver didn't move.

"I'm your worst damn nightmare," Sable said. "I'm the Trooper who'll blow your ass off if you don't do what I say. You got that? Now drop the damn knife."

"You've got one more second before I drop you." Carpenter had already taken a shooter's stance.

The knife clattered to the floor.

"On the floor. Your arms to the side and spread your legs.

As they cuffed him, Sable's first reaction was to grab Oliver by the throat and strangle him, but he used force of will to stop himself. After they had secured him, Sable met the girl's eyes. She was trying to hide her nakedness. "Are you okay?"

The girl barely nodded, while Carpenter covered her with a blanket.

Back at the detachment, they took statements from the girl they now knew to be Patti Dale. Apparently, Oliver had lured Patti to his home using the Internet. Now it was time to interrogate Oliver. The one part of his job Sable didn't like was that he, the interrogating officer, could lie or make as many false statements as necessary to trap or bring about the conviction of a suspect. Sable seated himself across the table from Oliver. Thinking back to earlier when he had seen Oliver with the girl, he tried not to dive across the table and strangle the creep. He'd been a cop long enough to have developed a good poker face. "With the evidence we have on you, are you willing to talk?"

"The girl told me she was eighteen."

"And she liked having a knife held at her neck?"

"I want my lawyer." Oliver, now dressed in orange inmate coveralls, folded his arms and leaned back in his chair.

"I have no problem waiting for your lawyer. When he arrives, I'll let him know that we are charging you for the murders of Jennifer Dawson and Timothy Slaymaker."

"You have no evidence." He was unruffled.

"Ah, but we have."

"You're bluffing." His blue eyes flickered slightly, but just enough that he knew Sable was on the right track.

Oliver's grin disappeared and Sable decided to leave him in that in that state of uncertainty.

Silence.

Oliver began to shift in his chair.

"Remember the cigarette that you ground out in your hand that day we visited?" Carpenter asked.

"So?"

"Well, I sent it to the crime lab. And the DNA from your saliva matches that of the skin and blood found under the fingernails of Jenny Dawson. I'm pretty sure that when we compare Timothy Slaymaker's samples that'll cinch it." Sable's smile went wide, but he kept his eyes flat and cold. He knew it was a lie, but he was sure the tests would eventually back him up.

Oliver was visibly troubled, his eyes grew wide, and his body shook.

Sable leaned forward, hunched his shoulders and placed his arms on the interrogation table.

"Look. I didn't kill anyone and I wasn't anywhere near the crime scenes. I'm willing to take a lie-detector test to prove it."

Sable arranged for the test to be administered, but during the interview, the needles had remained steady with the exception of when the examiner asked him about drug usage.

As Sable headed to the Golden Spike Bar, at the back of his mind he kept thinking about Oliver and the girl. At the back of the bar, he found a booth and ordered a mug of draft beer. He leaned back to consider the last few days. Could it be over? He knew it had to be Oliver. However, though the man's file stated he might be a pervert, he didn't seem he could be a psychopathic killer. Then of course he could be a Theodore Bundy.

Sable took a swig of the beer. Somehow, it just didn't taste right and he was about to leave when he looked up and saw Carpenter. She was wearing a one-piece jumpsuit that clung to every curve and nuance of her body, with the front zipper open far enough to show cleavage. Her hair flowed free over her shoulders while her brown eyes invited him to consider the possibilities.

"Want to celebrate?"

"Sure, but I'm not sure why." Sable raised his hand to signal the waitress. She stopped abruptly at their table and he ordered another beer. "I don't think we caught the killer."

"But we put another scumbag away for about 25 years for kidnapping, sodomy and rape."

"There's always another sicko to replace him." Sable took a sip of his beer. "I don't believe that Oliver killed or kidnapped the children."

"We'll get that guy too, if there is one." Carpenter leaned over the table and placed her hand near his. "Don't you ever forget work—you know, relax?"

"That's what I'm doing." Sable became unsure of himself and aware of her closeness. He moved his hand away, grasped the glass of beer and downed a slug. Though he thought Carpenter was a beautiful, intelligent woman and he was attracted to her, he couldn't afford to be intimate with a partner. Such things could be disastrous to a working relationship if anything went bad.

"You know what I mean." She smiled slightly, her lips quivering. "It breaks the tension and allows one to think clearer."

Sable could respond several different ways, but knew such a relationship wouldn't work. How could he let her down gently and not embarrass or alienate her? He was just about to tell her when the phone rang. He gratefully snapped it open and answered. "Sable."

"Sorry, Sabe. You're back on duty. We have a fresh kill," Benson spat out his sentences in a rhythm similar to rain hitting an old washtub.

"Where's the scene?"

Benson gave him directions. "Want me to call Carpenter?"

"Don't worry, I'll call her."

"Be there in 15."

Sable looked at Carpenter to see that her face was flushed. "I get the point."

"Damn. Now we know it's none of the scumbags we have in jail." In the back of his mind Sable knew that somehow Jim James was involved--*was he dead or alive?*

CHAPTER 10

Sable had quickly thrown on his uniform and headed to the crime scene. Carpenter had opted to dress in the back of the Suburban. While she maneuvered into blue slacks and a white blouse, Sable tried to keep his eyes focused on the highway ahead, though he caught a quick flash of a well-formed brown thigh in the rear view mirror. He took a deep breath and bit his lip. As he took a side road that lead deep into the forests, he considered that maybe Carpenter was still trying to push the issue of starting a relationship. The situation was so macabre he thought it would be the furthest thing from her mind.

A forest of alder, birch and brush closed in on the road, forcing Sable to slow. Occasionally limbs hit the truck, scraping down its entire length, yielding a high-pitched screech. As they broke out into a meadow, Sable saw two guardsmen, fully armed, on each side of the road. He shook his head. All he needed was for the National Guard to go vigilante on him.

Sable rolled down the window and leaned out, he said, "Where's the girl?"

The guardsman nodded and pointed. "Down the hill and to the right."

He parked next to a small grove of trees that sat in the center of the field. As they exited the Suburban, he took in the surrounding area. Around the perimeter of the crime scene were several soldiers standing guard. As they approached one, Sable said, "Tell me what happened."

The man just looked at him, his face still blanched.

"Why don't you answer me?"

The nametag identified him as Riker. "It's cold."

"Are you okay?"

"Hāde-anagut *(He comes).*
"Who are you talking about?"
"Auktelchnīk."
Sable looked at Carpenter, shook his head and motioned to another soldier, this one taller and heavy set. "What happened?" "We were out on a sweep when we saw Auktelchnīk. He was standing over the child with a knife. When he saw us, he turned, snarled and attacked." The soldier clenched his rifle against his chest as he haltingly spit out the words--as if he were still living the event. "We threw everything we had at him, M16s, 9 mms, . . . but the bullets seemed . . . to burst into flame."
"Uásse īdūe-ssakt *(what is your name)?*" It was just as he'd thought. Maroak had sent teams into the field to find the serial killer.
"Hanford Galek."
Sable pondered the situation. When the man with the knife attacked the guardsmen, they had panicked, their shots going wild. Also, the perp must have been wearing body armor and any of the bullets that hit him would have made him look invincible. The bullets bursting into flame was easier to explain. The soldiers had fired tracers.
"He wasn't alive. It was his tsige-káo *(spirit),*" Galek said.
"What did he look like?"
"He was tall, maybe 6-feet 3, very thin, long white hair, and a thin, oval face," the soldier said.
"What was he wearing?
"Traditional clothes made of moose hide."
"Was he a Yanayadel?"
The soldier shook his head.
Sable breathed a sigh of relief. "Would you work with a sketch artist?"
The soldier nodded.
"Thanks."
Riker waved his hands in the air and said in Tlingit, "There's a demon in our midst."
"Father bless us . . . ." The other soldier started to say as Sable walked toward Benson.

"The ravens are flying from the valley," Riker yelled after him.

Carpenter shook her head as she walked with him. "Dís yan yaawawát *(It's a full moon)*."

"What do you expect? These guys shot about a good hundred rounds at our killer and he didn't go down," Sable said, realizing how powerful the suggestion could be. "Woétsch ach-i-re-tán *(You speak to me)* Tlingit? Why didn't you tell me the other night at the council meeting?"

"A woman doesn't have to reveal all her secrets." Carpenter shrugged and smiled. "You have to be multilingual around here."

Sable cringed as he approached the body—a little girl, blonde, about ten years-old, wearing a yellow, flower-patterned dress and white sneakers. Soldiers had tromped over the crime scene destroying any fragile clue. Definitely he and Maroak had to talk. Sable nodded to Benson as he hunkered down over the girl and slipped on latex gloves.

"We aren't going to find any evidence this time." Carpenter joined him.

Sable looked around. The forest was silent, bereft of any noise from birds or animals. No breezes moved through the trees. And as a cloud moved overhead, throwing a long shadow and blocking the sun, he felt as if the entire sky was going to turn dark. He shook off the feeling and surveyed the child's body. The soldier's reaction to the killer made him recall from legends that the body of a shaman was not supposed to decompose. His essence was like dried salmon waiting only to be reanimated— brought back to life--through a ritual chant. But an evil Shaman or unclean person was deserted of his tu kinajek *(spirit)* or soul, so how could he come back? Sable jolted himself back to reality. If he didn't watch it, he'd start believing in fairies and dragons.

He blinked. The child didn't have a mark on her. She looked as though she was sleeping. He lifted her skirt but found the panties still intact.

"Looks like he didn't have time to cut out her heart. The guardsmen stopped him," Carpenter said.

For a split second Sable thought he saw her chest move. He laid his fingers along the jugular. "I have a pulse. She's alive," he yelled.

Carpenter checked the child's pulse too. "Damn. They saved one."

Sable withdrew his cell phone and dialed the detachment. "Lum."

"What chu' want, Sabe?"

"I need the chopper out at the crime scene ASAP. We got a live one who needs a medivac." Sable gave Lum directions.

****

Sable paced back and forth while waiting for Becky George, Jon's wife, to let him know how the little girl was. Becky, a physician's assistant, ran Kanashig Medical Center.

As Becky stepped out of the intensive care room, he asked. "How is she?"

"She's in some type of coma and I can't figure out why. At least I have her stabilized for now." Becky had a slightly turned-up nose and oval face full of light freckles, hidden by a light tan from her Cherokee heritage. Her shoulder-length, white hair was up in a ponytail.

"Thank God," Sable sighed. Even now, after all these years, he had friendly feelings for Becky, but for a long time the feeling wasn't mutual. Now she was married to one of his friends. A number of years ago, he had introduced her to his best friend, William Kincaid. After a long stint in the Alaskan bush, she had been lonely and fragile and had fallen in love with Bill. However, she mistakenly thought Bill was going out with other women behind her back so she had quickly ended the relationship. As Bill's friend, he was out of favor with her until a couple years ago when they had come to an uneasy truce.

She came over, put her hand on his shoulder and gave him a peck on the cheek. "You did good."

Sable thanked her for helping, told her to let him know if there was any change in the girl's condition and drove back to where they had found Jennifer Dawson.

Sable made it a point to visit each murder scene at the same time of day that the crime occurred. He hoped to get into the mind of the killer and get a better idea how the killer made his approach—where he had hidden. It gave Sable a feeling for what the killer had seen and felt. It was almost like looking through the killer's own eyes. Sable stared at the spot where Jennifer's body had been. He combed the crime scene again, though the forensic teams had scoured the area and all the evidence should have already been removed. Sable had stood in the midst of crime scenes that felt like this before. Murder sites gave off an aura of evil.

He remembered the challenge by Dan-e-wåk to use the tsāk-ssēt. He knew he had to come to terms with the amulet and its power. Though he'd never known it to lie, sometimes visions were presented as if they were hidden in the veils of clouds. Sable's hand began to tremble as he placed the amulet in it. He fell to his knees, as the darkness tried to consume him, body and soul.

Suddenly Sable was ripped from the present into a dark canvas. He saw Jennifer and tried to remember this was a dream, a reverse premonition of sorts, symbolic of what had happened. As Jennifer fought her assassin, Sable could only make him out as a shadowy figure. The knife plunged down, striking her directly in the chest and driving her to the ground. The child's eyes bulged as she stared unbelievingly, first at the knife and then at the man. The knife dropped forward and the girl helplessly watched the blade move up in a quick, slicing motion. She cried, screamed, tried to scratch him, then she tried to reach for the knife. As she tried to speak, to form words, the blood frothed from her mouth. The last thing she saw was the contorted face of the killer and the large, gleaming knife. The man leaned over her, placed his mouth over hers and drank her life force. The figure began rending her heart with his teeth, savoring each bite. Sable came out of the vision and at that moment realized that this thing that walked like a man would kill again. Why hadn't he been able to see the killer's face? He shivered and decided to go back to the office. He was barely able to push himself up and staggered back to the Suburban. Each time he used the talisman it weakened him, sapping his strength as though he'd been put in a washer and spun dry.

CHAPTER 11

Tūtsch-gūtsch tossed and turned on the small, wooden bed. His large frame hung over both ends of the old Army cot. Echoes of distant drums tumbled through his mind as he fought to keep Auktelchnīk's evil at bay, but all too often felt the shaman encroaching on his soul.

"Why are you doing this to me?" Tūtsch-gūtsch swung his legs over the edge of the cot as he listened to the crackle of the fireplace in a room that smelled of burning wood.

"You brought me back and now I'm repaying you. I'm going to make you immortal and since we have mixed our bloods, your journey has begun." Across the cabin, Auktelchnīk sipped coffee and grinned. His square face was crowned with a full head of white hair that he'd swept into a ponytail. He had a strong chin, with a deep-set cleft that emphasized the power of his body. He uncomfortably eased himself from the white man's chair. These hard-backed monstrosities had no place in the Indian's world. But Auktelchnīk wasn't Tlingit. He was something older, if he could only remember—Egyptian, Greek, or . . . he wasn't sure. "I like this coffee, as you call it."

"I was immortal before you came."

"After centuries, your so called virus will die. But I can give you what you want--immortality and power."

"I don't want it anymore."

"I know everything you think and feel. Remember, I've walked through your mind and know your worst fears."

"Not since that first time when I found your skull then brought you back." Tūtsch-gūtsch cursed the day he'd found the skull. Legend said that if you chanted the sacred words over the skull of a powerful shaman, you would gain his power. Just the opposite had happened. Auktelchnīk had come back and taken control over him, slowly at first and then stronger each day. Some days he found he had to pull himself from a fugue.

"I own you, body and soul." Auktelchnīk tipped his head back, his evil laughter reverberated around the room as his ponytail bounced from side to side.

"At least release the children. You don't need them anymore now our bloods have mixed."

"But I do. Do you think my power and immortality comes from just eating their hearts--it comes from drinking their souls and physical essence. Besides I need three more for the solstice."

"What then?"

"Then I'll take over the world and set it right."

"Of course, with your brand of evil."

Auktelchnīk laughed. "Evil. Your world today is more evil than mine was--than I am now. Greed, robbery, rape, murder . . ."

"Evil--your soul is . . ."

"Evil. Yes, but even I know how to treat mother earth with respect. You're--my descendants have let the others destroy mother earth: you rape the land for its minerals and leave nothing in return but deadly waste. You pollute seas with toxic waste, the sky with carbon monoxide and foul smelling hydrocarbons and acids . . ."

"My people don't do any of . . ."

"You drive cars?"

"Yes."

"Boats, planes?"

"Yes, but . . ."

"Recycle?"

"Rarely, but . . ."

"Take a stand against the defilers of the land."

"We've tried but we don't have the power."

"Power? You've always had the power." Auktelchnīk waved his hand and the cabin floor and walls shook. "But you have let others destroy the earth."

"What was that?" Tūtsch-gūtsch felt the ground under him waver and he clung to the cot he was seated on.

"Power." Auktelchnīk smiled and waved his hand again and the floor moved with a roll that rippled across the room. After the solstice, no one will be able to stop me. I will kill all but true bloods."

"What do you mean . . ." Waves of terror coursed through Tūtsch-gūtsch's body.

"Only pure blooded--the people . . . what now are called-- Indians."

Tūtsch-gūtsch didn't respond for he felt the encroachment of the dark times when he blacked out. Auktelchnīk had stolen his mind and body. At first, Tūtsch-gūtsch had blacked out for only a few hours, but now, his mind was taken over for days at a time. He couldn't remember what happened during the dark yet when he came to, he was covered in blood. He feared that the shaman had his soul, and soon there would be nothing left of him.

"I will use all my power to defeat you and release the children." Tūtsch-gūtsch mustered his courage.

A little girl moaned in her sleep. He watched in horror as Auktelchnīk's eyes glistened in anticipation. The little girl shifted against the bars of her wooden cage. In two other cages rested a boy and another girl. What heinous things would he do to these children on the solstice? He was almost glad that he didn't have to deal with the reality and was an unwilling participant when his mind clouded over. Although he had fed them and made sure they had enough water to drink, they seemed to be wasting away, their cries filling his nightmares.

Once, he had released two of the children, hoping they would get away, but he had blacked out within moments. Later, not knowing how much time had passed, he had stumbled to the cabin covered with blood. He had hoped the blood came from wild animals, but he knew better. In his twenty-four years, he had never known such terror as not knowing and not being in control. Once, he had escaped and made it to within a block of the police station but then Auktelchnīk had taken over his mind.

"Haven't you learned? You can't succeed."

"Somehow I'll defeat you." Standing, Tūtsch-gūtsch paced the floor of the old miner's cabin. As he came to the window, he looked up at the sun and moon, breaking through the clouds. Their light fell on the meadow in front of the cabin, painting a path of escape he knew he could not take. Though trapped for now, he'd find a way to resist until he could escape. All the spells Dan-e-wåk had taught him had been useless, so Tūtsch-gūtsch simply had to learn more on his own.

"Even when I am sleeping, I'm protected. Once, it took several shamen to kill me, but never again. Soon my powers will be beyond anyone, living or dead. The shamen of this time have lost too much power, too much knowledge." While he roared in laughter, Auktelchnīk's eyes changed from black to brown, then piercing green, then violet and back to black.

"I'll find a way."

"You? You're nothing more than a worm on the end of my hook. And your teacher's not much stronger."

"I don't believe you. Dan-e-wåk is very powerful." That was it! In the past, he had tried to contact Dan-e-wåk, but failed, but he hadn't tried during Auktelchnīk's shape shifting. Dan-e-wåk might not be able to defeat Auktelchnīk alone but if he brought help, they might be able to.

"So you say."

Less than a year before, Tūtsch-gūtsch had been the apprentice of the village shaman, but he had wanted to gain power fast. He called the fatherly man "SE" short for Silver Eyes behind his back, had said that in order to gain real power one must build on knowledge one step at a time. Each spell must be practiced over and over until it was letter perfect.

Dan-e-wåk had warned him against the dark side. According to him, it was very easy for even a good man to be seduced. In this case there was no seduction, but an outright takeover of his mind and body.

Auktelchnīk yawned. "I'm going to run with the wolves. Would you like to go?"

"No."

"Live up to your name sake, the Tūtsch-gūtsch, for I can
help you shape shift into any animal you want. It's exhilarating."
"No!"
"Tonight, I will run down a caribou and rip its throat out,
then drink its blood."
"I'll pass." This was his chance. Once Auktelchnīk shape
shifted, his power was reduced and Tūtsch-gūtsch could try to get
to Dan-e-wåk, but how? Could he make it to Dan-e-wåk's house
before Auktelchnīk returned? No, that was too dangerous, but he
could use mind talk. And when Auktelchnīk came back, he
wouldn't know what he had been doing.

Sitting cross-legged with his arms loosely relaxed on his
lap, Tūtsch-gūtsch began deep breathing. He took a deep breath
through his nose, held it and then let it out slowly. He began to
chant, taking himself down through the deep layers of his mind.
Slowly, his body tingled and lightened, giving him the feeling of
floating above the floor as he mentally reached out to Dan-e-wåk.

Tūtsch-gūtsch listened. Hearing no answer, he called again
and again.

A force pierced his mind and he was almost pulled from his
trance. Panic began to pull him upward. A calming voice he
recognized as Dan-e-wåk stretched out across the distance and his
mind, comforting him.

"I'm here, Tūtsch-gūtsch." Dan-e-wåk sent a series of
questions that flooded his mind, yet he was able instantaneously
to answer all of them, bringing his teacher up-to-date on what he
knew and suspected.

"I'll be there in two days, so hold on," Dan-e-wåk said.

Another force enveloped Tūtsch-gūtsch's brain and
massive flames seemed to cut deep, sending him spinning away
into darkness.

CHAPTER 12

The notes taken at the crime scene the day before lay in front of Sable. He took a sip of his warm Coke, which was already flat from the day before, and studied the notes. He was missing something. He had seen the girl before. A quick check of the photographs revealed the missing child and her name: Adonica Nash. Why had they found her now? She had been missing for about three months. It didn't make any sense. He took a deep breath and called the parents to let them know about their daughter and where she was. They were overjoyed. After putting down the phone, he looked around at his desk. Files, paperwork and books were strewn about. It seemed he was never caught up. He shuffled the paperwork on his desk, but had trouble concentrating. A number of reports needed to be written up and filed, but he wasn't up to it just then. Sable looked over at the map that had been recently placed on one of his walls. A red pushpin marked where each child had disappeared and green indicated where their bodies had been found. Sable stared at them trying to discern a pattern.

Lum knocked, came in the office and sank into the chair across from Sable's desk and started right in. "What do you think Carpenter'll do if I put a move on her?"

"You mean . . .?"

"Yeah."

"Probably call a trooper or better yet the FBI."

"She can call me anything or any time she wants," Lum said then held up a piece of paper. "This is why I really came. I think we have a live one."

Sable studied him as the trooper held up the artist's rendering. Lum shoved the drawing across the desk, put both feet on the edge of the desk and leaned back in the chair. "It's a long shot, but if I'm right, we can go home and catch some shuteye tonight."

Sable cautioned himself not to overreact, to remain calm.

"The medical examiner just called, he found something interesting."

"Okay, give."

"The ME thinks he has a DNA match. At least six bars."

"That's not much."

"But try this on for size." Lum shoved a mug shot across the desk. "Not only does this guy match the description, but he's the six point match."

"Damn, Albert Bosch. Now this guy's doing little kiddies instead of women." Sable sat straight up in his chair and sucked in his breath. Somewhere there was a murderer walking around, and they were closing in on him. *Here would be another sleepless night.* "Call for the warrant."

Sable and Carpenter stopped the Suburban about a block down a rutted narrow road. Tall birch guarded each side of the road. Though the warrant hadn't arrived, they decided to investigate. As they neared a clearing, they had a good view of the yard. In front of the house, the twisted remnants of several wrecked cars intermingled with rusty engine blocks and rotting tires. Waist-high weeds were strewn across the yard forming a confidence course. Sable and Carpenter, lulled by the pastoral scene, both jumped when a scream pierced the silenced.

"What the hell was that?" Sable asked as he checked his .40 for smoothness of the draw.

"Sounded like a woman screamed," Carpenter said. "We need to check this out." She started dodging the obstacles without checking for cover. Sable drew the pistol, following in her footsteps, jogging and dodging the engine blocks and tires. They cut a swath through the weeds. As they neared the building, Sable thought he heard another scream.

Sable nodded toward a ladder placed against the wall and near a window "Let's check it out." When he got to the top, he looked in and saw the back of a large man with his fist in the air poised to strike a cowering woman on the floor.

"I cleaned the house and cooked your dinner the way you like it," she whimpered and tried to push herself up. Instead, Bosch threw a kick. The blow caught her on the cheekbone and sent her back against the wall. She screamed.

"Look, bitch. You can't clean or cook. Whoever taught you did a lousy job." Before she could stand, he kicked her in the stomach.

She whimpered, "Please don't hurt me any more."

"You're not worth a damn thing." He yanked her up by the collar of her blouse, the material separating in his hands. He drew back his fist, ready to send another hammering blow. "You're also a lousy lay."

As Sable stood on the ladder, it began to tilt, sway and walk. He twisted to counter the ladder's movement, then leaped to the ground, landing on his feet and jolting his back and ankles. A pain shot up and down his back as he watched the ladder rock, bounce and clatter against the wall until it crashed. The woman's scream covered the noise.

Sable didn't even have to say a word. They both ran for the door. Dashing up the steps, Sable and Carpenter hit the door with their shoulders simultaneously. It splintered from its hinges and fell flat with a resounding thud.

"What the hell?" Bosch turned and looked at them in surprise. He had shoulders like a bull and burly arms with sledgehammer fists and legs like those of an elephant. The killer Sable was trying to find was driven to kill, and this man's personality matched the bill.

"You're under arrest. Now lay on the floor and spread 'em."

"You have no right to be here. You don't have a warrant, so get the hell out of my house."

"You're under arrest for domestic violence."

"I can do whatever I want in my own home."

"Buster, you've been misinformed. There are laws here in Alaska to stop that." Sable said, knowing that domestic

violence was taken seriously in the state. And if the judge didn't
protect her, he would.

Bosch walked toward him, his face becoming a mask of
rage. At that moment, the fists clenched at the man's sides
seemed huge as pile drivers. The man had to be insane to threaten
two cops with guns.

"We can do this easy. We can do this hard. It's up to
you." Sable felt his body tense automatically from years of
studying karate. Though Sable didn't want to fight and he was
sure he could take Bosch, there was a shadow of doubt at the back
of his mind.

Bosch's eyes were filled with hate and he raised his fist in
the air as though threatening to strike. "You'd better back off or
you'll get a taste of this."

"You want that fist shoved down your throat? Better yet,
hit me, let me kick the shit out of you, and I'll be able to get you 8
to 10 for assaulting an officer, that's unless my partner shoots you
first."

Carpenter moved to block Bosch. She brought her knee
up into his groin with every ounce of her strength and anger she
could muster. Bosch's eyes widened in surprise, his body lurched
forward, his jaw ramming into her knee and he slipped to the
floor. Carpenter whipped on the handcuffs. In spite of the cuffs,
Bosch drew himself into a fetal position, groaning in pain.

Sable looked at the woman. "Are you all right? Do you
need a doctor?"

She hugged herself and shook her head, then shakily
stood.

"This is FBI Agent Annelle Carpenter," Sable said as he
pointed to his partner. Though Sable flashed the woman a
concerned friendly smile, she regarded them with suspicion. Now
that he could see her, he saw that she was a pretty brunette in spite
of the blood flowing from her nose and the bruises and welts on
her face. Though she was dressed to show off her body, Sable
somehow suspected it was for Bosch's benefit. From the quick

glance at Bosch's file, he knew that her name was Charmaine. "And I'm Trooper Sergeant Robert Sable. We need to talk to your husband downtown."

"Yeah, he's probably going to be gone for a long time. He's suspected of killing a number of children." Carpenter said.

Just then Lum entered the room, picking his way over and around the fallen door. He raised the warrant. "I got it."

"Thanks you're just in time," Sable said.

"Good show, Sabe." The trooper looked down at Bosch then put his hand over his crotch and tugged. "Huevos grandes."

"The heuvos grandes are Carpenter's."

"Good show." Lum nodded to her.

"You don't need a warrant. As far as I'm concerned you can tear this damn house down." Charmaine folded her arms but winced from the pain. "And, when you're done with it, torch it."

"You bitch, you'll get . . ." Bosch said, but then screamed from pain.

Sable glanced at his partner suspiciously.

"It must have been something he ate." She smiled mischievously.

Sable shrugged, pulled a card from his pocket and walked over to Charmaine. Under his breath, Sable said. "Here. This is an address of a safe house run by a friend of mine in Fairbanks. She'll help you. And should your husband get out on bail, the house has fences and armed security." And these women would shoot to kill if their scumbag husbands were crazy enough to try to break in.

"Thanks." She smiled feebly as a tear rolled down her bruised cheek.

"In fact, they'll even come and pick you up." Sable turned and strode back to Bosch. "Let's get this jerk out of here." He grabbed him by the collar and with the assistance of Carpenter yanked him roughly to his feet.

Back at the station, Sable and Carpenter placed Bosch in the interrogation room with a series of photographs face down, spread out in front of him. They stood, staring at the man through the two-way mirror. Sable instinctively knew it was him. It had

to be. No, he wanted it to be him with all his heart and soul.
Then the killing would stop.

Through the mirror, Bosch leaned back in his chair, ran
his hand though dark, greasy hair that hung down to his shoulders
and then examined his nails. A slight smirk was plastered across
his face.

"I want the bastard bad." Carpenter slammed her fist into
her palm.

"So you want to be bad cop?" Sable asked.

She nodded and grinned. "Let's make it bad cop, bad cop."

"I thought FBI agents were always bad cops."

She glared at him then smiled. "Okay, point taken."

"You got the deck of cards?"

She gave him a questioning look. "Oh, I got it. We're
going to do some bluffing."

"Nowadays with the Supreme Court rulings,
interrogations walk a fine line."

"Well, we'll just have to be sneaky."

As they entered, Sable turned on the camera, stated the
date, subject and circumstances of the interrogation. He and
Carpenter sat down directly across from Bosch and for a few
moments didn't say a word.

Bosch gave them an amused look as if he had been through
the process a number of times and had no plans to tell them
anything.

Sable picked up one of the morgue photo he knew was of
Jennifer Dawson. He turned it over and slid it across the table.
The face that was once pretty and innocent was now gray, the lips
drawn in rictus. Her eyes were cloudy and lifeless and the large
wound that split her chest was dry and blood-encrusted.

"Christ." Fear flashed through Bosch's eyes and then they
became flat, cold and empty.

Sable offered him a cold smile, which carried all his
distain for the man. Unconsciously, he squeezed his hands into
fists.

"You knew her, didn't you?" Carpenter hunched forward, placing her hands on the table as though she was restraining herself from coming across it.

Bosch's jaw tightened giving Sable the answer he needed. "Your wife said you knew the girl."

"The bitch is lying." Bosch kept his voice even.

"Said Jennifer delivered your morning paper." Sable glared at Bosch giving every word force and intensity. "Said she even did odd jobs around your house. That you occasionally drove her home."

"Where's my lawyer?"

"Grown women were too threatening for you so you decided to start doing little kiddies." Carpenter's voice was taunting. "Making them scream, beg for mercy, cutting their hearts out for the shear joy of it."

"My lawyer. I want my lawyer," he said sullenly.

"She's coming." Sable straightened and smiled directly at the man's livid face. "But she won't be able to bail you out of this one." Sable shoved Bosch's mug shot and the artist's rendering across the desk. "You've been identified by three witnesses and your DNA so far is a six point match."

Bosch folded his arms and Sable noticed that his hands were visibly shaking.

"We've got you screwed, glued, tattooed and dressed up for life at one of Alaska's high security hotels." Carpenter kept her face deadpan though her voice had a smirk to it.

"Look," Sable said, forcing himself to stay calm. "You will talk after your lawyer gets here and she tells you the facts of life and murder."

Sable heard the door slam open and he looked up and recognized Doreen Lawson whom he guessed was Bosch's attorney.

"And what facts are those?" Lawson had sandy hair and warm, amber-brown eyes offset by a gentle, trusting face, but her voice was cold and professional.

They rose to shake hands with Lawson. Her hand was cold and clammy and when they shook hands, she gave a weak shake, but from her reputation he knew better than to size up an individual based on a handshake. She handed him her card, which he stuffed into his pocket without looking at it. He and Carpenter gave her a quick run down of the facts.

"What's with the Gestapo tactics?" She turned her attention to Sable.

"It's harassment, plain and simple," Bosch said.

"I need some time with my client—alone please." Lawson's eyebrows formed a deep vee and with a wave she inclined her head toward the door.

"Sure thing. Take all the time you need." Sable walked over to the camera, shut it off, and he and Carpenter left the room.

As they stood outside the conference room, Sable said. "This is going to be a nightmare when it hits the paper. I can definitely hold him on the assault and battery charges. The murder charges are not as tight as I'd like them to be."

"I'm sure I have enough for a conviction."

"Well, all the attorney has to do is challenge our witnesses who thought he was Auktelchnīk, some ancient evil shaman and our case goes right out the window."

"But the wife and the DNA."

"Lawson can say the wife has an axe to grind and for a true match we need more than six markers."

"Damn."

After Lawson came and got them, Sable started the videotape again.

"Well, counselor what does your client have to say about the charges?"

"He's going to cop to the charges on the domestic abuse, but he says he has nothing to do with any of the kidnappings or murders."

"And?"

"That's it."

"We have witnesses that place your client at the scene of the most recent crime," Sable said.

"Yes, I heard about that." Lawson smiled and waved her hand as though brushing away the charge. "Some wild man charging some guardsmen with a knife."

"Well, we also have . . ." Carpenter started.

"Nothing." She gave Sable a hard look. "My client has an ironclad alibi. He was in jail for the last three months. I would have figured that smart troopers like yourselves would have checked out that possibility."

Sable cursed under his breath.

CHAPTER 13

"It's too late now." Auktelchnīk watched Tūtsch-gūtsch pace the room. He had tricked the young man into calling his teacher. When Dan-e-wåk tried to displace his spirit from Tūtsch-gūtsch, he would drain the teacher's powers and destroy him.

"When you and Dan-e-wåk are fighting, I'll put a knife in your heart." Tūtsch-gūtsch placed his hands on his hips.

Auktelchnīk casually waved his hand and an invisible force lifted Tūtsch-gūtsch from the floor and threw him against the wall. He crumpled in a heap. "Haven't you learned by now that my powers are greater than, how you say . . . your damn teacher's--I like this swearing of your language."

"It's not my . . .," he choked.

"I know, it's the white man's." Auktelchnīk strode to the cages and rattled the one containing a dark-haired little girl. "How's my pretty tonight?" He fingered the knife on his hip, the one he had killed the other children with. He shuddered with delight as his hand came in contact with it, remembering it ripping through their bellies and up through their chests.

She whimpered.

"I need you." His eyes locked with hers and all emotion drained from her face. He smiled, opened the cage door and beckoned her.

She crawled forward and out onto the floor. Auktelchnīk motioned for her to stand and follow him. Then he turned his back on her and walked to the door and out onto the porch. A large stone table stood in front of the cabin, ringed by four fires, each aligned with the sacred directions he now knew as North, East, South and West. He began chanting an ancient song—words he knew but had forgotten the meaning of. With the precision of a coroner, Auktelchnīk thrust his knife into the child's belly, sliding it in a smooth motion toward the sternum. The girl screamed, her head swung to the side of the altar, blood gushing from her chest. There was a moment of soundless terror, helplessness, and shock. He forced her sternum apart and took her heart into his hands, watching it beat. With a quick flick of the blade, he sliced the arteries. Holding her still quivering heart, he leaned over, focused on her eyes and drank her essence. For a moment he was her, feeling her body shut down, her vision fade. It was like an adrenaline rush as endorphins released slowly at first, then in a cascade. He felt a surge of power within him. It was now so close to the solstice when he'd be all-powerful—he'd align with the magnetic forces of the sun, moon, earth and other planets. This solstice all the planets would be in perfect alignment and he would draw on that enormous reservoir of strength. He needed another child, a little girl, because they were so elemental.

CHAPTER 14

After contacting Tūtsch-gūtsch, a looming darkness stole into Dan-e-wåk's mind. Out of the night, he could feel its presence in his bedroom, watching him. Sporadically, cold, black tendrils slipped out of the cloud and fought to control him. Switching his nightstand lamp on, he looked around the room. Flitting shadows moved along the walls and disappeared in the brilliance of the light. The presence seemed to melt away. Cold sweat clung to his skin and the bed sheets stuck to him as a cool breeze whipped through the open bedroom window, caressing his body, swirling across his body, forcing him to shiver. Dan-e-wåk swung his legs over the side of his double bed, letting the sleep fall away. As his fingers rubbed the grit from his eyes, he stood slowly, stretched and walked to the window. He gazed out at the cool, gray dusk of early morning. Before closing the window, his gaze reached out through the trees and into the mountains, trying to sense Tūtsch-gūtsch's presence, but he couldn't. As another breeze hit his damp body, he slid the window shut.

As Dan-e-wåk headed to the bathroom to shower and shave, for the first time in years doubt entered his mind. Though he believed in the validity of legends, he knew that over the centuries they became exaggerated. Yet, the legend of the Auktelchnīk seemed too real, sending a sliver of panic to his knotted stomach.

Dan-e-wåk pushed the thoughts away and reviewed his options. He was a college man with degrees in psychology, parapsychology and medicine. Over the years, his training had to come to reinforce his belief in shamanism. Taught by a village shaman in the traditional ways, he added his own spin to the practice. Foremost, he was a doctor, not in the modern sense of the word. He was a doctor with an ancient tradition, using a holistic approach to healing. When modern medicine failed,

Dark Shaman 85

herbs, psychology and mental energy normally succeeded. Occasionally, he had to indulge the whims and beliefs of his patients, yet in his profession, the mind was a powerful entity that could do just about anything. In deep trances, he focused his thoughts and sent healing energy into his patients, and at the same time, Dan-e-wåk worked as an empathic conduit, pulling the negative feelings and energies from them. Once he had these energies, he refocused them and sent them into the earth. Of course, this didn't differ much from the theories of modern medicine relating to chemical and electrical imbalances of the body. The body was resilient with its own healing properties, if directed in the right manner.

Dan-e-wåk stepped from the shower, dried off, then he wiped the mist from the mirror. His dark eyes peered out from under white eyebrows. In spite of his white hair, he saw a youthful, angular face that belied his years and experience. This experience was his weapon as he faced his greatest enemy. Years of practice in the use of psychic power would destroy Auktelchnīk and that was his edge. He wished he could bring in his good friend, Chlawūch-tschāk, another shaman, but he was in the village of Taku in southeastern Alaska. Before he left, he'd have to warn Jon George and Chlawūch-tschāk of the danger.

Dan-e-wåk slid on jeans, a plaid shirt and good hiking boots, and headed for the kitchen. He switched on the lights of the kitchen and a musty smell invaded his nostrils. He frowned, knowing this was impossible, for he kept his kitchen immaculate. As he circled the room, he passed his ancient refrigerator, his white painted cabinets, the kitchen counter worn by age and his new stainless-steel sink. At each place, he performed a sniff test, but the scent wasn't coming from any one item.

Surveying the room, his gaze fell on the Formica-topped, kitchen table's center where words were broadly scrawled across it in what appeared to be blood. "Come and Die!" Dan-e-wåk touched the writing, feeling the moist stickiness with his fingers and before he could react, the writing faded away as if it had never existed. As he moved his thumb over his index finger, the tackiness remained. Slowly, he brought his fingers his nose and sniffed, smelling the odor of rancid blood that choked him and he dropped his shaking hand. Dan-e-wåk rushed to the sink and turned on the water, but the blood had vanished from his hands. He braced himself on the counter and took several deep breaths to steady himself. He had only seen this type of manifestation once before, long ago. As he reached over to the stove to reheat the coffee, the phone rang and Dan-e-wåk jumped back like someone trying to avoid an electric wire. The phone continued its insistent ringing as he walked over to it. Instinctively, he knew it was his friend, Chlawūch-tschāk. He picked up the receiver and hoarsely said, "Yes."

"Are you all right?" a concerned and familiar voice asked.

"That you, Chlawūch-tschāk?" Dan-e-wåk asked, his voice still shaky.

"Yes, Dan-e-wåk. What happened? I sensed something was wrong." Chlawūch-tschāk said.

Dan-e-wåk told Chlawūch-tschāk of Tūtsch-gūtsch and Auktelchnīk.

"Wait for me. I can be there by noon, maybe sooner."

"I can't—my student's in danger."

"Then take my nephew, Sable, with you. He has a powerful tsāk-ssēt."

"All right, I'll wait for you," Dan-e-wåk lied.

As Dan-e-wåk hung up the phone, he knew that he had to act now, before Auktelchnīk became all-powerful. He put the coffeepot on to warm and headed to the basement to pack his rucksack. It had been a while since he had been hunting, but this time the game he was hunting was the deadliest he'd ever encountered. As he scrutinized the weapons mounted on the wall, Dan-e-wåk ignored the rifles and modern bows, for they could not kill this evil. Selecting a finely hand-crafted bow and tschunēt arrows made with eagle feathers, he checked the tautness of the draw, then took it, along with a moose hide quiver to an old varnished table. He carefully examined each arrow's shaft and covered the tips of the razor-sharp titanium blades with plastic caps. He removed his grandfather's lance from its rack on the wall and laid it beside the bow. Its spearhead was coated in the purest gold and silver. His grandfather had told him he had it made in case Auktelchnīk returned. At the time, Dan-e-wåk had scoffed at the idea. No one had ever come back from the dead. He now knew his grandfather had been right.

Although he didn't have time to go the through proper rituals of washing in a mountain stream, using a sweat lodge or even clearing his mind with sacred smoke, each step had to be followed. His morning shower had to suffice for washing away negative energy. For the sacred smoke, Dan-e-wåk pulled out sage, birch and pine incense sticks from a rickety desk drawer. He drew one out, lit it and placed it into a holder. As the smoke rose into the air, the aroma invaded the basement and he took deep breaths, inhaling the scent. With his hand, he swirled the smoke over his face and body, chanting sacred words passed down from shaman to shaman over the centuries in a language before the Tlingit language. Then, taking his weapons, he laid them on an old frayed carpet in the center of the room. He sat cross-legged in front of the weapons and began taking deep breaths through his nose and slowly exhaling. The chant reverberated in his mind as he prepared for his journey, picking up each weapon, and blessing it as he pointed it to the four corners of Mother Earth.

After finishing the ritual, Dan-e-wåk stood, picked up the weapons, gathered up his pack and added several sacred items to his medicine bag. When he was done, the bag contained eagle feathers and claws, brown bear claws, fans made from raven wings and crystal stones to help focus his power. Now all he had to do was write a letter to Jon and Chlawūch-tschāk explaining why he had left alone.

Dan-e-wåk stood before Jon George's door, his hand poised above the bell. He opened the front screen door and placed a white envelope between the door and the jamb. As he walked through the gate, an icy-cold breeze cut through him, forcing him to shiver. He snapped his jacket closed, raised his collar as protection against the wind and then continued walking.

The breeze continued past him, swirling toward the house. The wind's momentum jerked the screen door open. As it swirled again, it picked up the letter, gently carrying the envelope on its currents into the air and toward the forest.

CHAPTER 15

Inside the crowded restaurant, Sable opened the morning edition of the *Anchorage Tribune*. On its front page a photograph showed Albert Bosch, along with his attorney, leaving the Token Detachment. The headlines read: RIPPER STRIKES AGAIN. VICTIM TOLL RISES. State Troopers are still at a dead end in Ripper Murders. He'd received even more bad news early this morning when he called the detachment. The fingerprints from the killings had been run through the Automated Fingerprint Identification System--AFIS with no matches. That meant the killer had never been in the service or in jail. Another dead-end. He cursed under his breath and surveyed the room. The restaurant rumbled with conversations about the children. He focused in on the table where two women were discussing Bosch.

"You think he murdered those children?" the heavy-set one asked, holding a fork loaded with pancakes dripping syrup, poised inches from her mouth.

"They released the damned molester for lack of evidence." The other's face he couldn't see but she had long, dark hair that flowed across her shoulders.

"He's a wife beater according to the article," the first said. "For that they should cut off his balls."

Sable cringed, then motioned to the waitress. She seemed to be in her mid-50s, maybe older, with sharp angular features and thin eyebrows. She tilted her head so her thin nose was pointed at him and her pen poised over the pad. "What'll it be this morning?"

He squinted up at her nametag. It said "Inga." "I'll take your 'Slam' and coffee." Sable saw his partner enter the restaurant and he waved at Carpenter. "Make that a double order."

"Got it. I'll be back with your coffee momentarily."

"Have you had breakfast?" Sable asked.

Carpenter shook her head.

"Good. I ordered for you, I hope that's okay?"

"Not a problem. I'm too tired to think this morning." She pulled up a chair and sat.

"Rough night?"

"Yeah. Can't sleep lately worrying about the kids." Her eyes were a web of red lines, and dark circles lined her eyes.

As Inga served their food and coffee, they momentarily ceased conversation. When she left, Sable said. "I hate to admit it, but I'm at a loss on where to go from here."

Carpenter looked into her coffee, then back at him and nodded knowingly. "It'll be our luck some young trooper will stop this guy for a traffic ticket and make the bust when he sees something out of the ordinary in the car."

"One can hope," Sable said. "I hate to say it, but I think we need to bring in NecroSearch. That's the only way we'll find the rest of the children." The nonprofit organization, based out of Colorado, assisted law enforcement in the search for clandestine gravesites, using dogs and modern scientific techniques. It was a gamble that might pay off.

She picked up her coffee cup and cradled it in her hands. "I'll give them a call when we get back to the office."

After breakfast, Sable stopped at the hospital to check on Adonica Nash, but her condition hadn't changed. He prayed that she recovered even if she couldn't tell them anything on her abductor. At the office, Sable put on the reading glasses he needed more often lately, pulled out his notes and the files to do another review of the case from the bottom up. Only a few days had passed since he'd picked up the case, but the trail was very cold with no new leads. Never before had he been involved in a serial murder case of this magnitude. He remembered that one of his friends had been in on a high profile case. The killer was a carpenter named John Bates. Bates became known as the "carpenter, cabinet, coffin maker." That killer had a similar track record to this fiend. During an eight-month period, the killer was averaging a murder every other week. How could someone not see the man, especially when Kanashig was spread over just a few blocks and Token and the other small villages and towns were about the same size?

A knock on the door drew Sable from his thoughts and he looked up to see Lum. "You got another suit from the Federal Bureau of Idiots outside. Claims she's a profiler. I thought I'd better check with you before I let her in."

Sable shrugged. "Send her in."

Lum waved to someone in the hall and stepped aside to allow her to enter the room.

Sable took off his glasses, folded the earpieces and looked up as a woman briskly marched in. She was about Annelle Carpenter's age, maybe a year or two younger, but not from the same generation. Her short, firebrand-red hair framed delicate features and challenging green eyes with a slight hint of blue. She hesitated, then extended her hand. "Agent Marsha Nutall."

Sable smiled, stood and reached across the desk. "Robert Sable."

"I know. I checked your bio out before coming. I'm from the FBI's Behavioral Science Unit at Quantico."

"Where's your trench coat?" Sable asked trying to interject a bit of levity into the meeting. At least Carpenter never wore one.

"Not even the FBI wears trench coats when it's sunny out." Her smile flattened, but she kept looking into his eyes. She looked at him as if she were trying to make up her mind if he was okay or not. He was not sure if that was mentally, physically, or otherwise.

Sable nodded and motioned for her to take a seat. It had finally happened. The FBI finally taken the situation seriously and with the governor's prodding had finally expanded the case. Bringing in the FBI's BSU forensic experts who were know for tracking serial killers throughout the country was a step on the right direction.

"I was requested to provide assistance."

"I'm glad to see you here." Sable hedged and sat back in his chair, his arms folded. These days one had to be politically correct.

"I want to make one thing perfectly clear before we start out. What I do is not voodoo science. It's based on . . ."

"I know that it's based on sound behavioral science and years of investigative cases and experience."

"Sorry, I normally get a raft of shit on what I do from small-town cops."

"I'm not a small town cop." Sable was starting to enjoy this.

"Sorry, I . . .," she seemed to search for the right words.

"Does anyone know you're here other than the governor or your chiefs?"

She shook her head.

"Good. Keep it that way. I don't want the press to know you're here. We don't want any hype we have another Jack the Ripper, Ted Bundy, Zodiac or Green River Killer on our hands," Sable said, then paused. "Now, what you do think we have?"

"He's white, maybe in his early 20s and 30s and is more than likely a blue-collar worker."

For a second Sable shifted his gaze to the window and out at the forest. Duh, and what type of person would be out in the wilderness of Alaska but a blue-collar, frontiersman type.

"He's powerful since he's able to carry his victims long distances. He has a medium build, with a broad, muscular chest. He's probably done this in other states to a lesser degree and moved to Alaska to get out of the limelight. The killer harbors a murderous rage towards the Indians and ethnic groups."

Sable nodded and noted to himself, 'tell me something I don't already know.'

"He could have observed the children from a distance. He undoubtedly plays out the scenarios he's going to do with them. He's seeking revenge for an implied or actual wrong. This is racially motivated since the majority of children are dark skinned or Native. What better way than to eradicate the Indians than to destroy their children? Or maybe it's that he believed some woman in his life--a girlfriend, a mother, a stepmother wronged him as a child."

"Or he could be like the paranoid schizophrenic in Fairbanks that thought he was saving the children by killing them."

Carpenter stood in the doorway and coughed. "Or the Zodiac Killer taking up residence in the Alaskan bush. I expect him to step out of some nearby trees wearing an executioner's hood and a black bib with a circle and cross--the symbol the killer used as his calling card. And just like the Zodiac Killer's victims, our killer leaves his bodies in remote locations near well-traveled roads."

Nutall's jaw tightened and she gave Carpenter a hard look.

"Do you know each other?" Sable asked.

"No," the women said a beat apart.

Sable introduced them.

"Back to your psycho," Nutall said." "He can't compare to Countess Elizabeth Bathory, who reportedly killed over 600 girls in seventeenth-century Hungary. She used their blood to bathe in to keep her young. And I understand that she was quite fond of torture. Some believe that 'Vlad the Impaler' and the Countess were the inspiration for Bram Stoker's 'Dracula.'"

Sable shrugged. "I think we all have an equal understanding of a serial killer's mind. He was most likely physically abused as a child. So he begins to withdraw from reality. From the outside he may appear to be normal, but inside his mind, he's a whirl of sick fantasies. He begins stalking his prey. He may be a Bundy or a Zodiac and lure his victim into his clutches. He enjoys his prey's terrified reaction as the hopelessness of the situation descends upon them. The murderer gets a psychological adrenaline rush and pleasure from the putting his victim to death. At that point, he might even be having an orgasm." Sable paused to take a breath.

Carpenter slid into the chair next to Sable's desk. "Yeah, it's just like drug addicts, sexaholics and alcoholics who try to prolong the pleasure, but it's transient. They can't. So they fall into a depression, an emotional let down, and then they need to start the cycle again. In other words, like an alcoholic needs booze, to feel normal, they must kill and kill again."

"Okay, I get it. You guys aren't dumb," Nutall said as she folded her arms. "I know my stuff. The reason I got into this field was to understand the criminal mind, especially those who kill again and again without remorse."

"Point taken."

"Bottom line: Since there is no penile penetration, my guess is that we're dealing with a sexually dysfunctional male."

CHAPTER 16

In her new red Mustang, Lisa Ridell turned off the Alaskan Highway to the village of Kanashig. When she had told her friends her destination, they'd said they had never heard of it. "It's halfway between Token and Tetlin," she told them. How little her Alaskan friends knew about the state outside of their own city. Kanashig's name was derived from the Tlingit-- yán-dei yaa kanashgit, meaning 'on the verge of darkness.' Why the Tlingits would use such a name for their village puzzled her. In fact, her greatest mystery, which none of her colleagues could answer, was why the Yanayadel clan lived so far north when most of the Tlingits lived in southeastern Alaska and Canada. Yanayadel, over the years, had been derived from yan a-ya-deil meaning 'to guard.' From myth and history, it seemed that a portion of the Chilkats and Chilkoots followed a trade route north to the Athabascans—the Koyukon, Hän, Tanana and Tanacross, then decided to remain.

Lisa stepped on the accelerator and felt the power of her new car as it surged forward. With the top down, wind whipped through her soft, long dishwater blond hair and the sun reflected brightly off the interior, giving her a new sense of freedom. Her first archeological dig was several miles up the Tanana River from Kanashig. Her interest in the Alaskan Indian ran deep. Being part Cherokee herself, she felt she had to help in the preservation and protection of Indian artifacts. Two years before, at the age of 23, she had graduated from the University of Alaska at Fairbanks with doctorates in archeology and anthropology.

A team from the University on an initial visit to the village had given a strange report. Kanashig was not the typical Indian village. Somehow the villagers must have amassed sufficient wealth to entirely rebuild Kanashig. One of Lisa's colleagues had unearthed records under the Freedom of Information Acts that purported of some type of secret settlement between the Army and the Yanayadel. Still, the strangest part of the report concluded the villagers had white hair and appeared not to be over the age of thirty. Rumors abounded as to the reasons for their longevity-- everything from their diet and use of rare herbs to their having found the fountain of youth. The group had spent a month in the village. The people were open and willing to discuss the cultural heritage, but not the reason for their youthful appearance.

In the distance behind her, Lisa saw what appeared to be a large white SUV headed toward her. As it approached, a red and blue light flashed ominously from its dash. "Oh shit." She felt her throat tighten when she glanced at the speedometer--it read 90. This time she wouldn't be able to talk her way out of the ticket. She took her foot off the accelerator and the Mustang slowed.

The driver of the Suburban flashed his headlights. She pulled to the side of the road and watched the Suburban in the rearview mirror slide in behind the Mustang. She turned off the ignition, feeling the heat rise in her cheeks, took a deep breath and waited by tapping her fingers lightly on the steering wheel.

She heard the slight squeal of brakes, a door slam and the crunch of shoes on gravel as the trooper, dressed in full uniform, neared. She rolled down the window. "Good day . . ."

"License and registration please," the trooper said, his face a somber mask. "Do you know how fast you were going?"

"Ninety," she croaked and dug her wallet from her purse.

"And you know the posted speed?"

"Sixty-five, sir." Then she unsnapped the registration from the visor and started to hand both to him.

"Please take the license from the wallet."

"Yes, sir." She glanced at his nametag--it said, 'Sable.'

"What's the rush?" He examined the documents and returned the registration.

"It was a lovely day and I didn't realize . . ."

"I should cite you for ninety." He opened the ticket book, laid the license on it and began writing. "But since you didn't give me a lot of excuses, I'm putting down seventy. However, the court will probably throw it out because it falls within the allowable tolerance. You can either pay the ticket or show up to the court to have it voided."

"Thank you, Officer Sable." Her voice was barely a whisper. What was this? She was thanking him for giving her a ticket. She felt a flush of embarrassment and slight anger come over her face.

"Please drive more carefully in the future." Sable handed her the ticket to sign.

By the time Lisa pulled into the village, her anger from receiving the ticket had dissipated. She realized the trooper had really done her a favor. A large, dark cloud crossed in front of the sun and she shivered from the sudden chill. It was as if someone was trying to warn her to turn back. For weeks after she was put in charge of the project, she had had the same nightmare each night--flames flickering on a cave wall lined with petroglyphs and strange chanting in a language she didn't understand. An Indian wearing a wolf mask danced around the fire, beckoning for her to join. Lisa had told herself it was only the stress of the new assignment.

Shaking her head, she looked in the rearview mirror at her slightly freckled and tanned face. She saw worry reflected in light-brown eyes showing small flecks of swirling amber and gold. Laughing to ease her nervousness, she followed a neat line of houses along each side of the road. As she passed them, she marveled at the neatly trimmed yards, the white picket fences and vines and flowers weaving up trellises. At the center of the town, she found the council lodge and as she pulled to a stop, a handsome young man stepped out of the doorway and approached her car. "Uásse-i-tú-eti," she said, trying to give the proper greeting but knowing that she was mispronouncing it.

"Ka-denchro-denik, chetsinach tuu chrat (*My heart is strong*)," he responded.

"Good afternoon, I'm looking for Jon George," she said.

"That's me," he said.

"But I thought . . .."

"A village elder would be much older," he chuckled.

As he opened her door, she slid from the seat, drew to her five-foot-eleven height and met his gaze squarely. Lisa couldn't help but admire his striking physique. Jon's skin was a light copper, as if tanned in the sun. He wore a white shirt and black slacks that his finely sculpted body filled out with ease. Although he was not stocky, he was definitely muscular. Maybe she could get to know him better . . . then her gaze fell to his wedding band. She flashed a smile. "I'm . . ."

"Doctor Elizabeth Ridell--I've been expecting you." He offered her his hand.

"You don't have to be so formal. I like to be called Lisa." She accepted the gesture and gave his hand a quick shake.

"Then Lisa it is. Just call me Jon."

"Is there an inn or motel where I can stay?"

"Sorry, we don't have a motel, but if you don't mind, you can stay at my house. My wife, Becky, has already made arrangements," Jon said. "You can use my granddaughter's room. She recently married."

"Granddaughter? You don't look old enough to even have a daughter."

"My mind was somewhere else. I meant my daughter's room."

"Okay, but I'd like to get out to the archeological site this afternoon," Lisa said.

"There won't be a boat until morning."

"Then I'll take you up on your offer," Lisa said. "Where's your house?"

"Two blocks north on the right--201 Main."

"What if I miss it?"

"In a couple more blocks, you'll drive into the Tanana River," Jon said. "Before you leave, I want to warn you. We're having a friend over for dinner and he considers himself an amateur archeologist. You might have an interesting conversation."

"Sure, sounds great," she said and pursed her lips. How could an amateur be interesting? They normally thought they knew everything. Lisa thanked Jon, got back into her Mustang and headed up Main Street. Within minutes, she parked in front of Jon's house, wondering what else the day would bring. This house was much different from the others, being a split-level, ranch style home, trimmed in white, with a soft, reddish-brown paint. Also, Jon's charm and hospitality had caught her off balance. She hadn't met anyone so neighborly in a long time. Before she could step out of the car a gorgeous young woman with medium-length, white hair ran down the walkway from the house, flashing a bright smile. Becky had a soft tan with subtle freckling. And as she drew closer, Lisa found the woman's eyes were much like hers. Stepping from the car, Lisa found herself taller than Becky by what she guessed was four inches.

"I'm . . .." Lisa said, offering her hand.

"I know. Jon and I were expecting you, Dr. Ridell," Becky said. She clutched Lisa's hand, giving it a hearty shake.

"Just Lisa." She returned the grip. Becky had a firm, dry, no-nonsense handshake. Although the woman was exceptionally beautiful, Lisa wondered about the white hair with such a young-looking face.

"Can I help with your bags?" Becky asked.

"Sure, they're in the back seat. But I'll take the heavy duffle bag."

As Becky started up the walkway, Lisa followed, trying to keep up with the woman's stride. "I understand that you are part Cherokee--well, so am I."

"Jon must have told you a lot about me. From your hair, I thought you were Kanashig Tlingit."

"No. It's just one of the hazards of working and living in Kanashig." Sadness came to Becky's voice.

"Would you care to tell me about it?" Lisa asked.

"About the job or the village?"

"Your hair."

"No," Becky said.

For a moment, Lisa was stunned. Here was a mystery no one wanted to talk about. What would kill the melanin in the villagers' hair? She had seen people's hair turn white overnight from massive heart attacks. And she had heard of an instance documented in a medical journal of hair turning gray from fear. But an entire village? Was it a chemical in the food or water, or could a strange virus have hit the village? No, she was letting her imagination run away with her.

"Well, then, how about your job?" Lisa asked, trying to break the ice again.

"I work as a physician's assistant at the village medical clinic. You'll be surprised because our center has some of the most modern technology for its size."

"Then your village has its own doctor and hospital?"

"The doctor only visits once a month and so I handle all the minor emergencies, but the center is not large enough to be considered a hospital."

"You'll have to show it to me sometime," Lisa said, pausing. "So that's how you met Jon?"

"Yes, I met him several years after I lost my husband . . .." Becky stopped as she pushed the door open.

"Several years. You must have married at a young age."

"Something like that." Becky smiled.

Lisa stepped into the living room and admired its simplicity and neatness. It was a large, inviting room with cream-colored walls, had a floral-design sofa and love seat, an easy chair, knickknack shelf and an entertainment center. Setting her bags down, she said, "I love the way you've decorated the room."

"I didn't do it, Jon did. You see, we're still newlyweds," Becky said and then motioned toward to the hallway. "Your room is the first one on the right."

"Jon said he had a daughter."

"Gran . . . I mean daughter from a previous marriage."

"Oh, by the way, you know, you don't really have to do this. I can drive back to Token and find a motel."

"It's over sixty miles—no way you're driving back. It's no problem to stay here. Besides, Jon and I like to have guests."

Pushing through the bedroom door was a task for Lisa. First the hasp on the frame caught the duffle bag's strap and then once she got it free, she stumbled into Becky. "I'm sorry . . ."

"I should've been looking where I was going. Can I help you unpack?"

"No, thanks. I normally live out of my suitcase." Lisa placed her duffle bag on the bed. The room was spacious with a large, double bed, desk and chair and a finely crafted chest of drawers. At first, she couldn't place the wall color, but it was a light, tangerine pink. Pictures were neatly placed on the walls and desk. She felt comfortable here, but at the same time she seemed an intruder in the daughter's room.

"Well, I'll leave you to rest. If you need to freshen up, the bathroom is across the hall."

"Thanks, but I'd like to watch the news on TV except I noticed that you don't have one."

"Well, not in the front room. Jon doesn't believe in television because it leaves nothing to the imagination and rots the mind. Reading and listening to the radio exercises the mind, he says. But don't worry, there's one in the den. I couldn't live without it."

"Same here."

"Dinner's promptly at six and I'd better warn you, we are having a guest," Becky said playfully.

"Who's the guest?"

"An Alaska State Trooper, Sergeant Robert Sable. He's a long time friend of ours and is interested in archeology."

"I know. Jon mentioned him." Lisa groaned silently. He couldn't be the same rat that had given her the ticket. "Is he married?"

"He's a widower. Why?"

Were Jon and Becky trying to set her up with one of their friends or was she just being suspicious? She wouldn't mind meeting an eligible man, though not a trooper, especially not the one who had given her a ticket. And romance wasn't her primary purpose for being here. "Just curious."

"Don't worry, we aren't trying to set you up," Becky said and then she slipped out of the room.

After getting settled, Lisa wandered into the den and turned on the TV, finding that she had missed most of the news. She slid into the easy chair and she pushed the chair into a reclining position.

When the announcer looked up from his notes, he stared into the camera. Behind him in a small-framed box, a picture of a small, longhaired child graced the screen. "Early this morning, Tanak children discovered the body of ten-year old Timothy Slaymaker of Kanashig," the announcer said. The picture was replaced with an outside shot of the Token State Police station. "We now take you live to Token trooper headquarters where correspondent Angel Murphy is on the scene."

"The State Troopers are continuing their investigation of the ripper serial killings." The TV reporter spoke into the hand-held microphone. Next to the correspondent stood a handsome young man with black hair she knew was Robert Sable. A chill ran down her spine as the camera focused in on the trooper's face. Something gave her a vague premonition he was somehow tied to her dreams of the wolfman. At least Sable didn't look as imposing on television or as good looking. He looked even better.

"With me is Sergeant Robert Sable of the Alaska State Troopers." Angel Murphy stuck the microphone into the trooper's face. "Sergeant Sable, can you fill us in on what happened to Jenny Dawson and Timothy Slaymaker?" The camera again focused in on the trooper.

The trooper stepped back from the microphone and folded his hands in front of him. "Early this week, two children discovered the nude body of Jenny Dawson. A couple days later, troopers found Timothy Slaymaker. A search of the areas has yielded no new leads. However, after the medical examiner makes a determination and forensic tests are back, there may be a break in the case."

"It's rumored that the heart was removed from the victims by the ripper." Angel Murphy pushed the mike forward.

"The medical examiner is still determining the cause the death."

"But . . ..?" Angel Murphy recovered. "Is there any progress in the case?"

"We're following leads. There's been some progress, but there isn't anything new to report." Sable momentarily looked away from the camera and then back.

"Has Adonica Nash identified her attacker yet?"

Sable kept his poker face and tried to appear unfazed at the question. *How in the hell had Murphy found out about the girl?* "No, Adonica's still in a coma."

"Is Albert Bosch the ripper killer?"

"Current evidence indicates that Bosch did not kill any of the children. Now I have to get back to work."

"The public has a right to know the full extent of the investigation. There's a madman out . . ."

"We'll release more news as it develops," Sable said, abruptly turning and walking into the detachment.

The news changed to the sports and another chill ran up Lisa's spine. She had a feeling something evil was right around the corner, that somehow by exploring the caverns they had unearthed an ancient evil. Of course, that was silly. With her education and background, how could she believe in such things? Feeling tired, she stood, switched off the television and headed to the bedroom for a nap.

Soon after Lisa drifted off to sleep, she began to toss and turn as dark shadows closed in from all directions. Suddenly, she stood in a large cavern, lighted by a ceremonial fire in the center, without knowing how she got there. Flames danced and shadows clung to the walls. Large boulders were scattered across the floor. Around the fire, a lone dancing figure in decorated buckskins sang and chanted in a strange language. The mask of a wolf hid the dancer's face. In the background, Lisa could have sworn she heard drums beating, but as her eyes searched the recesses of the cavern, she couldn't see anyone else. Occasionally a Tlingit word she understood crept into the chant. The language had to be an ancient version of Tlingit that no longer existed. But how did she know this if the language was long dead and no one should know it unless . . .. She felt the sting of the figure's burning eyes pulling her in, down and down.

In spite of her resistance, the hypnotic pull was more than she could tolerate and Lisa felt her body being dragged a step closer to him, bringing the wolf-like mask into focus. The figure slipped it off, dropped it and a contorted, evil, painted face smiled. She gasped and tried to run, but her feet were frozen in place. Now he came closer and closer as the beat of the drums became a frenzy. He reached for her and she felt his burning touch . . ..

CHAPTER 17

At Sable's office, he, Carpenter and Nutall poured over case files, bouncing ideas back and forth on who the killer might be.

"This creep has to be someone new." Carpenter looked up from one the pedophile's files.

"We could have inherited him from another state," Sable said.

"That's a possibility, but this pervert seems to know the area quite well, meaning he must be from here."

The phone rang and Sable answered it, dreading what the call might bring. It was as he'd feared--the murder of another child. "Well, it looks like you get to see one of the crimes up close and personal."

"Not another child." Marsha Nutall blanched.

Sable nodded.

On the way to the scene, a tractor-trailer rig barreled down upon them from the rear, blew past them and cut them off short, forcing Sable to pull to the side of the road. Behind the truck, propelled by its wake, several leaves rode the currents of the air, dancing and spinning along the pavement. He hit the siren and turned on the flashing lights, but the trucker was long gone.

"You aren't going to let that asshole get away?" Carpenter asked, steadying herself on the dash.

"No," Sable said, then called ahead to set up a roadblock for the trucker.

Turning off the road into a copse of trees, Sable drove down a one-lane road that led to an open gate and a line of chain-link fence that spread out in both directions and disappeared into the forest. Sable casually examined the fence, noticing the wires crisscrossed to form diamonds. Tied strips of galvanized steel reinforced each link. He wondered why anyone would have such a fence until he broke from the trees and out into a gravel pit that seemed be several acres square. As he came to a stop, he ensured he parked directly behind the lead cruiser.

When he exited the Suburban, he saw the body of the child lying 30 to 40 yards down the ridge, the body twisted obscenely almost into a pretzel. He looked down at the embankment for a safe path that wouldn't cause contamination. Finally he shrugged and motioned for the others to follow. As he neared the body, he saw her gray tongue protruded from her mouth and her once dark eyes were filmed over.

Sable nodded to Benson.

"Why is it I always wind up first on the scene?" Benson grumped.

"My god," Nutall began retching, but tried to control herself.

"Not here." He clapped his hands in front of her face, trying to distract her. "Focus on me."

She turned and ran for several feet, but got no farther. She fell to her knees and vomited.

"Dead bodies after meals aren't fun," Sable said, knowing Nutall couldn't hear him.

A thorough search of the crime scene yielded little or nothing. Again they had been thwarted. The killer had left nothing. Whoever they were up against was intelligent. But occasionally even the most intelligent killer made mistakes as with Jenny Dawson and Adonica.

When Nutall returned, her face was the shade of whitewashed stucco. "This killer's a class A psychopath."

"And after that trick he pulled the other day with the National Guard, he must consider himself a god," Carpenter said.

"Well, HQ doesn't like the papers saying that we have a psycho on the loose," Benson said.

Nutall coughed and Sable thought she was going to vomit again. "Maybe the press coverage will help us. We can use it to our advantage."

"And it might draw out our killer if we slant it the right way."

"Yeah, and let the press know the children's still-steaming, beating hearts were ripped from their chests. They'd have a field day over that," Sable said.

"We could leak that the killer has deliberately made this look not only like it was the work of a madman or Satanist, but that he is following the legend of Auktelchnīk." Benson took off his glasses, folded and stuffed them in his pocket. "That might give the press a better perspective of what we're up against."

"The damn press hasn't got the slightest idea what's involved in this investigation. We're already incompetent as far as they're concerned. So, why give them the rope they hang us with?" Sable's brow furrowed as he pondered the proposal. "Okay, who wants to put their career on the line and leak the information?"

Nutall waved a hand, dismissing the idea. "Okay, okay. Point taken. We'll plan our strategy a little better."

"Sabe, we've got another hot one," Lum yelled as he slipped and slid down the hill.

"Not another child."

"No. From all appearances Bosch offed himself."

Sable shook his head. He knew that there was no way Bosch would commit suicide. He feared that that meant only one thing: one of the parents of the missing children had exacted revenge. Sable and Nutall left while Carpenter had stayed at the child's crime scene to see if she could find anything useful.

Within minutes, Sable pulled into the Musher's Rendezvous Motel parking lot. The building was constructed of red brick, stained by years of dirt and soot. Sable had left Nutall, still queasy over the child, in the Suburban. He parked in a shady spot well away from the other police cars and walked toward the building. Sable dreaded walking through the feeding frenzy to make his way to the crime scene. The press and a number of thrill seekers were ringing the three cruisers, lights flashing, already circling the motel. An ambulance just departing, its lights no longer pulsing, forced the crowd to part. The dead didn't need saving.

One of the reporters, a tall, red-haired man who was exceedingly thin, blocked his way and shoved a mike in Sable's face. "Did the child killer leave a suicide note?"

Sable didn't recognize the man, but he put up his hand to block the microphone and gave him a cold, hard stare that caused him to step out of the way. He dodged through the throng and continued toward the building. He shook his head. Why did child molesters and serial killers intrigue so many people? But he answered his own question. For many, these modern-day ogres offered a perverse thrill.

The trooper at the base of the stairs nodded. "We've got the room sealed off and the forensic team from Fairbanks is already here."

"Good. Thanks." Sable brushed past the man and headed up to the room. A rookie uniformed trooper standing near the door nodded, saying little because of Sable's rank. Before he entered, he took the normal precautions--white protective shoe covers and surgical gloves--and went in. At the door, he checked both the locks and brass striker. Neither showed scratches, tool marks or dimple marks. He stood in the doorway to take in the whole picture. In the center of the room, Bosch continued to gently rock as though propelled by a breeze. Sable's eyes darted around the room, looking for clues, trying to get a feel for what had happened.

"What have we got?"

"A maid found him a little after ten this morning," Carson said. "Said the door handle had the maid service card out. She found the front door and windows closed, and locked; nothing seemed to be disturbed." He looked back at his notepad.

"Has anyone else seen the body?"

"Yeah, the motel clerk."

"Damn. I'll want to talk to him next." Sable took a deep breath. "The press is going to have a field day on this one. Find any note?"

"Nothing."

Sable looked up at the dangling corpse. There was something wrong, something missing in the picture. He needed to take it all in, piece by piece. His eyes continued to scan the room to find what was missing more than what was out of place. Scuff marks on the rug. Chair not tipped over. Someone had faked the scene, but who? Momentarily a bright light blinded him. Nearby, a photographer was snapping pictures of the dead man. Other technicians were taking measurements for the crime scene sketches. A number of wood and tile surfaces were smudged by fingerprint powder. Another technician was vacuuming the carpeting, chairs and sofas.

Sable brought his attention back to Bosch. Moving closer to the corpse, he saw bruises on the windpipe. There was nothing gentle or beautiful about death even when it was a scumbag like Bosch, but deep down there was a sense of satisfaction that it couldn't have happened to a nicer guy. The problem was that now, he'd have to find Bosch's killer and instead of pinning a medal on him, he would have to send him away for 25 to 30. Hopefully, this killer wouldn't go after the other pedophiles. Logic dictated that it had to be one of the parents. Unfortunately, no matter how evil Bosch was, Sable was honor bound to speak for the dead even when no one else would.

Nowadays the criminal never escapes. He or she always leaves something behind--a fiber or hair with which the killer could easily be convicted. The forensic team would carefully vacuum for fibers and hair, examine them under a stereoscopic microscope, a comparison microscope, a polarized light microscope and a microspectrophotometer. This evidence would provide the first important lead in the case, possibly the most critical evidence of the entire case. Each fiber could be tracked back to an article of clothing and sometimes even the bolt of cloth it was made from. And all the crime lab would need was one hair--that hair would give the DNA of the killer.

He drew in a deep breath and exhaled. Right now, he had more pressing matters and that was to find the child slayer. If a few bad eggs got broken along the way—well . . .

Sable entered the motel office. A high school student stood behind the counter. He was tall, blue eyed, and rail-post thin with dust-colored hair that looked like an exploded cotton ball.

"How may I help you?" His voice had an asthma wheeze to it. His nametag identified him as Roger.

"I need to ask a few questions about the murder last night."

"Okay."

"Who has keys or a master to the rooms?" Sable leaned forward on the counter.

Roger shrugged. "Well the owner . . ." He took a deep breath--more wheezing. "The maids, and of course the master key is locked in the safe, but . . ."

"But what?"

"Well, the maids turn their keys in each night and they're locked in the safe."

"Is there a list of the keys?"

"Nope. The boss memorized the list."

Damn. "So how do I find the boss?"

"His name's Meyers Lebhart, lives up near the Garner Peyton homestead." Roger scribbled the phone number and address on the back of a motel card.

Sable cringed at Meyers's name. It brought back dark memories. He accepted the card and stuffed it in his pocket. "Is there a time when the desk isn't covered?"

"Well, duh. I have to take a piss or a shit sometime." Roger smirked at his attempt at levity. "But I lock up when I do."

"Did you notice any strangers at the motel last night?

"Huh?"

"Have you seen any strangers going in and out of the building?"

"Hey, man, that's all we ever get here." He smiled at his joke.

"All right, what about people not registered?"

"Officer, my boss would kick my ass if I snooped. He has a standing order that I'm not to interfere with the lodgers."

"What about delivery or repairmen?"

"Yeah, several, but I didn't keep track of any of them."

"Do you maintain any surveillance cameras?"

"Hey, you got to be kidding. Out here in the wilderness we ain't got no crime." He raised his hands in mock surrender. "Well, at least not until now. Besides Lebheart's too damn cheap."

Sable turned to leave, but asked. "Who covers the desk when you're not here?"

Roger quickly scratched his replacement's name down on another card without comment.

Sable thanked the boy and headed back to the detachment. Along the way, he dropped Nutall off at her hotel.

CHAPTER 18

A knock on the door startled Lisa and she awoke in a cold
sweat and confusion, not recognizing the room. Her bed seemed
to rock and sway, forcing her to grab the headboard for support.
Finally she remembered she was staying at the Georges. She took
a deep breath and thanked God it had been only a dream. What
worried her was that it had seemed so real.

Another knock on the door brought Lisa fully awake. "Yes,
what is it?"

"It's dinner time." Becky's voice drifted through the door.

Lisa glanced at her watch. She had been asleep for several
hours, when she had meant only to take a twenty-minute nap. "I'll
be right out."

Quickly wiping the sleep from her eyes, she walked to the
vanity, brushed her hair and checked her herself in the mirror.
Not quite presentable, but it would have to do. Cocking her head,
she glanced one last time in the mirror, smiled and turned toward
the door. As she turned the knob, Lisa heard lively conversation
from the dining room. For some reason, she felt like an intruder,
sneaking up on a conversation she shouldn't hear.

Before she turned the corner, she paused to listen. The trio
talked in hushed tones.

"Anymore new outbreaks of the virus?" asked the young
man she assumed had given her the ticket. She felt as if a large
weight had dropped into her stomach.

"Oh, about every six months or so," Becky said.

"No one outside the village, I hope," Sable said.

"It no longer seems contagious and we've kept it
contained," Jon said.

"Have the children contracted it?"

"Yes, but it's latent until they reach puberty, some even as late 19 or 21."

Lisa couldn't help but wonder what virus they were talking about, but felt guilty for eavesdropping. Stepping back down the hallway, she coughed and then walked to the dining room. She entered and Jon and the young man stood. She recognized Sable immediately as he flashed a toothy smile and shrugged. Robert Sable had scrambled her senses. Her eyes told her that he was a stranger, a very handsome stranger, yet her heart told her something else entirely, that he could be more than a friend. She was about to seat herself when Sable came around the table and pulled out her chair and as she accepted the gesture, he gently pushed the chair in. She tried to remember the last time she'd met someone who practiced this quaint courtesy.

With a wave of his hand, Jon said, "This is Robert . . .."

"I know, we met earlier this afternoon . . .," Lisa said.

"Doctor Ridell, I presume," Sable said and chuckled nervously, wondering why he felt as if he were back in high school asking a girl out for a date. "I gave her a ticket for speeding,"

"You didn't," Becky said.

"I did—she was doing ninety . . ."

"I know you were just doing your job." She looked at Becky and Jon. "He cited me for doing seventy."

She turned to him. "I'm Lisa."

"Glad to meet you." He smiled, then offered her his hand, which she accepted grudgingly. "Jon already told me about you. And it's all good."

"Flattery still won't get you on my good side."

"Well, it's still a pleasant surprise in spite of the ticket. Until I pulled you over, Jon had me expecting a crusty old archeologist." When Sable realized he was still holding her hand, he released it.

"Well, then Robert . . .," Lisa said, feeling a little uncomfortable from the meeting. Suddenly, she felt light-headed and weak in the knees and she was glad she was seated. Her best guess was that it was her body's response to his pheromones. Why couldn't he be ugly? Ugly she could handle.

"Just plain Sable."

"Then Sable it is. I understand you consider yourself an amateur archeologist." Lisa sipped her drink, her eyes on Sable's face.

"Not really," he said, returning to his seat. "It's just that I've read several books on the profession and various digs."

"Well, what do you think of this most current site?"

"From what I hear, it's interesting and I'd like to visit it."

"I'll see what I can do," she said, realizing that she had been ignoring her hosts. She felt a flush of embarrassment come to her face. Looking from Jon to Becky, she added, "Of course, if it works out, you're invited, too."

Jon and Becky declined, begging off with other responsibilities, but, as she feared, Sable accepted, and it gave her both pleasant and uneasy feelings. Before she became too lost in thought, Lisa heard Becky say something about passing the food around.

"If you don't eat anything, we'll have to throw the leftovers to the bears," Jon said, grinning.

"Bears?" she asked.

"A form of levity around here," Sable said. He took a healthy helping of roast duck and passed the platter to Jon. His gaze kept returning to Lisa and he tried to pretend not to notice Lisa eyeing him.

From Jon, Lisa received a bowl of fried potatoes. She murmured her thanks and selected a small portion of the duck and laid it on her plate. Its enticing aroma suggested a special blend of herbs and spices--she wondered if they were Native American. After the duck, Lisa took a slightly larger serving of the asparagus, peas and carrots. She hated to be weight-conscious, but if she wasn't careful, it seemed everything turned into fat. Digging into her food, she ate slowly, trying to savor each morsel.

Dark Shaman

"I understand you graduated with several degrees. I've a friend who did the same thing," Becky said.

Lisa still felt a little apprehensive in her new surroundings and it seemed Becky was trying to draw her out. "Just the two--anthropology and archeology. But I have minors in chemistry, physics and mathematics."

Jon dabbed his mouth with his napkin and pushed himself away from the table. "Another excellent dinner, dear."

"You should know dear, you cooked it." Becky laughed, leaned over and whispered to Lisa, "Jon rarely lets me go near the kitchen."

Lisa raised an eyebrow--a man that could cook was as rare as finding ice worms in glacier ice. She hoped she would be as lucky in finding a husband, though she wasn't seriously looking. She had her career to think of.

"Let's have some coffee in the living room." Jon pushed himself away from the table.

They left the dining room and started down the hallway. Sable accidentally brushed against Lisa so closely he could feel her warmth and smell the sweetness of her perfume. He felt his heart skip a beat. Once in the front room, Lisa sat next to Becky while Jon sat in the Stratolounger and Sable sat in the love seat. The men continued to talk about hunting and fishing, Lisa found she was becoming a little bored.

As Lisa continued talking about her schooling to Becky, she heard Jon and Sable speaking in low tones about an ancient myth and the cavern her uncle and the university's archeological team were investigating. She tried to listen while still talking to Becky. She looked into her coffee, then at Sable.

"If I wasn't a rational man, I'd say that the spirits are angry at us for disturbing the peace of the caves," Jon said.

"I agree, but my uncle wouldn't," Sable said.

"I believe the cavern is the home of an evil ícht'a my people killed centuries ago, but I can't say whether the story is based on fact or not." Jon spread his fingers apart and examined his hands. "It all began at least a millennium ago. A shaman, Auktelchnīk, who sacrificed a number of young children. He

killed young children to drink their spirits and ate their hearts to
stay young. The villagers caught him and killed him. Over the
years the myth was embellished and added to until his powers
became extraordinary. According to the legend, he was immortal
until his people discovered his macabre practices."

A thought came to him that defied rationality--there was a
killer out in the Alaskan bush trying to live the legend of
Auktelchnīk. Sable asked, "Were the children's chests cut open?"

"I don't know," Jon said. "Like I said, he took the hearts
and used them in a special ceremony."

"Well, how about this? Someone, maybe Tūtsch-gūtsch, is
trying to mimic the legend to gain this power. Didn't you say you
believe he found the cave of Auktelchnīk?" Sable asked, then
paused, seeing a frown on Jon's face. "Go ahead with the story."

"The legend continues that the villagers, in secret, brought
in the most powerful shamans they could find from the outlying
villages to destroy Auktelchnīk. First, the shaman performed
sacred rites on the bows, arrows, lances and axes so the warriors'
aim would be true. Then each warrior went through a special
purification ceremony so Auktelchnīk could not cloud or
misdirect his mind. After a several-mile chase, the warriors
cornered Auktelchnīk on a cliff. The leader cut off the shaman's
head and the warriors buried the head and body separately."

"Did they ever find the skull?" Sable asked, doubt coloring
his voice.

"Yes, or at least I think Dan-e-wåk did, but I think he
reburied it."

"I'd like to see it sometime, maybe have the crime lab run
some tests. They could give a carbon dating on the skull."

"I don't think it should be disturbed," Jon said.

"Besides, it couldn't really be the shaman's skull for it
would have turned to dust by now," Sable said.

"Why not? Most Indians believe in the power of a shaman's
skull." Jon shrugged.

Lisa found it hard to keep track of both her conversation and Sable's. This was great--an ancient story the other team of anthropologists and archeologists hadn't yet cataloged.

"So your grant covers the investigation of the site for the summer only?" Becky took a sip of her coffee.

"Yes. Hopefully, the university will seek funding for next year, if we make good progress this year," Lisa said. She was disappointed because Jon and Sable had started talking about hunting and fishing. Maybe later she could entice Jon into telling other legends.

Whispering into Becky's ear, Lisa asked, "Aren't we going to have anything stronger as an after-dinner drink?"

"No," Becky said quietly. "Jon believes that alcohol destroys the mind, so we don't keep any in the house. The hardest drink in the house is either coffee or cola."

"Then make it a Diet Coke."

"Tell me about your job at the university," Sable said, catching Lisa off guard.

"I'm afraid it wouldn't be interesting to an outsider," Lisa said, pausing. "I'm an associate professor of archeology at the University of Alaska." A strange thought entered her mind--if she needed a drink so much, maybe she was becoming an alcoholic like her parents had been. She had stayed away from it while in school for that very reason and was now only a social drinker, using it on weekends to relax. Still, whenever she felt the need for a drink, she stopped drinking in fear of becoming an alcoholic. She tried to bury the thought and concentrated on Sable's face. Lisa was glad that she was sitting next to Becky. Sable's raven hair and steely gray-blue eyes enticed her and even his smile seemed perfect as he flashed her a grin. She definitely could get to like this man in spite of the speeding ticket.

"Actually, I believe teaching would be exciting--being able to mold students' minds into new ways of thinking," Sable said.

"Sorry, most of the molding occurs in the elementary school system. By the time a professor gets them, there's little chance to change what they believe."

"I disagree," Jon interjected, "As long as one is willing to learn, behavior patterns and learning can be changed. It's up to the teacher to excite the change."

"It's that I'd rather be in the field compared to being stuck in the classroom."

The conversation slowly shifted to politics, then religion, and then back to hunting and fishing. During a lull in the conversation, Becky brought out coffee and blueberry pie.

"Is that all you can ever talk about?" Becky yawned.

Sable grinned. "You're right and I have to be up bright and early tomorrow. What time do you want me here?"

Lisa looked at Jon and cracked an eyebrow.

"How about four in the morning?" Jon asked with a smirk. He had his elbows on his knees, hands out in front of him, cradling a large mug of steaming coffee.

"Remember, this is not a hunting or fishing trip." Sable stood and stretched.

"Okay, I'll give you a break. How about 6:30?"

"Only if that offer includes breakfast." Sable got a nod from Jon and then walked over to Lisa and offered his hand. "It was a pleasure to meet you."

As Lisa stood, she felt her knees weaken. Gazing into his eyes, she accepted his hand for a moment, fighting the urge to pull him near. She still couldn't get over how handsome he was. He probably had numerous women friends and wouldn't even consider giving her a chance.

"The pleasure was all mine," she said huskily.

"Then I'll see you bright and early."

CHAPTER 19

Auktelchnīk stepped naked into the night. He felt the cool evening air caress his face and breathed in the scent of spruce and birch trees. As he started running, his profile slunk toward the ground, metamorphasizing as fur covered his skin. It was good to be alive, for slowly but surely his power was returning and so was his memory. What he wanted was Tūtsch-gūtsch's body--to displace his spirit. The body was young, powerful, and handsome. In a few more rituals, he would have complete possession of boy's psyche. He'd have to wait until the summer solstice to accomplish the task, but that was only three nights away. The summer solstice--24 hours of daylight where the sun and moon would align in the sky with the other planets. The combined forces of the alignment would bring him to the zenith of his power. In ancient times, his power had been greatest when the sun had been in the sky all day. During the winter solstice, days of almost complete darkness made his powers weaken.

For several months, he had fought for the young man's body, but the boy's spirit had been very strong and he was unable to displace it. Over the last year his accomplishments had been great. By eating the beating hearts of young children, his body used the nutrients and hormones to gain control of his new life. The real power came from absorbing the energy of their souls and that energy would allow him to live another hundred years before he'd have to sacrifice again. Salivating at he thought of the children, he mentally replayed the act of ripping the beating hearts from their chests. At that moment, he recalled feeling the electrifying charge of the dance—the sacred words and the increase of power as he bit into the child's quivering heart.

The need to continue the killing was gone--modern science had made him virtually immortal. He knew everything Tūtsch-gūtsch knew, for the man's blood now flowed through his veins.

A virus--how it worked he did not understand--had escaped from some military laboratory, infecting an entire village. Although much of the basic concept escaped his mind, the young man's body was infected with it and had the ability to constantly repair any damage to itself. The only way he, Auktelchnĭk, could die was to have his head removed. It had happened centuries ago when the shamen from the neighboring villages united against him. After centuries of darkness, Tūtsch-gūtsch had brought him back to life in a special ceremony.

His anger flared as he remembered his enemies and past wrongs, but the smell of the caribou's hot blood brought him back to the present. He increased his speed to keep up with the frightened bull caribou, laughing and howling. He regretted his ancient enemies were not alive so he could enjoy his revenge. He was alive in a new era to explore and dominate. This time his sights were not set on an insignificant village, but on the world itself. He leaped and sank his fangs into the jugular of the caribou and ripped.

CHAPTER 20

Chlawūch-tschāk mulled over the conversation he'd had with his friend Dan-e-wåk the day before. He sensed Dan-e-wåk had lied. Looking at his watch, he saw it was 4:30 a.m. and knew he had to call Sable. Quickly, he dialed his nephew's home telephone number in Token, but his only reward was the insistent ringing of the phone and the metallic response of an answering machine. If Sable wasn't at home, he had to be at work. He clicked the receiver and dialed the trooper station.

After a few rings, a gravelly voice said, "Token Trooper headquarters, this is Sergeant Raferty. How may I direct your call?"

"This is Richard Gray Eagle, Sergeant Sable's uncle. It's urgent that I get a hold of him immediately."

"Just a second."

Chlawūch-tschāk heard only an occasional crackle of static on the line. He paced back and forth around the table, worrying the cord as he waited.

The phone clicked. "I'm sorry, Sergeant Sable is out for the weekend."

"Is there any way I can get a message to him? This is an emergency."

"The sergeant's out in the bush. You can leave a message and he'll get it bright and early Monday. Can anyone else help?"

"Please let him know that I will be going to Kanashig to see Jon George," Chlawūch-tschāk said.

"Sure enough. I'll personally give him the message."

"Thank you." Chlawūch-tschāk hung up the phone and mentally made a list of what he needed to take. He'd call Jon later in the morning from Fairbanks. Maybe Jon would know where his nephew was.

CHAPTER 21

Sable's digital watch flashed green at him with the time, 5 a.m. In an hour, he would see Lisa again. He'd awakened in the middle of the night, thinking about her. Whistling, he combed his shower-damp hair and looked at his reflection in his wardrobe mirror, feeling like a new man. Maybe it was the five-mile run he had just finished or his renewed interest in the opposite sex. In a way, Lisa reminded him of Amy and Janet, but he didn't want to fall into that trap again. Though Lisa was beautiful, he questioned her maturity. Sable stepped back from the mirror, adjusted the silver buckle on his belt and checked his attire--nothing spectacular, just a green plaid shirt, jeans and hiking boots. He was ready for the first archeological adventure since the death of his wife.

A chill suddenly went down his spine and he felt the pull of the tsāk-ssēt, drawing him to the drawer where it lay. He walked over to the dresser, opened the drawer, and picked up a light tan leather pouch that hung on a braided necklace. Though holding the pouch inches away, he realized that he'd never felt such an intensity of heat, letting him know that danger was extremely close. When he retrieved the stone, he pulled it from its leather pouch. He had never been sure what gave the talisman its power. Now, as he gazed down at the stone, he marveled at the swirling, colored lights flashing with different intensities. Were his mood swings linked to its rhythmic intensity? He wasn't sure. The talisman seemed to focus his extra-sensory powers, alerting him when evil was close by.

Early in his teens, Sable's shaman talents had begun to bloom. Then suddenly, he had dropped the shaman training to become a trooper. Though his uncle, the village shaman, had respected his choice, his mother hadn't and constantly nagged him every chance she got. For years, he had buried his talents, but since finding the tsāk-ssēt, his powers had begun to resurface.

Sable had found the tsāk-ssēt in a cavern south of Juneau, clutched in the mummified hands of an ancient shaman. Though he had left the stone where he found it, a ruthless criminal had stolen it from the tomb. Later, Sable recovered the stone and had meant to return it, but his uncle, Chlawūch-tschāk, had disagreed, believing rightful heritage was with a member of the village. He had then tried to give the stone to Chlawūch-tschāk, but he had refused because a link had already been forged with his nephew.

Occasionally, Sable had used it to aid him when he sensed danger. Now, it seemed to have a will of its own, as if it desired to be taken along. When he slipped the amulet into its container, the lights winked out but the stone's power continued resonating through his body.

In a matter of minutes, Sable stepped out his front door. The chilled morning air on his face invigorated him and offered a new adventure.

****

Before Sable could knock, the door opened, and in the doorway stood Jon. He was never sure how Jon sensed his presence, but somehow they were linked.

"You're late. It's about time you arrived," Jon said cheerfully.

"What do you mean late? I'm half an hour early," Sable said, glancing at his watch, then realized Jon had been pulling his leg.

"Come on in and make yourself homely." Jon flashed a broad smile, closing the door behind Sable, bowing and gesturing for him to proceed. "What did you dream last night?"

"I didn't dream," Sable said. "Is Lisa up and ready to go?"

"Not yet. I see you've already taken a liking to her," Jon laughed as he followed Sable to the kitchen.

"She's lovely, but just a little too young for me." Sable felt the heat rise in his cheeks and his mouth become dry.

"You know that age doesn't really matter. Look at me."

"But you're on your second childhood."

"It pays to be young at heart when you're over eighty."

"And only look twenty-five," Sable said mockingly as he seated himself at the kitchen table.

Jon grabbed a cup from the cupboard and then lifted the coffee pot from the stove. "But I was talking about you."

"If you mean am I going to ask her out to dinner or a movie, I'm not sure yet."

"You need a respite from your loneliness." Jon filled Sable's cup and placed it in front of him.

Swirls of steam rose from the coffee's black, shiny surface, bringing its aroma to liven his taste buds. Taking a sip of coffee, Sable paused and savored the flavor. "I'm not out to play the field or look for a serious commitment."

"That doesn't mean that you can't be friends."

"I'll consider it." Sable took another sip of coffee. "Well, where's the breakfast that you promised?"

"Consider what?" Becky asked, stepping into the room.

"Jon's trying to be a matchmaker again," Sable said as the frying pan Jon was working on began to sizzle.

"I don't blame him. You need a friend." Becky hugged him and gave him a peck on the cheek.

"I have lots of friends, including you two."

"That's different." Becky smirked.

"Don't tell me you're trying to pair me off too."

"Sure, why not?" Jon asked.

"I know when I'm outnumbered. You're hopeless," Sable said. Today would be interesting.

CHAPTER 22

The cabin cruiser sliced through the meandering Tanana water, its engines roaring and merging with the whine of its jet impellers, sending a low vibration through the deck plates and hull. A white rooster tail arched into the air at the stern of the boat, dividing the stern wake, the spray picking up the early morning rays of the sun and bursting into prisms of color in the air. Nonchalantly, the skipper guided the boat from cutbank to cutbank, following the main channel of the river. Oblivious to the piloting, Sable settled into his seat against the gunwale and enjoyed the passing scenery of forests that seemed to melt into meadows. The meadows merged into dense foliage that climbed high hills, and finally swept upward from the river. A large moose at the water's edge challenged their approach, inclined his antlers and took a few steps forward. Lisa, white-faced, was nestled next to him, trying to avoid the sting of wind from the boat's speed. Sable couldn't help but feel her nearness and while it warmed him. He shivered though he wasn't cold at all. It had been almost a year since he'd been this close to a woman. Sable leaned over and yelled, "Beautiful scenery, don't you think?"

Lisa looked back, puzzled, and yelled, "What did you say?"

Sable lifted a flap of her hearing protectors and repeated his question.

"It certainly is, but does he have to go so fast?"

"It only seems that way because we're on water. We're only doing 45."

"It still seems too fast."

The boat suddenly jagged to the left and Lisa was thrown across Sable's lap, where he caught her in his arms. As he held her, he could feel the warmth of her body through her thin, red windbreaker, while her alluring scent invaded his nostrils. As he looked down, her soft, brown eyes beckoned him. Realizing he held her too long, he gently pushed her upright. "Don't worry, we'll be there in a few minutes." He cleared his throat and ran his hand through his hair.

"It seems we're already here," she said.

The engine whine decreased and the skipper maneuvered against the deep bank, keeping the boat under sufficient power to nullify the river's current. As the boat thudded against the bank, the skipper announced, "We're here."

"Are you sure?" Sable looked around. Only a few scraggly spruce trees lining the edge of the riverbank were there to meet them.

"This is where I dropped off the last group. When do you want me back?"

"Five, Sunday." Sable removed the hearing protectors and handed them to the man.

"For both of you?" the driver asked, looking at Lisa.

"Just him."

"Well, the next trip will be next Saturday."

"Then next week it is." She lifted her pack over the gunwale and placed it on the bank.

Sable placed his pack next to Lisa's and vaulted over the gunwale. He offered his hand to assist her, but she waved him away. When they were safely ashore, the skipper turned the boat's bow downstream and began adding power. Quickly the boat leaped up on step and within seconds disappeared from sight.

"Where do we go from here?" Sable shrugged on his backpack. "You have the map."

"Five miles west, to the base of the mountains," she said, taking the map from her checkered shirt's pocket.

"Then let's go for it." After he snapped the buckles of his pack, he helped Lisa slip into hers.

As Lisa spread out the map and looked at the mountains, she selected a point on the map with her finger, and said, "I think we're here."

Sable looked over her shoulder at the map, took out his Lensatic compass and flashed a bearing to the mountain. "I thought archeologists knew how to read maps."

A blush rose to Lisa's cheeks, and she said emphatically, "We do."

"You're slightly off. We're here," he said, pointing to a river bend on the map that was a couple hundred meters farther south.

Her eyes flashed anger. "Only a couple hundred meters. What makes you think so?"

"Try this." Sable handed her the compass.

As she glanced up at the mountain, she took a bearing, compared it to the map and then snapped the compass case closed. "We're 'still' heading for the highest peak out of the three mountains. Now, let's go," she said, anger clouding her voice.

"It was an easy mistake to make. I'd have made the same mistake if I hadn't used the compass."

"I'll tell you the easy way, Mr. Trooper--follow the tracks."

"Ouch, that hurt."

A smile crossed Lisa's face. "Do you want to lead the way?"

"No. You do the honors."

"Good, then if I see any bears, I'll let you be the main course."

"No need to worry. I'm well prepared." Sable patted the .44 magnum on his hip.

They had taken only a few steps when a tremendous unseen force blocked Sable's way and he felt the talisman's heat vibrating through its leather pouch. A hulking Indian, wearing buckskins appeared on the trail, blocking his way. Streaks of black, white and red zigzagged his face. The stranger's white hair glistened in the morning sunlight with strange luminescence.

As Sable slid into a defensive karate stance, the Indian hefted and threw a spear. Sable retreated forty-five degrees, throwing a knife hand block to deflect the spear. His hand landed on empty air as the lance passed. The man rushed Sable and he leapt to the side, only to find that the figure had also disappeared. The ghost of a man he'd never met threatened him.

Lisa looked over her shoulder and called, "What are you waiting for?"

Still stunned by the apparition, Sable didn't answer for a moment. What was happening? Was his ESP surfacing or was it his imagination? Apparently, she hadn't see anything and of course, there was no need to worry her, though chills were still running up and down his spine. Clearing his throat, he started walking. Maybe he'd been working too hard with little sleep or food. If he didn't slow down, he'd be headed in one direction--the psychiatrist's couch. "Sorry, I was just thinking."

"If you continue that, I'll leave you behind." She was a strong-willed woman--like most of the women he knew.

For about twenty minutes they trudged through the low grass and brush in silence. He was still disturbed by the apparition of the Indian. What did it mean? It had been only a couple days since he'd used the talisman and had a horrific vision. Visions didn't just happen. They came when he had forebodings of someone close to him being in danger. It didn't make sense. Putting the thoughts from his mind, he tried to keep track of the trail and the possibility of surrounding dangers.

Occasionally, they neared a wet swamp and had to skirt the area, making progress slow and difficult. As the ground rose steadily toward the mountains, they walked through, around and over hummocks. Sable found himself starting to breathe hard, cursing the five-mile jog he'd run earlier. "You seem to be at ease in the field," Sable said, trying to control his breathing.

"That's what I trained for." Lisa didn't even look over her shoulder. "I also love to go backpacking, camping and fishing-- the more remote, the better."

"How long have you wanted to be an archeologist?" Sable pulled a handkerchief from his back pocket and wiped away the sweat forming on his brow.

"As long as I can remember."

"Have you had a chance to visit many sites?"

"My father was an archeologist and used to drag me and my mom to all his digs. In fact, he started when I was about four."

"Is that why you specialize in Native American artifacts and history?"

"It was my father's specialty."

"Did your father ever make any major finds?"

"He accidentally found a Viking warship buried in a large cave in Newfoundland."

"Accidentally. What do you mean, accidentally?" Sable glanced over his shoulder. The hairs on his neck began to prickle, giving him the feeling they were being followed.

"His expedition was excavating the remains of an Indian village when they found it."

"I remember reading something about that. Weren't the Vikings buried in full battle dress, standing or sitting at their stations?"

"Yes. It's still a mystery who buried them. There didn't seem to be anyone missing out of the ship's complement." Lisa stumbled over a clump of swamp grass, but caught herself.

"It's logical there had to be another Viking ship."

"That still doesn't explain how they died. There wasn't a mark on them and the forensic scientists didn't find a reason."

"Someday, I'd like to visit the cave and exhibition," Sable said and a chill ran down his spine. The air seemed heavy, cold, and stifling with the subtle stench of death. "Have you noticed anything strange with our hike?"

"No. Why?"

"I haven't seen any animals and for the last half a mile and I haven't heard a single bird chirping."

Lisa turned. "I hadn't noticed."

"What about the air?"

"It seems nice and crisp. Why?" She looked at her watch then she continued walking as though nothing was happening.

The closer Sable moved to the mountain, the more resistance he felt. He couldn't determine whether his perception was real or imagined, but he felt something was wrong. Around his neck, the talisman vibrated steadily, its warmth growing and resonating throughout his body. Controlling his voice, he said, "Maybe it's just me."

Lisa gave him a suspicious look and they continued on. The rest of the trip was made in silence.

CHAPTER 23

Although the sun was high in the sky, Chlawūch-tschāk still felt a morning chill. As he approached Jon's house, the aroma of cooking wafted through an open window. Inhaling deeply, he stepped to the door and knocked.

A surprised look crossed Jon's face as he opened the door and, slowly, his lips curled into a smile as he grabbed and hugged Chlawūch-tschāk. "I didn't expect you so soon. Only you and Dan-e-wåk can sneak up on me."

"Not true. This time I wanted to be invisible to your mind."

"Klēd-jēlch *(White Raven)*, Uásse-i-tú-eti?"

"Call me Jon. You know me—I'm good." Jon sighed. "You're in time for brunch. Becky went to the store for maple syrup—when she returns, she'll be glad to see you."

"And you're not glad?"

"Of course I'm always glad to see you. It's been a long time."

Chlawūch-tschāk stepped through the door, stepped back and scanned Jon. "You're a sight for sore, old eyes."

"As I told you before, I can remedy that. Become my blood brother."

"Become as young as you? I'd cheat my destiny." Chlawūch-tschāk frowned and moved to the front room couch. The offer was seductive, but to live forever was a great responsibility. What would happen if he became tired of living and wanted to die? Who would take his head?

"Your destiny hasn't been written yet. Just consider it," Jon said. "Let's go to the kitchen."

"Lead the way."

"To what do I owe the pleasure? You were kind of vague on the phone." Jon strolled into the kitchen and across to the cabinets. "Coffee?"

"Black." Chlawūch-tschāk sat at the table and brought Jon up to date.

"So you're looking for Dan-e-wåk and Sable." Jon poured the coffee and handed Chlawūch-tschāk a cup. "I can give Dan-e-wåk a call . . .."

"He's not home. He's gone out after Tūtsch-gūtsch."

"That's not possible, he'd have told me."

"I feel that he left you a message, but it never got to you." Jon appeared puzzled. "Sable, I can help you with. He's gone to an archeological dig up the Tanana."

"Where is it and how can I get there?" Chlawūch-tschāk cradled the cup in his hands and hunched over the table.

"I'll take you, but first I've got a little work to do on my boat."

"How long?" Chlawūch-tschāk was worried about both Dan-e-wåk and Sable. Somehow, he sensed his nephew was destined to clash with Auktelchnīk. He wanted to be with Sable when it happened.

"Only a couple of hours. Sorry, there's no faster way. Most of the charter boats are filled up this time of the year. Relax, have lunch with me and Becky."

****

Chlawūch-tschāk watched a large silver jet boat, pushed by the muddy-green waters of the Tanana, thudding gently against its mooring. Eddies in the current cascaded from the boat's stern as the water lapped by. Emblazoned amidships, above the gunwale was the name Silver Falcon. The boat reminded him of his jet boat he used on the Taku.

Stepping from the dock into the boat, Chlawūch-tschāk admired the construction. "I like your boat's name. It signifies grace, agility and strength."

"It's the fastest boat on the river." Jon's voice was muffled. His head was buried in the engine compartment and his body snaked over and around the engine.

"How much longer?"

"A couple of minutes." Jon raised his hand back over his shoulder. "Please hand me the flat tip."

Chlawūch-tschāk pulled a flat tipped screwdriver from the toolbox and laid it in Jon's hand. Jon turned a setting on the carburetor and pushed himself up. "That does it, we're ready."

Chlawūch-tschāk handed Jon a rag from the box, and he used it to rub the grease and oil from his hands. "As soon as you clean up," Chlawūch-tschāk chuckled and pointed to grease smudges on Jon's face. "You're well oiled."

"No matter. So long as it stays on the outside."

"A little grease and oil in one's diet never hurt anyone. It keeps you lubricated." The corners of Chlawūch-tschāk's mouth twitched.

Jon walked to the helm and switched on the blowers and turned the ignition key. "I figure you must drink at least a quart a day." Jon cranked the engine over several times, but it didn't start.

"What's wrong?"

"Nothing should be." Jon retreated to the engine compartment and pulled the distributor cap.

"Well?"

"Someone stole the rotor."

"Got an extra?"

"Yeah, sure," Jon said slowly. "What puzzles me is who'd steal it. At least no one I know from the village."

Within minutes, the engine roared to life. Jon maneuvered the Silver Falcon away from the dock and gradually pushed the throttle forward.

"Are you sure you know where we're going?'

"Do you really need to ask that question?"

"No." Chlawūch-tschāk stood next to Jon as the roar of the engine increased. He watched the RPMs rise. The stern dug deeply into the water as the bow pointed into the air, then breaking free, the boat leaped onto step.

CHAPTER 24

"It's about time you got here." A deep, jovial voice came from Sable's right as they entered a large clearing. Surrounding the campsite were several large tents set back about forty feet from the entrance of a large cavern. A large, hulking, dark-haired man wearing a gray shirt, jeans and dust-brown, scuffed hiking boots approached them.

Lisa shrugged off her pack, laid it on the ground, huffing. "I'm only a day late," she said, placing her hands on her hips. "As I recall you were late the last time . . ."

"It's good to see you." The man's hazel eyes twinkled as he bear-hugged Lisa, lifting her from the ground and swinging her around.

"Put me down!"

The man ignored her and gave her another swing.

"Uncle . . ."

Her uncle set her down and faced Sable. "Who do we have here?" The man's face became somber and challenging yet a twinkle remained in his eyes. "Let me guess." He stroked his chin. "Ah, I know a college boyfriend, no . . . a lover possibly."

"Please . . ." Lisa's cheeks reddened as she massaged her back where the pack straps had been. "He's not . . ."

Sable felt the heat rise in his cheeks as he pondered the idea.

"She protests too much. If Lisa won't introduce me, I will." The uncle stepped forward and offered Sable his hand. "Name's Martin Ridell."

"Doctor Ridell." Lisa corrected.

"Martin," her uncle said.

"Robert Sable—but just call me Sable." He took Martin's hand and grimaced as the man applied pressure; every bone in his hand seemed to be disintegrating under the vise-like grip. "I see archeology must be a family thing."

"For generations." Martin released Sable's hand, nodded to the .44, and smiled. "You're her bodyguard?"

"No. Just an amateur archeologist." Sable tried to casually flex his hand. Then he slipped off his pack and propped it against one leg.

Martin scowled at Lisa. "I told . . ."

"I know what you're thinking, but he's a friend of Jon's and a state trooper. He gave me a speeding ticket."

Martin's smile returned and he said, "Ah now I see. He's kind of cute and you're trying to fix the ticket."

"Can't I get any respect . . ."

"Not since I became your surrogate father."

"Really, I'm just here as a casual observer." Sable shrugged.

"You'll have to forgive my . . ."

"Forgive, nothing. Lisa and I banter like this all the time." Martin roared with laughter. "And forget that casual observer stuff. We can always use an extra pair of hands. Since you're here I'm going to work you until your hands bleed."

"I'd be glad to help."

"But he might . . .," Lisa protested.

"Nonsense. He'll do just fine." Martin said, then motioned to Lisa. "Why don't you put your gear away and I'll show him his tent."

Sable grabbed his pack and followed Martin to a large rectangular, blue-green nylon tent. Martin had to fold almost in half to pass through the flaps. Ducking, Sable stepped in and looked around. A row of cots lined the far wall, each with its own footlocker. "Army issue?"

"Possibly. It's not the Ritz--university funding, you know."

"That's okay, I've seen worse. Which is mine?"

Martin nodded toward the bunks at the east wall. "You can have any one of the three at the end."

"Thanks." Sable tossed his pack and gear on the one of the cots.

"She doesn't seem to like you very much." His grin widened.

Sable didn't know how to respond to the comment. It could be taken several ways.

Lisa poked her head through the door flap. "What's taking you so long? I'm ready to see the cave."

"Give the man . . .," Martin said.

"No problem," Sable said. "I'm ready. Lead the way."

"You'll be surprised at the dig." As Lisa was about to enter the cavern, she looked out over the forest, her eyes trying to transcend its depths. She stiffened as she saw the shadow of a man moving in and out of the trees in the dimness. Occasionally he stopped, looked as though he was watching her, then continued on his way. As she continued to watch the figure, she saw something that looked like a bow and arrow. Lisa froze. Ahead of her, looking out from behind a tree was an Indian dressed in buckskins. She vaguely recalled seeing him elsewhere, but couldn't place it. His dark, tanned face observed her as if she were his next meal.

"You okay?" Sable asked.

She glanced at Sable. "Did you see . . ." Her voice trailed off.

"See what?"

She looked back and the Indian was gone. "Nothing. I thought that I saw something."

Sable studied the cavern's opening. It was an elliptical shape with a massive pile of boulders on each side. "How many did it take to move that one?" Sable pointed to the largest one, which could have doubled for a full-size station wagon.

Martin frowned. "That's the mystery. Three months ago when I visited there was only a small opening and when we arrived last week all the stones had been moved to where you see them now."

"So the villagers moved them for you?"

"They claimed they didn't."

"Oh." Sable scanned the ground between the opening and the pile. It was undisturbed. "How do you think the stones were moved?"

"You got me. I figured that whoever did it used logs, much like blocks were moved to build pyramids."

"Strange," Sable said. "There are no logs, tracks, bark or wood splinters."

"I guess I hadn't really thought about it."

Sable stepped into a glare of artificial lights and felt a sudden dizziness. A generator hiccupped and the lights flickered, dimmed and then the engine sputtered, raced and the lights brightened, then dimmed again.

"I guess I need to feed the beast some gas. Look around, but wait for me to take you back into the cave and don't touch anything," Martin said, then turned and walked away.

Sable turned to see Lisa step into the light. Her brown hair glittered with hints of red and blonde. Sable studied her, again feeling the physical attraction and longing he'd noticed at Jon's. She had long brown hair, so soft it seemed to float over and off her shoulders. Her brown eyes were thoughtful, gentle, and seemed full of innocence and excitement for what the day would bring. He smiled feebly at her and walked to the first of several large tables. "How, where did the table come . . ." The table was lined with brightly colored pottery with a myriad of designs. Each item had a catalog number taped on it.

"Flown in." Lisa moved next to him and ran her hands over the pottery, outlining the drawings. "This is a great find--only a few chips and cracks in the artifacts. It's almost as if . . ." Her voice faded out.

"If what?" Sable moved to the next one and frowned. A quiver of arrows, a bow and several lances of different lengths with intricate designs either etched or painted on the shafts lay carefully arranged on the table. At one time, Sable guessed that the designs held some special meaning.

"Time seems to have stood still. These artifacts seem perfectly preserved," she whispered in awe. She suddenly felt the déjà vu of having been in the cavern before, but knew she hadn't. "Wait until we get a carbon dating on these artifacts; then we will know how old the site is."

Sable caressed the leather quiver that was supple to the touch, but should have been dry and brittle with age. He picked up a lance--the wood appeared fresh. The lights flickered again and he felt a chill run up his spine as the amulet vibrated, sending a slight shock wave through his body.

"Don't . . .," Lisa started to say.

"These weapons can't be from early Tlingits."

"What do you mean?"

"These are like new. See?"

"Huh . . ." Lisa ran her fingers gently over the object. "You're right; the leather should be mummified, cracking . . ."

Sable heard light footfalls behind him and he began to turn.

"Like our little display?" Martin had moved beside them with panther stealth.

Martin continued, "I too find it hard to accept their pristine condition. It looked like the dig had been salted, so scrapings have been sent out for carbon-date testing. Let me show you the rest of the find." Martin moved off at a fast clip.

As the cavern closed into a small, semi-darkened passageway, Sable took a couple deep breaths and almost gagged, for behind the mustiness was hidden the subtle smell of death. As fuzziness tried to spread through his senses, he fought it while scanning the narrowing corridor and vacant walls. "I would have expected some drawings."

"You'll be surprised by the next room."

As they stepped into a much larger room, Sable shielded his eyes from the brilliance of the high-intensity lights mounted on stands scattered throughout. The room was almost the size of a Roman amphitheater, with tiers of circular steps cascading down into a large circle. In the center was a stone altar. He didn't need to guess its purpose. Petroglyphs and large drawings covered the walls from top to bottom with such sophistication that the ancient artist could rival those of today. It was all here: a history of the Tlingit's travel across the land bridge separating Alaska from Siberia, hunting parties defeating the woolly mammoths and saber tooth tigers, and wars against neighboring tribes. Sable stopped scanning and looked at the documented history of sacrifices. The altar was in each picture. Around the room were several members of the team who he guessed were college students, some taking photographs, others painstakingly drawing on sketchpads while trying to accurately reproduce the artwork.

"This is wonderful," Lisa ran to a painting and began studying it. "No, this is extraordinary."

Martin closely followed as Sable began to circle the room studying the paintings. Approaching one painting, Sable stroked his chin. He felt an immense power emanating from the drawing. He had to step back to take it all in. The sun, moon and stars were all in the sky, reminding him that the solstice was in three days. "Is this the complete dig?"

"Yes. As far as I can tell."

"Do you have any idea who . . .?" The talisman vibrated and the heat from it began burning Sable's chest as if it were trying to tell him that there was more. A draft brushed his face through a crack in the rock and he ran a hand over the painting, which seemed flatter than the rest, his fingertips following the breeze.

"Have you found something?"

Sable felt the outline of what could be a door. "There's something behind . . ." Positioning his hands on the edge of the painting, he pushed. "This wall," he grunted. "Help me."

Martin assisted and there was a slow, steady, grinding sound of rock on rock that reminded Sable of removing a stone lid from a sarcophagus. The large slab grudgingly moved inches, then broke free and spun open on an axis, yielding darkness that absorbed all light.

"I'll be damned," Martin said, peering into the void. "Get some lights."

CHAPTER 25

As Sable scanned the murky depths and waited, a cold
breeze rushed past him into the main cavern, dropping the
temperature several degrees and forcing Sable to shiver. Could
this be a crypt? Behind him came sounds of scurrying and
shuffling across stone as the students returned with lights.

"What is it?" Lisa said, looking over Sable's shoulder. Her
presence removed the chill.

"Another way in," Sable guessed.

"Possibly an antechamber or tomb," Martin said. One of
the students handed the trio flashlights. "Thanks Peter. Have the
others set up lamps behind us."

"Well, aren't you going in?" Lisa turned on her light almost
simultaneously with the others.

"Sable gets the honor for discovering the room. I'll
mention you in my next paper." Martin motioned to Sable to
proceed.

Sable took a deep breath and swept the beam across the
floor, but it only cut into the cavern a few feet. "Well, I guess this
is it." As Sable stepped through the doorway, the cold dark
crushed down on him, trying to engulf him. The essence of death
seemed fresh, though Sable knew it had happened long ago.

"Shouldn't we get some rope just in case?" Lisa asked.

"Not necessary if we're careful," Martin said and followed
Sable.

"We need all three lights," Sable continued to sweep the
beam from side to side as he moved forward. Lisa soon joined
them. Behind them, the clatter of metal lights being assembled by
the students and staff echoed in the chamber.

She laughed nervously. "This is larger than the amphitheater." Lisa's voice echoed as the first set of spotlights flickered on and illuminated a small portion of the room. Another bank of lights ripped more darkness away. "Wall drawings?" Lisa's beam pointed to irregular shiny ripples running across the rock face of one side of the chamber.

"No, gold," Sable said.

"I agree," Martin said.

As another set of lights kicked in, the room burst into a kaleidoscope of colors. There was a simultaneous gasp from all. On the north and south sides of the cavern, several foot-wide swaths of gold formed an arrow that disappeared into the stone. Under each were stacked rows of skulls on top of neatly piled bones. Across each forehead were intricately drawn symbols whose meaning seemed long forgotten.

Sable shivered. He recognized the symbols. They were the same ones that had been painted on the foreheads of the dead children.

"My god. Nothing in the Tlingit history ever indicated human sacrifice." Lisa's voice was strained.

"Tlingits never practiced human sacrifice." Sable felt the pain, suffering and sorrow of the long dead. This was the work of the original Auktelchnĭk. "It may be just a burial chamber."

A staff stood in the center of the chamber on a dais. A crystalline orb topping the staff was held in place by a pair of spread golden wings. Two serpents coiled around the shaft below the wings.

"My god. It's a herald's wand—a caduceus," Martin shouted as he rushed toward it. "It's similar to the one carried by Hermes."

"I thought the wand carried by Hermes or Mercury was myth." Sable almost had to run to keep up with Martin. As he recalled, Mercury was a Roman god stolen from the Greeks. He served as messenger to the other gods. What Martin was suggesting was next to impossible. He stopped short.

Martin's flashlight lit the orb and a myriad of colored hues began to resonate from it. Simultaneously, across the room on

the east wall, a halo of light emanated from a circular opening
lined with different colored crystals.

"I've never seen anything like it," Sable said, feeling some
type of power emanating from both the orb and crystalline
chamber. "The light must have activated some type of
piezoelectric chain reaction in the material."

Martin whispered. "It looks like an invitation to me."

"I agree." Sable quickly closed the distance to the portal
and as he looked in, he swung the beam in an arc in front of him.
The crystals, lining the wall in a myriad of colors, lit up in fiery
brilliance as if the parties' light beam were charging up an electric
capacitor. When he stepped into the room, bolts of light and
thousands of tiny electrical charges hit Sable from all directions,
sending charges through his body. As the darkness consumed him
and his knees folded under, he felt the amulet, radiant hot, burn
into his chest. Before he lost consciousness, he thought he heard
someone yell to pull him out.

"What in the hell is happening?" Martin grabbed for Sable
and was thrown back. "Damn, a self-generating, electrical
chamber. That's . . . impossible."

"Hurry! The chamber is killing him." Lisa's throat
tightened and she fought for breath.

"Someone get a pole and rope." Martin yelled. He pushed
himself up to one knee and stood, but collapsed.

Peter brought a rope and spear and offered it to Martin.

Lisa turned to Peter. "Forget about Dr. Ridell. We have to
get Sable out of the chamber."

"What do you want me to do?" Peter unfolded himself to
his seven-foot height and ran his hand through his mousy dark
brown hair that was prematurely streaked with gray.

"You lift Sable's leg with the lance and I'll lasso his leg and
then we both pull him out."

"Got it." Peter stepped to one side of the chamber away
from the electrical arcs, then froze, for Sable's body was shrouded
in a yellow glow.

"Move, dammit!"

"Ah, okay," Peter said.

"God, he's heavy." Lisa huffed as she tried to lift the ropes on Sable's legs. "It seems as though the room doesn't want to give him up."

"Pull harder." Martin ordered as he finally pushed himself up.

"I'm doing the best I can." Peter's voice was strained.

"Let's get some help over here."

Several students cautiously joined in, grabbing the rope and within seconds, they pulled Sable to safety.

Martin pulled himself across the floor to Lisa's side. "Is he still alive?"

Lisa placed her head on Sable's chest. "Damn! He's not breathing and there's no heart beat."

"I know CPR." Peter knelt next to her.

"I'll start his breathing, you do the compressions." Lisa tilted Sable's head back, extended his jaw and pinched his nose.

CHAPTER 26

For a while, Sable floated above himself watching everything that was going on, then everything went dark.

Chlawūch-tschāk strode into the cavern with Jon following behind. Within a few minutes they'd found the archeological group. When Chlawūch-tschāk saw his nephew lying on the floor, he rushed to his side, knelt and felt for a pulse.

"How long has he been dead?" Chlawūch-tschāk placed his head on Sable's chest.

"Just who the hell are you and what are you doing here? This is a restricted dig." Martin stepped toward the pair but Lisa moved to block him.

"Ten to fifteen minutes. There's no way you can save him now." Lisa raised her hand to her uncle. "This is Jon, one of the Kanashig village elders."

"If he's a village elder then I'm the white rabbit from *Alice in Wonderland.*"

"Hush, Uncle Martin."

"How did this happen?" Martin shrugged and pointed to the chamber and caduceus, then explained what had happened.

Chlawūch-tschāk ignored Martin and looked at Jon. "You know what to do."

"Are you sure you want to do this? All human beings must die." Jon pulled a folded hunting knife from his pocket.

"Not this young. It's the only way while the door is open."

"He will be with you forever."

"What do you think you're doing? You can't bring back the dead with your Indian mumbo jumbo," Martin shouted.

"Back off." Chlawūch-tschāk walked over to the caduceus and picked it up. The crystals lit up, burning with the intensity of a focused spotlight.

"Now see here. That's an important artifact." Martin started toward Chlawūch-tschāk.

"Begone." The shaman waved his free hand and an invisible force threw Martin back about twenty feet. The students tried to converge on Chlawūch-tschāk, but met the same fate. A multicolored, swirling glow bathed Chlawūch-tschāk as he stepped into the chamber. With each second and pulse of light, the caduceus's orb glow turned amber.

While his friend was busy, Jon hunched down over Sable, opened his shirt and moved the tsāk-ssēt aside. He ran the blade of his knife across the chest just above the heart. As a fine line of crimson began to bead, Jon cut his palm and laid it over the wound for several seconds then replaced the amulet.

Jon stood and said a silent prayer. "I'm ready."

Chanting in an ancient language far older than Tlingit, Chlawūch-tschāk, his hair crackling with blue fire, strode from the chamber to Sable's body. He placed the caduceus within a foot of the tsāk-ssēt and the room exploded into a blinding flash. Spotlights around the room exploded in a chain reaction as Sable's body arched and relaxed, then went into a massive epileptic seizure. The light went nova and faded into darkness.

Sable grunted, groaned and tried to focus his eyes. "What the hell happened?"

"Uásse-i-tú-eti (*How are you?*)?" Sable recognized his uncle's voice somewhere in the background of cheers.

"Xat kaawadzás (*Exhausted*)." Sable took a painful breath and shook his head.

Lisa rushed to Sable's side and slid her jacket under his head. "I'm glad you're okay."

All Sable could manage was a sheepish, painful grin.

"Don't you know it is forbidden to touch the medicine man's things, my friend." Jon hunched down over Sable and began buttoning the shirt.

"I didn't . . . "

"He is really obstinate even after he's been dead."

"What about the room, the archeologists . . ."

"Don't worry. I'll take care of that."

With the power of the staff, Chlawūch-tschāk erased the short term memories of all involved, hid the chamber, and removed any evidence the trio had ever been at the site.

CHAPTER 27

After the three men left, Auktelchnĩk watched the woman
from the shadows of the trees. He studied her face, trying to
remember where he'd seen her before. Then it came to him: his
wife of so long ago. The face was the same, but somehow softer,
and the hair was now a sort of light brown. Her friends called her
Lisa, but he knew her as Takat-kĩjá (*Hummingbird*) because of her
flighty nature. He was now reborn and he must make her also
remember. Occasionally, he paced back and forth waiting for the
camp to go to sleep so he could kidnap her. Why the group had
invaded his sanctuary still mystified him. Tũtsch-gũtsch had told
him they were archeologists--people who studied ancient races by
digging up their bones. He found this somewhat ridiculous. The
dead were dead and of no interest to him. He listened to the
conversations but they made no sense.

****

Martin folded his arms, placing his feet shoulder width
apart. "I still don't understand how we lost 24 hours of memory,
or how you got here." Martin glanced at the date on his watch,
then gestured toward Lisa.

"I don't even remember coming here or arriving," Lisa let
out a sigh. "In fact, I was supposed to bring a guest, Robert Sable,
but I don't remember if he came or not." She told the group about
meeting Sable at the George's. After I went to sleep, everything's
a blank."

"And what happened to all our lighting and cabling?"
Jarod Gibson combed his thick black hair. It looked grizzled and
sharp as the hairs on a moose's back.

"That's going to set the project back about $15,000,"
Martin grumbled. "$15,000 we desperately need."

"What are we going to do about it?" Eric Williams was
thin but much taller than Martin.

"Who's going to cook tonight?" Christy Frost had the figure of a 21-year-old Barbie doll whose exposed cleavage and tight shorts were enough to distract any young male from concentrating on the dig for hours.

"I'll take care of it," Peter Atkin stammered. Whenever Peter was in Christy's presence, he stuttered like an uneven and improperly timed machine gun. "Now, let's get back . . . back to the topic at hand."

As the camp began shutting down and the archeological team began drifting off to sleep, Auktelchnīk glided toward his sanctuary, keeping in the foliage and close to the rock face of the nearby cliff. To increase his power, he had to get his staff, the staff of ages, and recharge it in the crystalline chamber. There were only three more days to the solstice. He had lost one girl and now needed to replace her. He preferred young girls because they were more elemental—they had a more powerful essence than boys. With one last quick glance over his shoulder, he slipped into the cavern. He waited until his eyes adjusted to the dark. On a table near the entrance were two flashlights. While he stared into the darkness, he vaguely recalled the purpose of the device from what he had learned from Tūtsch-gūtsch. He picked up one, hit the switch, shook it several times, but it didn't respond. Auktelchnīk picked up the second one and snapped it on. Within a matter of minutes, he stood before the portal to his secret power chamber. On the rock walls were his drawings of the Tlingit's history.

Though they were not his people, he had documented their travel to the new land along with the trials and tribulations they encountered. He ran his hand affectionately over the wall and gently pushed. It opened slowly, silently, and swiftly as though it glided on a cushion of air. He swung the beam to the left where skulls and bones of the children lay. He'd sacrificed them as he had others countless centuries before. The beam came back to the center of the chamber and froze. The dais where his staff had sat was empty, while behind it the dull radiance from the crystalline chamber was ebbing. His hands trembled. Without the staff of ages, he couldn't complete the final ceremony. It had to be the men he'd seen earlier in the day. They had taken the staff he'd been given by Hermes. Though most of the people of his time believed him a god because of his strength and supernatural speed, Auktelchnīk knew better. Hermes had come from the stars to study man in a strange chariot that rode on a cushion of fire. People of this time called this type of explorer an astronaut. Explaining he'd traveled in some type of spacecraft from a planet just like earth to study man, Hermes had befriended Auktelchnīk, asking the shaman to assist him. At the time, Auktelchnīk hadn't understood all the concepts of space travel, but he knew he wanted Hermes' staff and power—so he killed him. A half a world away, that spacecraft lay hidden deep the bowls of the earth in a cavern similar to this one. One day, Auktelchnīk had thought of returning to the ship to see if he could control it—use it, but now that dream was lost. Without the staff, he could not complete the ceremony. He had to get the staff of ages back before the solstice and kill the thieves. But where were they? First things first. He'd take his wife, Takat-kījá, back to his cabin. It might take a while, but she'd remember their past together.

As he stood at the back of Takat-kījá's tent, he pulled a large hunting knife from its scabbard and drew up a line in the seam. The nylon fabric peeled away silently as if it were cut with the blade of a samurai's katana sword folded 300 times. Lightning split the sky, throwing his shadow over the tent, forcing him to freeze.

He slipped through the opening and let his eyes adjust to the dimness. Across the tent, he saw the sleeping form of Takat-kījá. As he was about to step forward, the woman sat up on the cot.

****

The tent was dark except for the occasional flash of lightning. Lisa's instincts told her that someone was in the tent. As she scanned the wall, she thought she saw a shadow slip across it. She reached for the .44 magnum bear gun that sat on the stand next to the bed and took aim. The shadow—the man was big and husky, stood over six feet tall, and she didn't recognize him.

"Don't move or I'll blow you away." The gun wavered in her hand.

The next thing she knew the man snatched her gun from her hands. A large arm reached out and snaked around her neck. She futilely clawed at her attacker's arm, but found her fingernails tearing at some type of buckskin. Using both of her arms, she forced his arms out, set her teeth on the wrist, and drove them in, tearing, rending flesh and drawing blood.

"Hush, stop struggling, Takat-kījá." The man brought his knife to her throat.

"Who, who are you?" Lisa's voice was barely a choked whisper.

"You don't remember it now, but you soon will. I'm Auktelchnīk, your husband."

Lisa sucked in a quick breath. She remembered the name and the story Jon told. This couldn't be the ancient shaman that they had been talking about. The man in her tent was made of flesh and blood—real blood. She felt the warm sticky fluid run from his arm down her throat to her cleavage. Though the intruder believed he was the reincarnation of Auktelchnīk, she knew he had to be insane.

"Let's go now." He motioned for her to stand.

"But I need my clothes." Lisa slipped out of her sleeping bag and shivered.

"Leave them. When we get to my cabin, I will find clothing more suited to your new life."

"I'll freeze traveling cross country in only my underwear."

"The summer night air is warm. You'll survive." Auktelchnīk jerked Lisa out into the cool evening dusk.

Several hours later and what Lisa guessed was about twenty miles, constantly surrounded by a fog of mosquitoes, feet bloodied, with scratches that seemed to cover every inch of her

body, fatigue closed in on her as she stumbled and collapsed.
Gasping she said, "I can't go any . . . farther."

"All right, we'll take a rest, weakling." Auktelchnīk folded
his arms and looked around at their back trail that consisted of
what appeared to be an impenetrable forest, and then at the
morning sky. Birds flitted from tree to tree, singing their songs.
The archeologists would soon discover that Takat-kījá was
missing and send out search parties, but with no success.

"I need water." Lisa's voice was barely audible.

Auktelchnīk picked up some pebbles from the ground.
"Use these. They'll help until we find a stream."

Lisa tried to push herself up to take the stones, but fell back
to the ground.

A child's scream shattered the air, sending the birds flying
in all directions.

"It sounds like a little girl," Lisa mumbled.

"Ah, just what I need--another girl for my collection."

"Huh?" Lisa was feeling woozy.

"Takat-kījá, you stay here while I investigate."
Auktelchnīk began to walk away but stopped. Over his shoulder,
he said, "If you run, I'll find you. There no place you can hide
from me."

After a number of minutes, she wasn't sure how many,
Lisa looked around and listened. At first she began to crawl, then
she used a birch tree to pull herself up and began stumbling
forward. She wasn't sure where she was going but she couldn't
head toward the dig. Auktelchnīk would certainly look in that
direction. She knew that if she headed west she might run into a
highway or river she could follow. Lisa lunged up the steady
grade of the mountain, stumbling over exposed roots, logs and
fallen limbs. Then her foot caught in a root and she went down,
her knee cracking against a stone that was buried deep in the dirt.
A searing pain ran thorough her leg. Limping, she attempted to
continue running. But as fear shrouded her mind, it began to
paralyze her. She gritted her teeth and pushed her legs forward
beyond their limitations. Perspiration and tears streamed down
her face, blurring her vision. With each step her breathing became

more labored and she could feel the sharp pain grow in her chest. She felt a sob rise in her throat, but she tried to stifle it. If she cried out, Auktelchnīk would hear her.

****

Auktelchnīk stood next to the cabin door, listening to the sobbing of the girl. He shook his head, then kicked in the door. To his right, a tall thin man held a large hunting knife to the throat of a small dark-haired wisp of a girl. They were both naked and lay on a small metal-framed bed. Next to the girl were her soiled, wrinkled and bloody clothes.

The man looked up and quickly slipped off the bed, taking a combat stance. "Who in the hell are you?"

"Your death." Auktelchnīk drew a large hunting knife. As he raised it, the highly polished surface reflected yellow from the morning sun that flooded through the windows.

The man backed toward a rifle, leaning against the wall. "You're not invited to the party. Now, get the hell out before I kill you."

Auktelchnīk closed the distance as the man seized the weapon. As Auktelchnīk knocked it from the man's hands, the rifle exploded, and the hot wind from the bullet caressed Auktelchnīk's cheek. His eyes blazed as he drove the razor sharp blade into the man's solar plexus and lifted the blade in a sawing motion up through the sternum. As blood gushed over Auktelchnīk's hands, a low moan escaped the man's throat and he sagged to the floor. Behind Auktelchnīk, he heard the girl run out the door. He cursed, but knew she couldn't escape. He would find her and collect Takat-kījá, after he'd taken the man's heart.

CHAPTER 28

An insistent ringing phone brought Sable from a troubled sleep. As he reached out for the phone, every muscle in his body seemed on fire. He pushed away the covers from his bed and sat up. He scanned his room. It looked vaguely familiar, but every detail seemed fuzzy and out of reach. His mind felt as if it had been blended in a Mixmaster. "Okay, give." Sable's voice was raspy and his throat exceedingly sore. What had happened over the weekend? He couldn't remember how he'd gotten to his room.

"We've got a missing perp." Sable barely recognized Carpenter's voice through ears that seemed to be stuffed with cotton.

"Which one?" Sable struggled to keep the phone steady because of the weakness in his hands.

"Matthew Farley went off the tracker last night. Looks like he skipped."

"And we're just hearing about it now?" Sable carefully stretched, then yawned. "I'll meet you at his house in 30."

"Sable," Carpenter said.

"Yeah."

"Our perp may have kidnapped a woman. Last night, a member of an archeological team disappeared."

"What's her name?" Sable felt a lump rise in his throat.

"Lisa Ridell."

For a moment, Sable was unable to speak. Somewhere in the back of his mind he knew he had spent time with Lisa but he couldn't place where and when. Then he remembered that he'd pulled her over for speeding just before the weekend. That had to be it. Yet there was something more and he couldn't put his finger on it.

"Sable?"

"Put Benson on."

After Sable gave Benson instructions to bring in the National Guard to help in the search, he quickly showered and started shaving but found it hard to do in the fogged mirror. Using his arm in a broad sweeping motion, he cleared the glass and froze. Staring back at him was a stranger. His face was haggard and pasty, but what gave him the most pause was his hair, which had turned completely white. Briefly, the events of the weekend coalesced, but then disappeared. He shook his head and began shaving again. Right now, he couldn't deal with the implications of the cavern.

As Sable left the bedroom, Chlawūch-tschāk blocked his way. "You're going nowhere."

"I have a job to do." Sable tried to squeeze past him but failed.

"Yesterday, you were dead. You need to recover your strength. Do you have a death wish? You certainly act like it."

"I feel fine." Sable straightened to his full height and squared his shoulders, but his uncle towered over him by several inches. *Dead—he didn't remember that.*

"Once you recover, we have more important things to do. We have to make plans to stop Auktelchnīk."

"We can deal with this mythical, dead shaman later." Sable arched an eyebrow, then leaned against his bedroom doorjamb for support. "We're trying to do the same thing. Right now, I'm trying to find the copycat." Sable took a deep breath. "Besides you can't believe a dead shaman can come back to life?"

"You did."

Sable knew he'd lost an entire weekend, but refused to consider the scenario his uncle proposed. Had he gone on a bender? Not likely. This didn't feel like a hangover. He inclined his head toward the hallway and raised his car keys in the air as a symbol of defiance. "I need to go."

"You're going nowhere." His uncle snatched the keys from his hand, but Sable reached out and snatched them back.

"Uncle, you know better than to push me."

Chlawūch-tschāk shrugged and stepped from Sable's path.

****

Sable met Carpenter in Farley's driveway.

"Hell, you look like shit, but I like the hair. What happened to you?" Carpenter asked.

Sable used a forefinger to rub the sleep from his eye. "You know how it is. It was one hell of a party. Someone bleached my hair as a practical joke after I passed out." Sable felt the lie grate on him.

"Why wasn't I invited to this party?" Carpenter's eyes twinkled with mischief, in spite of the seriousness of the situation. Sable could see she was still very much interested in him.

Sable shrugged.

Carpenter drew her gun and Sable followed suit. They headed toward the entrance and pressed the button. Muffled chimes from inside played a haunting melody Sable didn't recognize. "State Troopers, open up!"

Only silence met them.

He pounded on the door, waited a few seconds, then pounded again. "State Troopers, open the door!"

Nothing.

"Good, I get to kick in the door," Carpenter said, taking a karate stance.

Sable shook his head. "Let's try the easy way first." He turned the knob and the door opened with the grating sound of wood on wood. Sable moved to the right while Carpenter went left. The door's hinges squeaked loudly as it closed behind them. They stopped in the front-room-combination-dining-room, listened and called Farley again. There was a musty smell that hadn't been there the last time they had visited. The curtains were drawn, leaving the room in darkness and Sable squinted to see. Carpenter found the light switch and turned on the lights. Sable was blinded, but then the room came into focus. On the dining room table sat a half-eaten pizza, still in the box, with crumbs scattered around it.

"Farley's housekeeping sure as hell degraded in the last few days." Sable scanned the room. Clothes and unread newspapers lay helter-skelter on one of the couches. On the coffee table were empty whiskey and gin bottles, mixed with empty beer cans of several brands.

"He's probably in his bedroom, drunk as a skunk."

Each took one side of the hallway and stealthily started moving toward the back of the house. The door to the bedroom was closed. The first thing that hit him even before he saw the body was the horrible smell. Sable gave the high sign, slipped his pistol under his armpit while he snapped on the latex gloves. With his gun at the ready, he opened the door with his free hand. As he drew a deep breath, he gagged and then covered his mouth. Farley had been dead for a number of hours.

"You got any Vicks?"

Sable nodded, pulled a bottle of Vicks Vapo-Rub from his pocket and dabbed it beneath his nostrils and then offered it to Carpenter who did the same.

Across the room, he saw Matthew Farley's mouth twisted and deformed with teeth bared. As they approached the body, he could see that the eyes were open and filmed to a dull gray-black. Farley was stark naked and gutted like a salmon on the slime line. The chest was laid open just as the killer had done with the children—cut from the pubis up, almost to the throat. His mouth had been sliced open so that his heart could be stuffed into it. Blood had soaked into the sheets surrounding the body with some of it spilling onto the carpet.

"Give me your gut reaction. Is this the work of our serial killer or a crazed parent?" Sable asked, already knowing the answer as his eyes prowled the room.

"It's got to be a psycho parent."

"That's all we need on top of everything--a vigilante." Sable slid his .40 back into the holster.

"Yeah, but whoever it is, is cleaning up the trash."

"When do you think he died?" Carpenter asked.

"From the lavidity, I'd say late last night. You want a closer guess, you could estimate the core temperature."

"No thanks. I'll let the ME take care of that."

Sable frowned, then used his cell phone to call the detachment and request a forensic team. This time the murderer had left no doubt that the death was not a suicide. One of the parents had killed again. But which one? Was he killing for revenge or was he trying to find his missing child? Under the pretext of garnering more information on the missing and murdered children, he and Carpenter would have to visit the parents.

After they did a cursory search of Farley's house and found virtually nothing, Carpenter dropped a pile of pornographic magazines on the coffee table. "Look what I have."

"If he were still alive, you couldn't arrest him for that. You know that the Supreme Court has ruled people can read any intellectually stimulating reading material they want. Just so long as it isn't kiddy porn."

"Okay, let's leave this to the techs and see what else we can drum up."

Once the forensic teams arrived, Sable and Carpenter headed to Kanashig and Jackson's house. Sable wondered which of the pedophiles this new killer would murder.

CHAPTER 29

Rain hammered down from an iron-gray sky, nailing water spikes into ground and forming pools in the ruts. Carpenter had left her cruiser for one of the investigators and teamed up with Sable. They'd agreed to interview the parents of the still-missing children and then the parents of the murdered kids. Sable pondered the clues of the last few days, trying to link them together. He almost drove over the yellow line. A solid-black Jeep dodged for the edge of the road and the young man driving raised a fist and flipped them a bird and shouted an obscenity Sable couldn't hear but guessed what it was.

Sable reduced his speed and pulled off onto a winding, mountain road that reached back into the wilderness. Along the sides were intermittent stands of trees. As they went higher in the mountains, his ears popped. The rain, now calmer, continued from darkened clouds, gently tapping the windshield and setting a percolating rhythm like a snare drum. Through the trees and rain, Sable was barely able to make out the vast, horseshoe lake in the valley below. As they progressed, the sun came out and the clouds evaporated as quickly as they had arrived.

Finally, after scanning the sides of the road for a couple more miles, Sable found the turnoff to the Jackson's house. As he came around the curve, he saw the sloping roof outlined against the blue sky. It was just a few minutes before noon when he drove through an opening in a wooden, crisscrossed fence. He pulled up next to a dark blue Impala parked in the driveway. The A-frame house was a combination of log and stone, with the high-pitched roof coming within a few feet of the lawn. And nearby, a babbling brook lazily ran down to the lake that was less than a couple hundred feet from the house. As they got out of the vehicle, he felt wet cold air heavy with the expectation of snow, but couldn't believe it likely with the sun just out. As they neared the house, Sable reviewed the case file on Betsy Jackson's kidnapping. Before Sergeant Nicholas Kelly's disappearance, he had interviewed the parents about the kidnapping of their daughter, but found few if any leads. He hoped this interview would go better.

At the door Emily Jackson managed a feeble smile as Sable and Carpenter introduced themselves. Emily was a slender, young woman, pretty in a soft way, with violet eyes and blond hair that ran past her shoulders. She looked directly at Sable then her eyes lowered until she was looking at the floor as though she knew that her child had not been found. "Have you found Betsy?"

Sable cleared his throat.

"My wife asked you a question," Benjamin Jackson hurled the words at Sable. He was a square-shouldered man with an olive tan and white hair. He was tall, well-built and in his forties, but looked like he was in his early thirties. He wore a plaid shirt and stonewashed jeans. He had his hands in his pockets as he stood behind his wife.

"Sorry, but we haven't," Sable said.

"Then why are you here?" Jackson asked, frowning.

Emily took a quick and nervous look around the room.

"We're requestioning all the parents of the missing children," Carpenter offered.

"And in some cases they're brothers and sisters," Sable added.

Sable looked into the front room. Hardwood floors reflected the late-afternoon sun's rays onto the painted walls, turning them from white to light amber. The living room was off a central foyer and took up the entire side of the house. There were several paintings by Alaskan artists depicting outdoors and mountain scenes. A brick fireplace stood in the in the center of one wall with two flowered sofas flanking it. The larger of the pair had a glass-topped coffee table in front of it. On another wall, bookshelves made from painted plywood and glass block held an impressive collection of modern and ancient classics.

Next to these was an extensive collection of jazz and blues records.

"Have a seat." Emily motioned toward one of the sofas. "Do you want something to eat? Some coffee or tea?"

Sable and Carpenter looked at each other, then shook their heads. Carpenter must have felt that something was off with Benjamin just as he did.

Emily slid gracefully onto one end of the sofa and tucked her legs beneath her. She tried to sit still on the couch, her hands tightly clasped together as if trying to maintain composure, but with little success.

Jackson cut Sable off before he could seat himself. "Are there any suspects in the case?"

"Not at this time. We've eliminated several suspects and are still collecting evidence."

"Could we please see your children?" Carpenter asked, placing her hands on the lounger's arms and feeling the texture of the material. "Then we'll talk afterward."

"You don't need to talk to the kids. It'll start their nightmares again." Jackson tapped his fingers on the arms of the sofa and his jaw tightened.

"Benjamin, be nice to our guests."

"Yeah, whatever." Jackson pressed his lips into a fine line. "Jesse, Barry, get your backsides in here."

Sable could hear the children scurrying down the hall and when they entered the room, the first one stopped short, causing them to collapse into a jumble. He quickly recognized them from their file photographs as they untangled themselves and stood. The taller of the two boys, Sable guessed was nine and had to be Barry, while the younger was about five. Both had straight black hair and brown eyes that went wide when they saw Sable and Carpenter.

"They aren't here to arrest us. Are they?" Barry looked from his mother to his father.

Sable shook his head and smiled his most friendly, disarming smile. "No, we're not. We're here to ask you a few questions."

"Good, cause we didn't do nothin." Barry squared his stance and placed his hands on his hips.

Jesse tried to imitate his brother. "Yeah, nothin."

"We came to ask about your sister, Betsy, and her disappearance." Carpenter's voice was low, melodious as a southern belle with a faint, tinkling quality.

"Okay." Barry's voice broke as he tried to look brave, even smile, but it didn't work. His eyes had that watery look that people get just before crying.

As Sable looked at him, he realized that few days ever passed that he didn't think of Amy and Bobby—especially with all the killings. He wondered what kind of young man his son would have grown into. Thinking that the trooper must be okay, Jesse sidled up to Sable's chair and grinned at him. He was pretty sure the child didn't know what was going on. Sable ran his hand against the boy's hair. It was soft and dark like that of Tlingit children.

"Barry, I know this is hard, but I'd like you to remember the day your sister disappeared. Can you tell me about it?" Carpenter's voice slightly wavered as she asked the question.

"Yeah, I guess." He took a deep breath, sounding like a woman with asthma.

"I remember too," Jesse added.

"Let's let Barry tell the story." His mother cautioned.

"We were all outside. Betsy was doing her thing." He stopped, looked out the bay window and then at Sable. "And I was pushing Jesse on the swing." Barry let a big sigh, stopped and looked at his mother, for support.

"Take it easy. You're doing fine," Sable said softly. He could see Barry's legs were vibrating heavily.

"Dad was in the house watching TV."

"What was Betsy doing?"

"Playing house with her dolls."

"Yuk," Jesse added. "Boys don't play with dolls."

Sable bit his lip as he recalled his son telling him that his toys were not dolls--they were action figures--and that only girls played with dolls.

"Then what?" Sable asked.

"The bad man came."

"Can you describe him?" Carpenter asked.

Barry frowned and looked from Sable to Carpenter then back again.

"She means, what did he look like?"

Jackson's jaw tightened. "Who would ever do this to a child?"

"Dear, hush," Emily said quietly and leaned slightly toward her husband.

"He was big and tall."

"Yeah, he was gargantuan," Jesse piped in, smiling slightly for using such a big word. "He had a mean, snarley face."

"What was the color of his hair?" Sable asked, shifting in his seat.

"White."

"What style?" Carpenter asked.

"How did he wear his hair?" Sable translated.

"He had one of them 'whatchu-me-call-its'—where the grownups tie their hair up."

"You mean a ponytail?" Carpenter asked.

"Yeah, that's what is was, a ponytail."

"That's what it was, a ponytail," Jesse giggled and plopped himself on the floor.

"What about his clothes?" Sable asked.

"They was all brown. They was like, you know . . . the kind the Indians wear on TV."

"Buckskins?"

"You got it." Barry joined his brother on the floor. "With all sorts of colored drawings on it. Just like a girl's shirt."

"Yeah, like a girl." Jesse smiled slightly.

Sable shook his head. They had to have meant that the clothing had been decorated in colors or beads. The psycho was really trying to copy the legend of Auktelchnĭk.

After several more questions, Sable and Carpenter came to a dead end and sent the children off to play.

"Have you heard that some of the suspects have been murdered?" Sable watched Jackson's body language carefully for a response, but the man didn't even bat an eyelash.

"No," Emily said.

"Nah, but I'm glad to hear it." Jackson popped some Cheetos in his mouth and chewed for a moment. He'd been listening to the conversation with the barest hint of a smirk. Then he said, "Good riddance to bad garbage. They need to give the guy who's doing this a plaque and awards banquet as Token's citizen of the year."

Sable waited while Jackson popped some more Cheetos into his mouth. "Have you heard any rumors as to who might have done this?"

"No. But if I do, do you think I would tell the law?"

Sable's smile returned. "I need to know where you were last night."

Emily leaned forward. "You can't believe that Benjamin has something . . ."

"Get the hell out of my house," Jackson roared. His eyes locked with Sable's in an intense stare as though realizing what the other's guess was. "And don't come back."

"Benjamin, shut up. I don't think that they meant . . ."

"Wife, shut up."

"But Betsy, they need to find Betsy." Emily began rambling and sobbing.

Sable went to her and placed his hand on her arm. "We'll do everything in our power to find her."

Jackson leaped up and began heading toward Sable when Carpenter tripped him and he went skidding across the floor. For a moment he was quieted, but after a few seconds he began to groan and stir.

Sable wanted to hug Carpenter.

"I'll be talking to you again."

As Jackson looked up from the floor, a shadow of discomfort crossed his face. Sable linked the look to his revelation Jackson might be killing the pedophiles.

Once out of earshot, Sable said, "I think we got our man or at least he's a good suspect."

On the way to the back to the office, Sable noted to himself the temperature seemed to have risen by twenty degrees and the sky was almost a clean slate. As he scanned the sky, he looked for some type of promise the horror would end, but he knew it wouldn't. His task would have been unpleasant even under the best of circumstances.

Sable placed around the clock surveillance on Jackson since he had now become their prime suspect in the pedophile killings. Things were falling into place, all things considered, at least on one case. He needed only a little more time to tie up a few loose ends. He also needed sleep, though he should have felt rested. He dimly recollected he'd almost had a permanent one—somehow he'd died and returned.

CHAPTER 30

After another sleepless night, Sable had gotten to the office early, reviewed the case files again and checked over his notes. Nothing seemed to jump off the page at him. He switched gears and buried himself in the administrative paperwork of being acting commander. After he finished, he called Carpenter and Nutall, arranging to meet for brunch. With Nutall, Sable explained why he was calling, then gave a brief summary of what they'd found out about Jackson and asked if she wanted lunch. As he started to leave the office, he stopped by the fax to pick up one from the Washington troopers and smiled. He rolled the dossier up and slapped it on the side of his leg. It was the first real break they had had in months.

Sable entered the Arctic Bear Restaurant and scanned the interior. In a secluded corner he saw Carpenter. Dodging a number of closely packed tables, he made it to the table. He tossed his hat and jacket on the vacant chair.

"What's for breakfast?" he asked, slipping into a chair.

"You still look like shit. You need some coffee in you." She was wearing a black sweater and matching black slacks and hiking boots. She looked like she was ready for anything.

"I feel like shit." Sable casually brushed the hair from his forehead. He detected a low-grade fever. He was still trying to recall what had happened during the weekend. Everything seemed a whirl of missing pieces that were slowly starting to fold together.

Carpenter cocked her head to the side and arched an eyebrow as she studied him. "You seem somehow younger today, I hardly recognized you." Carpenter beckoned to the waitress. "I still like the white hair—that must be it. It makes you look distinguished, but still not older."

The pretty waitress smiled and winked. "What can I get for you?"

Sable ordered coffee and a hamburger topped with eggs and bacon. Carpenter ordered a salad.

After the waitress left, Carpenter said, "That stuff's loaded with fat, cholesterol and salt. You know that's not heart smart."

"Do I look fat?" Sable shrugged. He shook his head. A low vibration began to course through his muscles. A tingling started at the back of his neck and crept forward over the top of his skull, as though his blood pressure had either dropped or increased. He braced himself on the table. "Where's Nutall? She should be here by now."

"Yesterday was pretty rough on her. This morning, she must be having a pretty hard time getting going."

Sable punched the number to the motel where Nutall was staying, but found she'd already left. "She's on her way."

The waitress returned with their drinks, placing them on the table as Nutall walked through the door. Sable nodded toward Nutall and asked the waitress to wait a moment. Nutall was wearing a blue business suit, miniskirt and black high heels. Sable shook his head—her outfit wouldn't work if they needed to go into the bush.

As Nutall slid into her seat, she ordered tea and a salad. Sable noted her complexion was near the color of white chalk.

"I finally meet someone that feels worse than I," Sable said.

"Don't worry, you'll get use to it." Carpenter looked squarely at Nutall, then picked up her teacup and cradled it in her hands.

"I've been on scenes before but not when it involved children." Nutall placed her hands on the edge of the table as if trying to steady herself.

"Don't worry. Even after all my cases, I still can't get use to it—any murder." Sable took a large swig of coffee hoping the caffeine rush would hit him soon.

"We're all in the same boat." Carpenter took a sip of her tea.

Nutall nodded weakly. "Thanks."

The conversation momentarily ceased while the waitress slid the hamburger in front of Sable and the salads in front of the women.

"Have you come up with a new angle on our killer?" Sable asked.

"I had a thought, but you wouldn't like it." Nutall stirred her salad in almost a dream-like state.

"And why's that?" Sable and Carpenter asked almost simultaneously.

"Well, have you thought about the lack of evidence and forensics at all the abductions?" Nutall asked.

Sable shrugged. "Sure. Well, give."

"I think we might have a cop or someone who was a cop." Nutall shook her head and hesitantly took a bite of salad.

"Okay, that's an option; though I don't like to think about that, we'll have to look into it."

"Or . . ." She went silent, seeming to be lost in thought.

"Well, we have a new possible by the name of Caleb Nicodemus."

Nutall pushed her plate aside and took the lemon placed next to her cup and squeezed it in the tea. "How much do you know about him?"

"That he likes little kiddies and he was a suspect in several killings in the King County area. But they never could pin it on him. He left for Alaska a month after his last interrogation." Sable gulped the warm coffee, held it his mouth for a moment to savor the taste, then swallowed. The caffeine rush still hadn't hit him. It seemed as though his body was fighting against it.

Carpenter leaned forward on the table. "Why haven't we heard about him before?"

"Well, the Washington troopers notified the Anchorage detachment last summer."

"And the children started the disappearing last fall." Lisa checked her watch. "Well, what are we waiting for? Let's go check him out."

"Nicodemus is out of town right now, but he should be back later in the week." Sable's back began to ache and he shifted in his chair.

"That doesn't mean we can't scope out his place," Carpenter said with a wink.

"Okay let's go." Sable drained the last of his coffee and got to his feet. "But first we have to stop at Farley's and see what the team found."

Nutall's dress rode up her long, shapely legs as she stood and Sable turned his head, trying not to notice.

When the trio entered Farley's home, a trooper from the crime scene unit was snapping pictures of Farley's bed. Another had a camera on a tripod, focusing on a footprint in the blood on the carpet. Alongside the impression was a ruler that gauged the shoe size at about eleven. Around the room, a number of wood and tile surfaces were smudged by fingerprint powder. In a corner, a technician vacuumed the carpeting in one-foot swaths and recorded his accomplishments on a clipboard.

Fingerprint technicians were scattered throughout the house, pumping dark powder with flitguns on tables, doors, knobs, jambs and windowsills, looking for latent fingerprints.

Sable waved Lum over. "Have you found anything yet? Latents?"

Lum was about to answer when Sable's cell phone rang. He flipped it open. It was Zerck. "What have you got?" Sable asked.

"Caleb Nicodemus' truck was found abandoned." The line went silent.

Sable took a deep breath. He'd learned silence was Zerck's way of building suspense. "And?"

"His truck's dead center of all the abductions and kills."

Sable breathed a sigh of relief. Maybe they were getting somewhere after all.

Zerck gave Sable directions to the vehicle.

When Sable finished writing them down, he looked at Lum. "I've got to go--an important lead."

"Well, we don't have anything significant yet. I'll let you know if we can find something solid."

Turning off the highway, Sable headed down a narrow gravel road, leaving a plume of dust in their wake. In his haste, he took the curve too quickly, spraying gravel that hit the guard railing in a machine gun rhythm. As they started up the mountain, houses grew farther and farther apart. The trees began to crowd in on the road and it narrowed further into one lane. Just as he passed a large meadow with tall grass and bushes sweeping up to the tree line, he saw something large and brown. Just inside a copse of trees, stood a large moose with an antler spread he guessed was at least seventy inches.

"You've got to see this," Sable said, pointing to the moose. After glancing in the rearview mirror to ensure no one was following him, he slowed, pulled to the side of the road and stopped. He rolled down the window and leaned forward so that Nutall could see the majestic animal.

"It looks like a big horse with antlers." Nutall chuckled slightly and Sable noted the color was beginning to come back to her cheeks.

"And just about as good eating," Carpenter said.

Sable arched an eyebrow and laughed. He recalled his parents telling him they had eaten horsemeat during the hard times in the fifties and found it quite tasty.

When the moose finally slipped back into the trees, Sable rolled the window back up and continued their journey.

As they neared the location where Zerck had said the vehicle was, Sable saw a birch deadfall lying across the road. He shifted the Suburban down into 4-wheel drive, ran up on the side of the road and over the top of a fallen birch. Suddenly ahead, the forest parted for a large meadow of waist-high grass and fireweed.

"There it is!" Nutall pointed toward the center of the meadow.

Sable remained silent.

"The guy must be color blind," Carpenter said. A brilliant-red aluminum shell covered the bed of the blue Chevy pickup.

"Just a sec, I need to put on a pair of Rebocks. I didn't think I'd have to go for a hike today," Nutall said.

"You're not hiking anywhere in that mini," Sable said.

"I agree. It's Alaska, sweetie. It's always a hike." The smirk on Carpenters face was priceless.

"I can solve that." Nutall ripped the side seam of the miniskirt almost to the waist. "I'm ready."

"And so you are," Carpenter observed.

Sable tried to stifle a chuckle. Damn, Carpenter would make one fine trooper, he thought.

They stopped about a hundred yards from the truck. Both Sable and Carpenter drew their weapons before they left the vehicle. As they approached the pickup, Sable noted a silver decal on the rear hatch window stating that it had been installed by the Call of the Wild Shell Company in Fairbanks. From what he could tell, the vehicle had been vacant for at least a couple days. An undisturbed, thick layer of dust covered it from the fenders to the roof. Cupping his hands over his eyes to reduce the glare from the sun, Sable surveyed the interior. There were two toolboxes, a hydraulic jack, a spare tire and two rolled sleeping bags. When he checked the cab, he found a rifle rack with a 300 Remington magnum.

Carpenter was the first to break the extended silence. "What happened to him? Could he have gone on what the Aussies call a walkabout?"

"He might have a cabin around here where he keeps the children. We should check it out."

"I agree, but I think we should take his rifle just in case he comes back for it."

"No problem. Got a Slim Jim in the back of the Suburban," Sable said.

"What about a warrant?" Nutall asked.

"He's a felon in the possession of a weapon—no warrant needed," Sable said. "And besides the rifle is in plane view."

It took Sable less than a minute to break into the truck and they were on their way. Carpenter gave Nutall her piece and kept the rifle. They spread out to each side of the road—Sable on the left and the women on the right. The meadow became brush that merged with the trees as they started up a slight incline. Sable's eyes darted over and through the birch and alder, looking for any type of movement as the trees closed in on the road. Within a hundred feet, the road abruptly ended, but just to the right was, Sable guessed, a heavily traveled moose trail that went up the mountain.

They hiked up the path while threading around ruts well-worn from the hooves. Dried bushes and twigs snapped under their feet as they ducked under the low hanging branches of the trees. A row of bushes lined the trail and just beyond them, at the bases of the trees, were patches of velvet-smooth moss. The trio scrambled over fallen logs, through brush and devils club and around huge boulders. When Sable reached the top of the first knoll, a small clearing spread out before them and in the center sat a small, square log cabin.

Sable motioned for the group to get down. "I think we've found our quarry."

"How do you want to do this?" Carpenter asked.

"I'll go in and you and Nutall act as my back up." Sable looked for places of cover and concealment. Strewn across the clearing were stumps, piles of logs and an occasional bush or two.

"Damn. You get to have all the fun." Carpenter drew the bolt back on the rifle to check the chamber.

"It's my state." Sable chuckled.

"But I outrank you on this team." Carpenter said.

"All right, I surrender--we both go." Sable took a deep breath and looked at Nutall. "You get to be back up."

"I can handle it."

"Can you use one of these?" He nodded to Carpenter, who handed Nutall the .300 Remington. Nutall returned Carpenter's .38.

"Hey, I was born on a farm and had three older brothers. I can hit a mosquito at three hundred yards." Nutall opened the bolt to make sure a round was seated, then slammed it in place.

"Iron sights or a scope?" Sable asked.

Nutall laughed quietly. "Iron sights."

"Then let's do it--cover us." Sable leapt up while trying to stay hunched over and began dodging left to right through waist-high grass that set a rapid high-pitched swishing sound. Carpenter followed suit. Half way across the meadow, Sable dove behind a stump and Carpenter behind a bush. While trying to catch his breath, he peered around the stump at the cabin, but detected no movement. Taking a last deep breath, he gave Carpenter a high sign. Sable raised three fingers and did a count down, then vaulted toward the cabin while trying to maintain the same zigzag pattern. Within a matter of seconds Sable was at one side of the cabin door and Carpenter on the other.

Sable brought his pistol to the ready. "Caleb Nicodemus, Alaska State Troopers, open the door."

Silence.

Sable nodded and they both hit the door simultaneously. Sable went right and Carpenter left. They stopped. Caleb Nicodemus's naked body was nailed in the center of the floor spread eagle, his filmed eyes staring up at the ceiling. His pale face, once handsome, sported a well-trimmed Errol Flynn mustache, but on his forehead an intricate pattern of fine lines and symbols had been cut with the delicate point of a sharp knife. His tongue protruded between his teeth and was off to one side. His chest lay open, the heart removed.

"Yeah, but it couldn't have happened to a nicer guy." Carpenter slammed her pistol into the holster and nodded toward the clothes. "Do you think the child's safe?"

"Shit! And I thought for once we had our perp. Some one beat us to the punch," Sable grouched. "Jackson, you think?"

They surveyed the cabin. It was just one-room. To the left was a wood stove, hand water pump and kitchen counter with makeshift shelving that was packed with canned goods. Against the far wall stood a homemade table and chairs. To Sable's right, soiled, wrinkled and bloody children's clothes covered an old Army style bed.

Sable shrugged. "If it was Jackson or another parent who did this then I'd say yes. If not, well . . ."

"Where's all the blood?" Carpenter asked. "There has to be more somewhere."

"Not if you take the pump—the heart. Without the pump, you won't find massive quantities of blood. That is unless it's removed post mortem." Sable raised a hand to end the conversation, walked back to the door and waved to Nutall, then called Benson, telling him what they'd found.

For several seconds, the line seemed dead. Benson recovered from the news and asked, "What the hell's going on? All of a sudden the area's one big blood bath."

"Your guess is as good as mine," Sable said then paused. "What about Jackson? Has he left the house?"

"We've got full surveillance on him and the guy just stands there, looking out his window."

"Damn. Well, maybe he got Nicodemus yesterday."

"I doubt it." Carpenter was kneeling by the body. "The stiff's only a few hours old."

Sable shook his head, then told Benson how to get to the crime scene. "We're going to see if we can track this desperado. If we can't, we'll need the dogs."

"I'm on my way." The phone went dead.

Sable folded his cell phone, slipped it into his pocket, then looked at Nutall. "Can you hold down the fort until Benson arrives."

"Sure, but I think I'll wait outside."

Outside the cabin, Sable began following a hard-packed trail to the north while Carpenter covered the south. Several minutes later, on the edge of a small pond, Sable found a deep impression of a moccasin in the mud.

"I found it," he yelled.

When Carpenter caught up, they followed a small stream that ran down the uneven trail. Maintaining his .40 at the ready, his eyes darted over the foliage and trail ahead, scrutinizing every shadow for potential danger. The rivulet left puddles bordered by muskeg, weeds and brush, forced them to walk in the water. With each step, their shoes made a sucking sound that made Sable cringe as they moved up the muddy trail following the footprints. To Sable, only a stampede of woolly mammoths could make as much noise. Then he saw it. Dead ahead, just over a small ridge, stood a thick stand of alder next to a wide canyon--and the footprints headed directly toward the canyon.

Sable moved left into the tree line and motioned for Carpenter to do the same. She gave him a high sign and nodded to the open area between them and the canyon. Sable shrugged and gestured toward the trees surrounding the clearing. Sable and Carpenter moved as stealthily as they could. If the situation hadn't been so serious Sable might have smiled. He recalled an adrenaline-charged trek he and Janet Blaine had taken through the wilderness of Southeast Alaska. Though they'd been running for their lives from David Meyers' henchmen, they'd fallen in love, or so he'd thought.

At the edge of the canyon, they stopped. Nowhere was there any movement. The canyon walls and the trees on its edges cast ripples of dark shapes and shadows across the canyon floors. A sliver of sun glittered blindingly just above the rim, forcing Sable to shield his eyes with his palm.

"He's not here." Carpenter broke the silence.

Ahead in the shadows, Sable saw something white glistening in the dirt. He motioned toward the spot and slid his gun back into its holster. Taking one final glance around, Sable strode to the object and hunkered down.

"Auktelchnīk?" Carpenter asked mockingly.

"Nicodemus more than likely. This has to be child zero."
He pulled on his latex gloves. He brushed away some of the loose
leaves and soil and found what looked like a small human skull
with the cap and patches of black hair still attached. As he
continued, a shattered rib cage appeared. He drew a deep breath
and struggled to control his disappointment. Sable closed his eyes
for a moment. The sound of thunder in the distance brought him
from his thoughts. He scanned the sky. Even though none of the
nearby clouds looked threatening, he knew that a storm was
coming. He could feel it. So they needed to get back to the cabin
and get the dogs before the trail was washed away.

"It still doesn't answer the question of who killed
Nicodemus. Jackson was under surveillance, so he couldn't have
done it."

Sable gently pushed the skeleton to one side, but it
disintegrated. "Your guess . . ."

A low moan cut the silence from somewhere nearby.
Sable scanned the rock face of the canyon wall.

"What was that?"

Sable raised his index finger to his lips and then pulled
the .40.

Sable headed toward where he thought he'd heard the
sound, but knew he was walking to what appeared to be an
impenetrable wall of rock. The moan was clearer and more
distinct.

As he neared the edge, something stung his cheek and the
rock face of the wall exploded, sending shards in all direction. A
moment later, he heard the vicious crack of a rifle and he dove
behind a large bolder for cover. As he peered from behind it, he
saw that Carpenter had found her safe haven behind a fallen tree.

"Can you see anyone?" Sable asked as he studied the
surrounding terrain.

"I think I see him—he's up on the ledge, but there's no
way I can take him out." Carpenter aimed her pistol and fired
several shots in rapid succession.

From Sable's position, he couldn't see anyone but he
heard gravel cascading as the man scrambled up the canyon wall.

"Damn. He's gone." Carpenter stood and approached Sable while reloading her .38.

Behind him Sable heard the sound again. He looked over his shoulder. From this angle he could see a cave with an opening so small he couldn't have seen it even if he was standing next to it. He pulled a Maglite from his belt and clicked in on.

"Let's do it--ladies first." Sable gave a sweeping gesture with his arm.

"This time I'll let you do the honors." Carpenter shrugged. "Sometimes I believe males should be chauvinists. Especially when walking into a darkened cave."

Sable aligned the light with the barrel of his pistol, crouched and carefully slipped into the entrance. The passage was only a few feet wide with a hard packed dirt floor. He molded himself to the cavern wall, moving forward step by step. As he traveled deeper into the cavern, Sable sensed someone was nearby. Just ahead, the tunnel opened into a chamber. He quickly scoured the room with his light. It was clear except to his right. There, he saw the huddled nude body of a woman pressed against the rock wall. It took a moment to register with Sable that it was Lisa.

"Don't hurt me." She covered her face with her hands from the blinding light.

"You're with friends," Sable said soothingly.

"Bob?"

"Yes. I'm here." Though the use of the nickname grated on him, Sable let it pass. He rushed to her side.

"Thank God." Her shoulders convulsed while she tried to conquer her emotions. She took deep breaths as she tried to stand and steady herself, but she fell.

"What happened to you?" Carpenter moved up behind him.

Lisa stared at Sable as he spoke, her eyes wide and unblinking. Sable was conscious of her nakedness, the slight tan of her skin under the bloody scratches and dirt. She had

contusions on the shoulders, neck, and legs that were most likely
finger imprints. Her hair tumbled across her shoulders and her
full breasts lifted and fell rapidly with her uneven breathing.

"He . . . It was so terrible."

"Caleb Nicodemus?" Carpenter asked.

"I thought he was a myth, but he's not. He's real."

Sable waited.

"Auktelchnīk!" Her voice cracked. "He said I was his
long dead wife Takat-kījá reincarnated."

Sable raised an eyebrow as he looked at Carpenter who
only shrugged. He could only guess at the horrors Nicodemus had
subjected Lisa to. Surely she couldn't be in her right mind,
believing her kidnapper had been Auktelchnīk.

"Water," she said. "I need water."

Sable lifted Lisa's head gently, took his canteen from his
belt, and gave her a sip. "Slowly, very slowly."

Lisa nodded and Sable, with Carpenter's assistance,
helped her up. Lisa stood motionless, her senses suddenly alert.
Cold sweat began running from her armpits. She began babbling
about her capture and her ordeal.

"You're safe now," Carpenter gently brushed a stray hair
from Lisa's face, but she flinched.

"I'll never be safe from him. You can't stop him . . . He
can do things that you wouldn't believe." Gradually, tears
rimmed her eyes, then ran down her cheeks. She seemed unable
to speak.

"A .38 can put a big hole in any man," Carpenter said.
Sable stripped off his shirt and helped Lisa into it. As they left the
cave, Sable shivered. He scanned the area to the horizon. He had
to get Lisa back to the cabin and soon before hypothermia set in.
At dusk, the mountain air slipped to 40 degrees. An overcast
evening leached into the sky, bringing in the ever-gray dusk and
leaving everything without shadow.

The wind was cold and unyielding. Carpenter flapped her
arms against herself and stamped her feet to generate some heat
against the cold.

All of a sudden, the hair on the back of Sable's neck prickled. Something moved on the periphery of his vision and he went for his .40. As he looked out over the wilderness, he saw an apparition melt into the shadows of the trees. A shiver ran up his spine. Somehow he knew the apparition was the man they were looking for and Dan-e-wåk was in trouble. He needed to get back and talk to Jon and Chlawūch-tschāk.

Back at the cabin the medics took care of Lisa's abrasions and evacuated her to the Kanashig Medical Center. The area surrounding the cabin was a tumult of investigators. Sable stood off to one side, jotting down impressions of the crime scene in his notebook. Lab techs were carefully vacuuming the room and rummaging through cabinets, drawers and boxes searching for evidence. Brilliant camera strobes lit up the scene in an endless series of soft electronic whispers and whines.

"You look like death warmed over. You should go home and get a good night's sleep." Benson stood behind Sable, looking over his shoulder.

"You're not my mother."

"Well, if you won't take my advice, at least try this. I brought you some coffee." Benson offered him a steaming paper cup of dark liquid.

"Thanks. I also need one for Lisa." The coffee was bitter, but hot. He was still chilled from the mountain passes. Somehow, he felt better than he had in the morning—stronger, more energetic. "Have you ordered the dogs to track the child?"

"Don't worry about it. Go home and get some rest."

"Sure, okay." After jotting down a few more observations, Sable headed back to the detachment and called Lisa's uncle.

CHAPTER 31

After several days wandering through the wilderness
north of Kanashig, Dan-e-wåk finally had found the cabin where
he believed Tūtsch-gūtsch was being held captive under
Auktelchnīk's control. From his vantage high on a forested knoll,
nothing seemed out of place. He leaned against a birch tree and
focused the 7x50 power binoculars on the cabin. Smoke swirls
lazily drifted from a stone-laid chimney into the sky, until finally
dissipating into small tendrils.

Dan-e-wåk patted the chīlta (*knife*) on his hip, set his pack
down, then checked his weapons. He unslung his bow, drew three
arrows from the quiver, uncapped them and ran his finger
carefully over the razor-sharp titanium blade. Placing the spare
arrows in the loop of his knuckles of his bow hand, he notched
one, then crept forward. While trying to stay within the trees, he
carefully avoided stepping on twigs. He closed the distance to
about three hundred yards when he saw him--the Auktelchnīk of
legends—tall, thin, but well muscled. Auktelchnīk led a young,
raven-haired lad Dan-e-wåk guessed couldn't be more than 12
years-old toward a large square stone altar.

Auktelchnīk laid the boy on the altar and began chanting
words that Dan-e-wåk didn't understand, but guessed was the
prayer for ritual sacrifice, granting the priest not only power over
the victim, but taking the lad's essence as well. Dan-e-wåk took a
solid archer's stance and drew the arrow back until he felt the
eagle feathers caress his face. Auktelchnīk raised the knife in
preparation to strike as Dan-e-wåk silently said an ancient Tlingit
prayer and released the bolt. He notched another and fired again.

Auktelchnīk screamed in pain as both arrows drove deep
into his back a second apart. He spun around and dropped into a
crouch. The third and fourth arrows, the shaman effortlessly

caught in his hand, letting each drop to the ground in preparation for another onslaught.

For a moment, Dan-e-wåk was stunned his arrows hadn't taken the shaman down.

Auktelchnĩk pulled the arrows from his back and raised them in the air, then jogged toward Dan-e-wåk. "Dan-e-wåk, I've been waiting for you. Do you think you can kill me with your measly stingers?"

Auktelchnĩk closed his fist and the ground rumbled and shook. Dan-e-wåk staggered into a nearby clearing and regained his balance, yanked his chĩlta from its scabbard and took a karate stance. In one-on-one combat he rarely lost. He had been taught karate by the best. As Auktelchnĩk neared, Dan-e-wåk squared off with him. He cautiously followed Auktelchnĩk's moves, adjusting his stance to maintain the balance between them. The ancient shaman charged. In his hand the highly polished hunting knife blade reflected the sun as it moved from side to side. Dan-e-wåk blocked the knife, blade on blade, then drove a spear hand into the man's throat. Auktelchnĩk staggered back choking and tossed the knife into his left hand. The ancient shaman weaved back and forth, looking for an opening. Dan-e-wåk did likewise, constantly changing his stance. Auktelchnĩk dodged to the left and to the right then hurtled himself with his blade arm outstretched at Dan-e-wåk. Dan-e-wåk danced out of the way, blocking the thrust, threw a sidekick to Auktelchnĩk's solar plexus, following the tactic by driving his blade deep into the ancient shaman's side. Stepping back in surprise, Auktelchnĩk screamed a series of curses, took a deep breath and shook his head. He eyes blazed, turning dark amber. He lunged forward and Dan-e-wåk stepped to the side, but the blade caught Dan-e-wåk's upper arm, piercing skin, muscle, and ramming into the bone. Dan-e-wåk gritted his teeth but the shriek came through anyway. A fist came seemingly out of nowhere, glanced off Dan-e-wåk's jaw and spun him to the side.

Dan-e-wåk recovered, stepped quickly back but his opponent followed, lunging with the knife and counter punching with the other hand. Dan-e-wåk didn't see it coming. The blow came from the right, crashing into his skull and snapping his head back. With his senses reeling, his legs buckled and he crumpled to the ground. The knife flashed again, but this time with crimson dripping from the blade. In a last-ditch effort, Dan-e-wåk drove his blade into Auktelchnīk's heart. The ancient shaman fell back and collapsed into the brush.

Struggling to his feet, partially stumbling, swaying, he stood. Dan-e-wåk knew Auktelchnīk was not dead and he had to escape. He reached down to pull the blade from Auktelchnīk's chest, but decided against it. From the ancient shaman's white hair, he knew the virus had infected Auktelchnīk, giving him virtual immortality. He wasn't sure how to kill him. Cut off his head maybe. The villagers of Kanashig had done that centuries ago and still the evil shaman had returned. For now he had to rescue the boy and Tūtsch-gūtsch, then regroup, bringing in Jon, Sable, and Chlawūch-tschāk. He took a tentative step toward the boy, then another and another, lurching from side to side.

CHAPTER 32

After being treated at the medical center, Lisa was released into Sable's care. He'd found her temporary lodging at a local hotel where his men could easily guard her should the kidnapper try again. Lisa refused to go into the room unless Sable checked it out first. Lisa stood in the hallway while Sable entered the room. Rays from the setting sun broke through the venetian blinds, striping the room in bands of dusty light. When he'd confirmed that no one was in the room, he waved her in.

"You'll be safe here until morning. I'll have a trooper guard your door."

Lisa grimaced, then squeezed his arm. "I'd like it if you'd stay with me."

"I can't. I have to get back to the office and finish writing reports."

She walked nervously to the window and tossed a nod. "He's out there somewhere waiting for me."

"You're safe from him now."

"I won't be until you catch him and put him behind bars." Lisa sighed and tried to smile but failed. She frowned.

"You're safe," Sable said softly. He reached out and took her hand.

Lisa's frown dissolved into a smile. Then she saw the chain around Sable's neck. She reached out and took the small leather pouch in her hand before he could stop her, untied the drawstrings and slipped the bag off the talisman. As she held it in her hand, the translucent rock, set in finely detailed and crafted silver, instantly began to glow. The colors appeared to swirl, blend, and radiate multicolored lights and warmth "This is gorgeous. I've seen this before, but where."

"I don't know how you could . . ."

"A shaman's amulet–a tsāk-ssēt. And you were wearing it this weekend when you died." She let it drop on Sable's chest.

"God." Sable stepped back from her as the searing heat from the talisman drove through his chest to his heart. A blue flame leaped from the center of the stone, and it began to vibrate with an intensity Sable had never felt before. Images from the weekend cascaded through his mind, and he grabbed the arm of a nearby easy chair and collapsed into it. Now he remembered everything—all the missing pieces from the weekend. It seemed so surrealistic.

"Are you all right?"

"Yes," Sable croaked.

"How could I have forgotten?" Lisa sat on the edge of the chair, gently placing her hand on his face. "Oh, yes. Now I remember. Your uncle mesmerized us with the caduceus."

Likewise, he reached up, laid his hand gently against her cheek and pushed back a strand of wayward hair. He photographed her with his eyes, wanting to burn the image forever into his mind. In spite of the scratches, nothing marred her radiance. As she leaned forward and kissed him on the forehead, his breath caught in his throat. Sable felt as if he couldn't speak.

He cleared his throat. "I'd better get back to work."

"I want you to stay . . . "

"Well, just a little while longer."

"I want you to stay," she paused, "all night."

Sable was suddenly so tired. "I'll stay for a while until you fall . . ."

She took Sable's face gently in her hands, brought her lips to his and kissed him deeply. He felt his heart thumping against his ribs as a shiver passed almost simultaneously through their bodies. Sable was transfixed by Lisa's scent, the warmth of her skin, and the feel of her body against his. When they parted, slowly, Lisa started unbuttoning his shirt.

He put his hand hers to stop her. "This might not be such a good idea, especially after your ordeal. You're confused . . ."

"Hush. I'm not confused and I know you want this as much as I." Her lips quivered as she placed her hand directly over his heart.

"I . . ." She kissed him again deeply while she ran her hands over the hairs on his chest.

She was beautiful, her cheeks glistening with her tears. She slumped against him, burying her face in the hollow of his shoulder. It was as if she were drawing the pain of his past existence away from him, wiping his life clean.

Sable's finger traced the outline of her lips. He kissed her firmly, a gentle pressure that shaped her mouth to his. As his tongue slipped inside seeking hers, a tremor shook his body. He lightly ran his hand from Lisa's face and neck and down her arm.

"Ouch. Careful—I'm covered with scratches."

He pulled his hand away. "Sorry."

"Don't be." She said. They separated and stood. She moved toward the bed, slipped off her panties, and threw them at him. He caught them, felt the soft fabric in his hand, and tossed then on the chair. In spite of her assertiveness, underneath there was almost a girlish quality to her actions he found disarming. Sable followed her, took her hand, interlaced fingers, and with his other hand slowly undid the buttons of her blouse. As he kissed her open mouth his tongue searching, touching, and intertwining, he wrapped his arms around her, pulling her into him. As their bodies molded to each other, he continued to probe her mouth deeply. When they parted, he slipped off her blouse and began kissing her, starting with her forehead, ears, down her neck to her breasts. He gently unsnapped her lace covered brassiere, slipped it off and let it fall to the floor. He gently took a nipple into his mouth kissing it and kneading it with his tongue. Lisa's breasts were firm, round with a slight curve ending in small perky nipples. Their clothes seemed to dissolve away piece by piece, appearing as small heaps scattered across the floor until they reached the bed. He slipped his arms around her as she slipped onto the bed. He tried his best to stay away from her wounds. As he lay beside her, he outlined her face with his fingers and continued tracing the curve of her neck, arms, and hips. Slowly, carefully, gently, he entered her. In a caressing, urgent, rocking rhythm, they began to move as one--as if they had shared each other's body for a lifetime.

Lisa's eyes glazed over, her checks reddened, her breath came in short spurts and she arched her back to meet his thrusts. He increased his urgency to meet hers, his heart racing wildly in his chest. They both came in an almost violent explosion, and he collapsed on her. They made love again. When they were completely spent, Sable cradled her in his arms.

Tears began to slip down Lisa's face. "I'm glad I found you."

Sable put a finger under one of the tears and caught it. "And I you."

When her breathing deepened, Sable realized she had finally stopped crying and had fallen asleep. He then tucked the covers around her and gently brushed the strands of hair covering her face aside. He thought he would lay next to her for while before going back to work, but slipped into a deep sleep.

The ringing cell phone pulled Sable from a stuporous sleep and he grabbed at it, forgetting where he was. "What is it?"

"Just checking in to see if you're okay." Sable recognized Carpenter's voice.

"Yes." His voice was barely a whisper.

"The woman?"

"Lisa's fine."

"You're on a first name basis."

"I met her at Jon's—it's a long story. I'll tell you about it later."

Before Sable left the motel, he tore a page from his notebook, wrote Lisa a note and propped it on the nightstand.

****

Lisa's eyes snapped open and she screamed, her sleep disappearing instantly. Had she heard a noise? Her eyes fearfully searched the darkened room looking for Sable. The window across the room was open and the cool morning breeze pushed the curtains back and forth in a rhythmic dance. Though it was quiet, her heart went cold. She knew she hadn't opened the window before going to bed. As she stared at the shadows on the bedroom ceiling, she stretched under the warm blanket, trying to figure out where she was.

A figure, dressed all in black, filled the doorway.

She pushed herself up and against the headboard, wishing she'd talked Sable into leaving her a gun.

"Are you all right, miss?"

"Who, who are you?"

"Corporal Rick Lum. Sergeant Sable assigned me to watch you. He told me it'd be my ass if anything happened to you."

"I'm fine. Thank you."

She turned on the nightstand light, her hands shaking. She picked up the note and read it. "Lisa, you're very special to me. I'm sorry I have to leave, but duty calls. I'll see you tonight. XXX OOO Sable."

CHAPTER 32

The first thing the next morning, Sable drove to the
detachment. His uniform was rumpled from yesterday. There
were a lot of telephone messages and a pile of letters on his desk
he spent time prioritizing. The murder cases seemed to be getting
out of hand, and he desperately needed another viewpoint—
Masters'. Sable was about to pick up the phone and call Masters
when the secretary knocked on the open door. "Come in."

Linda Talbot leaned around the jamb. "I've got a real
character out front who wants to talk to only you. Says he knows
you."

"Well, who is he?"

"Lester Ward."

Sable laughed. "You're right, he is one heck of a
character. Sure, send him in."

Minute's later, Les Ward, a man of medium height,
scruffy, with an unruly thatch of thick graying black hair, walked
in to the office. He still had the same square features Sable
remembered when he had first met Les about twenty years ago. It
seemed the man hadn't aged at all. He owed Les for saving his
father's life and he knew it was payback time. During the
Vietnam War, Les had covered his father when he had seen a
grenade hit nearby. The man had gotten off easy. The shrapnel
had torn into his back only an inch and several places in his
backside.

Sable stood, reached across the desk and offered his hand.
"How's it going?"

"Happy as a clam except some bastards are using my trap
line cabin." Les had a slow gravelly drawl.

"And you want me to kick them out, right?"

"Yup, I'd sure like it." Les pulled a cigarette from the pack and tapped it on the arm of the chair, tamping the tobacco tightly together.

"Can I get you anything to drink?" Sable pointed to the 'no smoking' sign on his desk.

"I'll take one of those diet drinks you used to like as a kid."

"You got it." He stepped over to the office refrigerator, grabbed two cans of Diet Coke, and popped the lids. He handed one to Les, walked back behind his desk and took a swig.

"Thanks, I need that."

"Tell me about these desperadoes." Sable slipped into his chair and took another swig.

"Well, I know one these fellers, Jim James, and that's what makes me so cussed mad."

"You mean Tūtsch-gūtsch?"

"Yeah, that's him, but the other fella's tall, got white hair and a pony tail. And he wears only buckskins."

Sable's eyes narrowed and sat straight up in his chair. He didn't believe in coincidences. "How long have they been there?"

"Since last fall, I think. I figured it was temporary, but they haven't moved out."

"Why didn't you approach them and ask what's going on?"

"Well, when my partner, Wyatt Richards, disappeared, it kind of spooked me. After that I gave those folks a wide berth."

"Why didn't you tell anyone about your friend's disappearance?"

"I told that nice Sergeant Kelly and he got real excited. He told me he'd get right on it, but I never heard from him."

As a message came in and the computer beeped, Sable hesitated and glanced at the screen.

"He got real excited when I showed him on the map."

Sable pulled out a map and spread it out on the desk, then handed Les a pencil. "Where's your friend's cabin located?"

"His is here and mine's there." Les marked each location with an 'x.' "See, they're only about a ten miles apart."

Sable studied the map for a moment and shook his head. Nicodemus' cabin was central to the other cabins--finally he'd found a solid link. "Thanks. I'll get on this right away."

While Sable and Les passed a few pleasantries and Sable caught Ward up on what his father was doing, he couldn't help but feel antsy about getting on this newest piece of information.

When Les left, he closed the door to the office and contemplated the case.

Sable dialed Carpenter and explained the situation. "We're going for a plane ride."

While waiting for Carpenter, Sable polished the windshield of his 1977 Cessna turbo 210 Centurion and did the preflight checks from tires to engine, oil and fuel. After Carpenter was seated, Sable settled back in the seat, then hit the ignition switch. The engine chattered, coughed, wheezed and fired again. The engine's rumble set up a low vibration throughout the fuselage. "Ready?"

"I have to warn you I'm afraid of small planes." Carpenter clutched the edges of her seat.

"Why's that?" The wheels and struts creaked as they began to move.

"They don't have parachutes."

Sable couldn't help smiling. "Neither do large airliners."

The corners of Carpenter's mouth tried to lift into a smile, but failed.

"Tower, this is November Zero Five Six Alpha. Request permission to take off."

"Roger, permission granted."

"Are you sure you have a pilot's license?" Carpenter asked.

"You need a license to fly these things?"

"You're not very reassuring."

"I have it somewhere." Sable held the wheel by the pressure of his knees and began patting his pockets.

"No, that's okay. I'll trust you."

Sable taxied the Cessna out on the runway, and began gently increasing the throttle as he pulled back on the wheel. As the asphalt rapidly disappeared, the plane shimmied gently, lifting off, barely clearing the trees that lined the end of the runway. Beyond were the rolling forests of the bush that eventually swept up into the crags and snowy mountain slopes. Once he reached altitude, he banked toward Richards' cabin, set the GPS, and began watching the track heading.

Within minutes, the Cessna banked over a small cabin, turned and lined up with a rough country road. A couple of minutes more, and they were down. The plane hit the rough road, bounced a couple of time, then continued rolling down the road, bouncing over the chuckholes and rocks. Sable taxied the Cessna to the front of the building over an unkempt grassy yard that looked like a meadow. Behind the cabin was a copse of trees and brush that swept up and into a vast expanse of rolling hills. Sable opened the door and jumped down from the plane. Carpenter followed suit.

"Let's see if we can find Richards or some bad guys." Sable headed toward the cabin.

Carpenter wiped the sweat from her upper lip. "I think you should give your license back to the FAA."

"Well, I got us down in one piece, didn't I?"

"That's debatable." Carpenter hugged herself and briskly massaged her neck to dissipate the tension.

"Looks like no one's home." Sable pulled his .40 and stepped to the left of the jamb while Carpenter took the right— much the same as at the Nicodemus cabin.

"Wyatt Richards, this is the State Troopers. We need to talk to you." Sable brought the pistol to the ready and molded himself to the logs.

Silence.

Sable reached for the doorknob, cautiously twisted it and pushed the door open. He glanced in and nodded to Carpenter. They went through the door only a beat apart. There were no signs of life anywhere. Undisturbed layers of dust covered bookshelves, tables and chairs. A dried blood trail led from the front door to a back room. A squirrel scurried across the floor and up one of the support beams, the scratching of tiny feet across wood echoing in the empty cabin. Sable dropped to one knee and followed the movement.

"Hey there country boy. We going to have some fried critters tonight?"

Sable chuckled slightly as he pushed up. "Whal thar darlin', you get to skin and cook 'im."

"You shoot 'im, you cook 'im."

When they entered the back room, they found broken lamps, shattered glassware, overturned furniture and a bed filled with bloody blankets that said Richards didn't go easily. Dried maroon blood spatter lined the walls and in the center of the floor was a large stain that could only be blood with a trail that led out a side door.

"He sure as hell put up one hell of a fight." Carpenter slipped her .38 back into its holster.

"Yeah, but where did he go? That's the question."

"Another one: which blood trail is Richards'? It looks like the perp mortally wounded him, went out the front and Richards went out the back."

Sable followed the trail out a side door that was partially ajar. As Carpenter stepped out on the porch with him, he knelt down to see if he could make out the direction Richards might have crawled. Rain and snow had washed away any trace of the trail. He studied the brush and tree line about fifty feet behind the cabin, remembering his flight with Janet through the mountains from mob henchmen. "If I were trying to get away from a relentless killer, I think I would head that way." He inclined his head toward the trees.

Carpenter nodded.

"We need to do a sweep. I'll head north and then meet you half way." Sable motioned for Carpenter to go left.

Sable carefully moved the limbs of the bushes aside, looking for where Richards might have hidden. Progress seemed slow while he checked each possible path. Time was of an essence in checking out Ward's trap line cabin.

"I've found him," Carpenter yelled.

Sable jogged toward her and then saw what they had been looking for—Richard's skeleton. Animals had scavenged most of the body. Only the skull, with a partial thatch of gray hair and the bleached bones of a right hand curled around the hilt of a large hunting knife remained.

"Well, it looks like we've found him." Sable hunkered down over the meager remains.

"How can we be sure that it's Richards or the desperado that attacked him?"

Sable caught the glint of silver-gray metal under some leaves. He reached over and picked up a set of dog tags from the dirt Richards must have worn. He brushed the dirt away revealing Wyatt Richards' name embossed in the metal tags. He handed them to Carpenter. "Yup, that clinches it. It's Richards'"

"Want to bet James or the Auktelchnīk wannabe did this."

"In this case, I'm not betting."

"Going to call this in."

"I don't think the cell can reach from here. We'll call Benson once we're in the air."

****

Sable spotted Ward's cabin in a large meadow about two miles ahead. Smoke drifted from a typical stone chimney and the cabin looked nonthreatening. He cut back on the Cessna's throttle and banked toward the cabin. "It looks like there's someone home."

"I guess that we'll just have to come back with reinforcements." Carpenter had stopped gripping the seat for support.

"Why don't you take the wheel and I'll scope it out." Sable pulled a set of binoculars from under the seat.

"You got to be kidding. I don't know how to fly a plane."

"You just need a few instructions." Sable gave Carpenter a quick overview of the features of the Cessna 210. When he looked out the window, he found that they were over dense forests and the cabin was several miles behind them. While carefully monitoring Carpenter, Sable let her turn the plane around. On the second pass, Sable saw the man who haunted his dreams. He focused the binoculars in on the face, trying to study it in detail though the distance was great. The man with a white ponytail reached up into the sky and clutched his fist as if he were strangling someone or something. Suddenly, Sable felt a hard pressure in his chest. His heart raced, feeling as though it was shifting up and down through the gears of a Mack truck without using the clutch. Suddenly, the plane's engine coughed, sputtered, and died.

"What did I do wrong?" Carpenter's hands froze on the wheel.

"Nothing. It could possibly be a vapor lock in the carburetor." Sable lied, trying to keep his voice calm as he grabbed the wheel. "I'll take it from here," Sable paused, took a deep breath and said, "Please let the wheel go."

"Oh." Carpenter pulled her shaking hands back and folded them tightly on her lap.

The engine whined as it turned over, but didn't start.

"Looks like were going in dead stick." Sable trimmed the Cessna out and headed toward Richards' cabin while trying to restart the plane.

"What does that mean?"

"We have to land the Cessna as though it were a glider." Sable clicked the mike. There was no static or sound. "Damn, even the radio's dead. I can't even send out a May Day."

"We're going to die, aren't we?"

"Don't worry. I believe I can land this. If we can find a clearing . . ." As the wind whistled past the cabin, Sable watched the air speed indicator drop. He did some quick mental calculations: air speed versus time and distance. It was approximately six minutes or more back to Richards' cabin and the road.

"What do you mean you 'believe' and 'if' we can find a clearing?" Sable detected something in Carpenter's voice--panic. "There's the cabin." Sable gambled and hit the ignition one last time. The plane's engine caught and the RPMs finally came up as they began to land. Before setting down, Sable called the detachment and told Benson to meet him at Richard's.

"What happened to the engine, the power?"

"Sable shrugged. "Your guess is good as mine. But I should be able to easily fly the plane back to the airport." *The white-haired man couldn't have caused the systems to go out. Could he?*

"You just lost a passenger. I'm going to wait for Benson and return with him." Carpenter sighed and wiped the perspiration from her forehead. "I think it's safer to ride back."

As Sable taxied to Richards' cabin and cut the engine, he saw two men and a boy emerging from the woods and moving toward them.

"Isn't that Dan-e-wåk with one of the missing children? The other man I don't recognize." Carpenter grabbed the strut and jumped down. "And Dan-e-wåk's got blood all over him."

"The boy is Bobby Mills and the other man is Jim James, aka Tūtsch-gūtsch." She reached for her gun and Sable raised his hand and stopped her. "Let's hear what they have to say."

As Dan-e-wåk neared, Sable spread his feet apart and looped his fingers over his belt. He carefully studied the shaman's clothes. The blood on the clothing was Dan-e-wåk's and the holes more than rips or tears. Sable guessed they were from a knife, but he didn't want to say anything in front of Carpenter, knowing that Dan-e-wåk's wounds were by now mostly healed. He feared one day that the village's secret would be discovered. "What the hell happened to you?"

"Knife fight." Dan-e-wåk leaned over, placed his hands on his knees and took several deep breaths. Tūtsch-gūtsch stood off to one side with a blank look on his face and his eyes glazed over. "I rescued the boy and Tūtsch-gūtsch from your killer."

"Do you need help?" Carpenter motioned toward the blood.

Dan-e-wåk shook his head and pushed the boy toward Carpenter. "He needs water."

"You haven't answered my question."

"I met him."

As if she knew Sable wanted to talk to Dan-e-wåk privately, Carpenter took the boy aside and began checking him over.

"The serial killer? You know who he is?"

"Yes."

"Not Auktelchnīk again."

"Yes. I killed him, but he won't die."

"We need to get you and the boy to the medical center, but I'm going to have to take James in for questioning." Sable shook his head. He was on the verge of believing Dan-e-wåk but reasoned the killer had survived by somehow becoming infected with the Army's virus. He surmised that the only way to take out this Auktelchnīk wannabe was to do a *Highlander* on him—in other words, remove his head.

"I'm fine but the boy and Tūtsch-gūtsch need help more than I."

Sable shook his head. "If Tūtsch-gūtsch is involved in the kidnappings and murders, I have to take him in."

"It won't do any good. He's no longer here," Dan-e-wåk said. Sable knew he meant Tūtsch-gūtsch was in some type of mental fugue.

Just then Benson, Lum and Nutall drove up in a dark dusty Suburban and stopped next to the plane. As the trio left the vehicle, Sable nodded toward them. "We'll talk more about this later. Just don't mention you think this guy's Auktelchnīk. They'll fit you for a straight jacket and send you to Alaska Psychiatric Institute. You don't want to spend the next several years on tranquilizers at API."

Dan-e-wåk shrugged. "Jon, Chlawūch-tschāk, you and I need to talk about handling this situation."

"Okay, we'll get together early tomorrow morning," Sable hedged. After I send in the Swat Team, he thought. Benson and

Lum took Carpenter and the others back to town. Sable flew the
Cessna back to the airport.

While he waited for the SWAT team to arrive from
Fairbanks, Sable drove to Lisa's hotel to take her to dinner.
When, she met him at the door, however, one kiss led to another
and before they knew it, the kisses had turned into an hour of
lovemaking. Sable finally took her to the Arctic Bear Restaurant.
While they waited for their dinner, Sable brought Lisa up-to-date
on the case.

After the waitress brought them their coffee, Sable watched
Lisa add two packets of Equal to hers. He sipped his scalding,
black and unsweetened.

"You might think you have him cornered, but you don't."
Lisa reached across the table and laid her hand on his.

Sable turned his palm upward and gently clasped her hand.
"Don't worry. After tonight, your kidnapper will be in jail and
you'll be safe."

Lisa just looked into her coffee, then back at him and shook
her head.

CHAPTER 33

Slightly before midnight, dusk settled in darker than Sable had seen in a long time. A mass of dark thunderclouds hung thick in the sky masking the full moon. Though tomorrow would be the solstice, the longest day of the year when the moon and sun would be full in the afternoon and evening sky, it didn't seem evident tonight. He scanned the few members of the SWAT team that had been flown in hours before from Fairbanks. He vaguely recognized the team members from the wall of honor in the Fairbanks' detachment. They were dressed in black from head to toe with body armor and helmets. Each carried an M-16 rifle and had a .40 on his hip for backup.

Heading the team was Staff Sergeant Eric Valera. His rough square features, barely visible through the black and green camouflage paint, were hewn from years in the outdoors. Second in command was Sergeant Paul Tiggs. Though shorter than the normal trooper, Tiggs' frame rivaled that of Atlas. The others-- Dave Gallagher, Roger Edwards and Marc Clinton—had already spread out in attack formation, about a hundred feet apart.

They had an excellent position on a high knoll overlooking Ward's trapping cabin. Hunching down behind a large clump of bushes, Valera talked into a thin wire VOX communicator mike that came down from his black helmet. On his own radio set, Sable listened in on the conversations as Valera gave directions to his men. Sable watched Valera focus the binoculars and intently study the cabin. Flickering light from a window was the only sign of life inside.

Sable shook his head. He wasn't sure how Valera's men could make it undetected to the cabin because of the large meadow surrounding it. About a hundred feet from the cabin a large object caught his attention. In the dimness, he tried to make it out. It was large, square and had deep grooves running down from each corner. Then something occurred to him and he pulled his compass from a jacket pocket. As he sighted in on the object, he realized it was perfectly aligned with the cardinal points of the compass—a sacrificial altar.

Sable heard a twig snap and as he looked up to see a tall slender man move up next to him and begin jotting notes. Valera had earlier introduced Ferris Yeager as a team evaluator. He knew Yeager wasn't really needed, for it was common knowledge that Valera's team was the best in the state, having collared some notorious criminals and winning several national competitions.

Carpenter moved up behind Sable and whispered in his ear. "I want to be in on the kill."

"It's Valera's call, but if he won't let me go in with him, he definitely won't let you."

"Thanks, but no thanks." Her face screwed itself up in anger and she retreated into hostile silence.

Valera let out a rough sigh. "Damn log cabins, there's always only one way in. At least this guy's not the Unibomber."

"I wouldn't underestimate the man. He took on a squad of national guardsmen and came out the victor," Sable said.

"Yeah, but he wasn't dealing with my team." Valera face hardened as he raised his hand in the air, then said into his mike, "Ready to rock and roll."

A series of rogers cascaded over the radio net.

Valera motioned and he and his team moved forward slowly down the hill.

Darkness seemed to close in on Sable. He tried not to move but found his muscles beginning to knot up from crouching so long. As he glanced at the luminous dial of his watch, he couldn't believe that it was the solstice—here it was the beginning of the longest day of the year with almost 24-hours of uninterrupted light, yet it was still dark at 12:15 a.m.

Sable had been following the movements of the SWAT team as it closed in on the cabin. By now the team lay some eighty feet from the structure. Three team members prepared to go in the front door and two covered the window. When the three hit the front door with a battering ram, there was a loud crack of splintering wood as the door exploded inward. Several rifles simultaneously spit a hail of bullets. The echoes of the barrage, the breaking glass and bullets thudding into the log walls seemed to Sable to be as loud as if he were standing in the middle of the action.

A brilliant black light with a blue corona exploded from the cabin almost blinding Sable. Its force threw the men covering the window some 30 feet into the yard, then everything went quiet and dark. The earth rumbled and shook.

"Valera, you okay?" Sable asked into the mike, while steadying himself, but only heard the static of an open radio channel. Carpenter moved up behind Sable and pulled her .38. "Valera, this is Sable. You okay down there?"

"Explosives?" Yeager asked, his voice shaky.

Sable shrugged and drew his .40. "Your guess is as good as mine."

"You guys aren't going down there?" Yeager asked.

Sable looked at Carpenter and smiled.

Carpenter smiled back. "Let's do it."

"You guys are nuts. I'm staying here."

With about fifty feet between them, Sable and Carpenter cautiously headed down the hill. Ahead of them lay the cabin, dark and silent as the souls in Tūtsch-schiā-nách (*black valley*) with its unending moonless nights. The going was slow, but they finally stood at each side of the doorjamb, hardly breathing. Sable pulled two Maglites from his belt and tossed one to Carpenter. He held his light parallel to the barrel of the .40 and nodded to Carpenter when she was ready. He had started a countdown by nodding his head when a tall white-haired man burst from the cabin. Sable spun around, centered his sights on the man, took a deep breath and began to squeeze the trigger. The man's shape became a shadow, then a wolf that disappeared into the darkness.

"Did you see that?" Carpenter leaned against the cabin for support.

"I'm not sure what I saw." Sable took a quick breath. "At least I'm not going to mention this in any report." He didn't want to believe it—not the paranormal. Everything told him not to believe it. And for the first time in his life he was frightened—no terrified. Auktelchnīk had really returned, he thought.

"Then, how do we write this up?"

"I'm not sure. I'll have to think about it."

Carpenter clicked on the light and swung the beam through the open doorway. She drew a quick breath and held it. Their comrades' bodies lay crumpled in heaps, not moving. "I think I'm going to take a couple days off, head to Fairbanks, and get very drunk."

"I need you here. You can just as easily get drunk here."

"I'm afraid I'll lose it. I really need to get away from here and this case."

Sable nodded. "Okay, but I have to follow this through."

"I wish you luck, but I don't think any power on earth can stop Auktelchnīk." She stumbled over the name. In the dusk, Sable saw her hands were still shaking.

When Sable got back to the detachment, he called Nutall and told her she was no longer needed on the case. "We've finally got the bad guy," Sable lied.

"You mean Nicodemus?" Nutall's voice was doubtful. "Then who killed him?"

"One of the parents. It shouldn't be too long and we'll have him too."

"Well, what happened to the child who escaped from Nicodemus' cabin?"

"I'm afraid she's still missing."

"Please let me know when you find her."

"I will, just let me know where you'll be."

"Do you know what happened to Carpenter? She just called me and asked me to go with her to Fairbanks."

"I believe the stress of this case finally got to her."

"Well, I'll check on the case in about a week and see how it's going."

After exchanging good-byes, Sable dialed home and his uncle. Auktelchnīk had to be stopped.

CHAPTER 34

Ahead lay a winding dirt road. Sable reduced his speed and entered a narrow dirt drive that led from the highway to Jon's hunting lodge. Each fall, Jon served as a hunting guide for tourists as well as Alaskans. During the summer, he took tourists camping, white-water rafting and jet boat touring.

Approaching the lodge, Sable parked the Suburban off the edge of the road. Surrounded by trees on three sides, the two-story lodge faced the valley on the south. The smell of burning wood from the fireplace hung heavily in the morning air. Sable turned up his collar against the wind as he cautiously circled the building. From a large black Ford pickup, which he recognized as Jon's, he heard howling and yapping dogs—hunting dogs. The dogs had been placed in a large camper-shaped kennel that was subdivided into a number of wooden cages that held each animal. Just beyond the truck was an Olympic-size swimming pool fed by a frothing mountain stream. He shivered, wondering how anyone could swim in near freezing waters.

As Sable stepped up to the front door, Jon opened it, poked his head out and motioned for Sable to enter. "It's safe. We've already checked it out."

Sable stepped into the lodge, scanned the room and shook his head. This was a side of Jon he'd never seen. The room had all the trappings of a standard hunting lodge—comfortable furniture and wall-to-wall trophies—from large king salmon, silver salmon and king crab to bears, moose and caribou. Above a stone-laid fireplace hung a moose head that sported a record rack; Sable guessed it was close to eighty inches. In one corner, a huge stuffed grizzly bear stood, its feet apart, front paws outstretched in a fighting posture—claws bared, its mouth open wide, lips curled,

and long white fangs ready to snap an unsuspecting hunter's arm
in two—if it had still been alive.

"Nice place," Sable said, keeping his voice neutral.

"It's hype for the tourists. Advertising, if you will. The
visitors go gaga over it." Jon flashed his white teeth in a broad
smile. "It puts food on the table and that's what counts."

"What's with the pool? I don't know anyone who would
swim in it."

"I only heat it when the tourists show up."

Sable nodded. "Okay, where's the rest of the gang? We
need to get this operation going."

"In the workshop."

As Sable stepped into the room, he realized that it was more
than a workshop. A variety of carpentry and automotive tools
hung on the west wall. On the north wall, a large picture window
seemed to open up a portal to the wilderness with its snow-capped
rugged peaks and dense forests.

Sable found Dan-e-wåk and his uncle huddled around a
workbench. In front of them were polishing cloths, funnels, a
scale for weighing powder, and several presses so they wouldn't
have to continually change the dies. Were his friends creating
some type of dumdum bullet? His knowledge of the finer points
of reloading was shaky, but the process was simple. He knew
brass could be reloaded over and over. It was a simple process:
push out the fired primer, resize the brass case, insert a new
primer, add the right amount of powder and seat a new bullet in
the case.

"It's good to see you, Xhoots'een." Dan-e-wåk
momentarily looked up from his work.

"Glad you could join us. Please chip in." Chlawūch-tschāk
handed Sable a polishing cloth.

"Sorry I'm late." Sable picked up a .40 case, inspected it
for defects such as head separations, excessive bulges and defects
and began wiping it clean. He had to exercise care to prevent dirt
from scratching the case and, in turn, the resizing die.

"You're later than you know." Jon joined them and began weighing the power charges he had placed on small square pieces of paper.

"All right, dammit. I'm sorry I didn't believe you guys." Using a brush, Sable started cleaning the cases with a light coating of lube. "Okay, using the SWAT team was a bad idea."

"Well, maybe not. You may have given us the time we need. Auktelchnīk expended a lot of power fighting off the SWAT. So, Valera and his men didn't die in vain." Dan-e-wåk took a shiny silver bullet, held it to the light and carefully examined it, then held it over the case mouth. With his other hand, he lowered the press handle while easing the case and the bullet up into the die.

"But we have to find Auktelchnīk by tonight." Chlawūch-tschāk inserted the pointed end of a deburring tool into the case to remove burrs and chamber the case mouth. When he was finished, he fit the other end over the case mouth and removed exterior burrs.

"And why's that?"

"Tonight's the solstice, when Auktelchnīk will be at the zenith of his power. He probably needs to make several more sacrifices. My guess is he has to fill out a baker's dozen."

"But he has no children and he's on the run." Sable put the cloth down. "Besides we'll never find him."

"He will find the children," Dan-e-wåk said. "And we'll find him."

Or he'll find us. To amplify his power, he needs the caduceus. Chlawūch-tschāk momentarily looked up from his work.

"Did you bring the clothing from the cabin?" John asked.

"Yes. It's in the Suburban."

"The tsāk-ssēt?" Dan-e-wåk asked.

"Yes." Sable unconsciously reached for the amulet, feeling its warmth sear into his skin.

"Good. With the combined power of your tsāk-ssēt and the staff of ages, we can defeat him."

Sable watched Dan-e-wåk hold another round up to the light. As the bullet caught the fiery brilliance of the sun, the light dancing from its curved surface split into a rainbow of colors. Sable held back his disbelief. *Dāna--Silver bullets.*

"Good, Jon has the dogs out back."

As if Jon were reading his mind, he shrugged and grinned. "I'm using my dāna and dāna coin collections I've been saving for years, but it's going to a good cause."

"It's time the weapons are li-xeitl *(blessed)*." Dan-e-wåk placed the last round and then wiped the perspiration from his forehead. He carried the tray of bullets to a table covered by a traditional red ceremonial dance blanket, bordered with white fringe. In the center of each was a large, symbolic portrait of a klēd-jēlch *(white raven)*. Several rifles and pistols were already on the table. Chlawūch-tschāk went to a corner and uncloaked the caduceus of power and brought it back and placed it also on the table. Jon returned from another room and placed down the ancient case he had told Sable about. Jon carefully opened it and drew out a large golden ax, which was similar to the headman's axe of early Britain, and laid it on the table with the rest of the weapons.

"Where'd you get the atu-tē schenagóje?" Sable ran his hand, palm down, in a circle several inches above the blade. Even at the distance, he felt an overwhelming hit of blistering power, radiating from it.

"It's been in my family for at least a millennium. It's said that the first Klēd-jēlch, a leader of the Yanayadel, cut off Auktelchnīk's head."

"We're all here from the Jēlch clan," Chlawūch-tschāk said.

"Klēd-jēlch clan," Dan-e-wåk corrected.

Sable shook his head. He thought there was only one raven clan.

Dan-e-wåk walked to one end of the table and Chlawūch-tschāk the other. Chlawūch-tschāk raised the caduceus staff and its orb while Dan-e-wåk spread his hands out with palms down over the table. They began chanting in a language that sounded to Sable almost like Tlingit but not.

When they finished, Chlawūch-tschāk said, "May the ancient ones and the Lord bless us."

"We're ready for the sweat lodge," Dan-e-wåk said.

"Alone each of us must seek his own vision."

Instead of a sauna in the back of the lodge, Jon had a tschāsch-hit (*sweat lodge*). In the traditional manner, grass and dirt covered it, forming a large mound. Like the sanctity of a church, the sweat lodge to Native Americans was just as sacred. Dressed only in a terrycloth towel, Sable ducked through a small opening covered by a blanket. In the center of the room, a mound of rocks pulsed with a dry heat. Each man took a point of the compass and sat cross-legged facing the center. Dan-e-wåk drew a ladle of water from a galvanized metal bucket and poured it over the rocks, yielding the unmistakable hiss and crackle of steam being created.

Though it seemed ages since he'd been in a steam bath, Sable found this much hotter. After a while, a white solid mist blanketed the entire room, clogging his sinuses, throat, and burning his eyes. The tsāk-ssēt weighed heavily on his chest as he tried to relax and concentrate. He unconsciously took a deep breath, burning his lungs, and choked. He bit his lip to keep from cursing. Then, taking a slow breath, he felt time expand into a void of nothingness. He was about to give up and leave when the tsāk-ssēt began to vibrate and glow, and the whiteness parted. He found himself at Ward's cabin. On the altar, a young child lay spread-eagled. Auktelchnīk stood over her with a long gleaming blade in his raised hand. Sable reached out to stop the shaman, but the scene disappeared into circular waves that progressed outward as if he'd plunged his hand into the surface of a mirrored lake. He now knew where Auktelchnīk would be--they didn't need the dogs. He struggled to stand, his legs rubbery. Swaying from side to side, he took a few tentative steps, then stumbled from the tschāsch-hit into the coolness of the Alaska outdoors.

"It's about time you came out. We've been waiting for almost an hour." Chlawūch-tschāk slapped him on the back, and motioned to the swimming pool. "Now you need to jump in the pool."

"The water's ice cold." Sable shivered at the thought.

"It's part of the ceremony."

Sable shrugged, walked to the edge, untied the soaked towel, let it fall to the concrete and jumped. As he hit the water, he gasped--the cold came as a shock to his system, numbing him and robbing him of his breath and strength. It continued to crush in on him, trying to pull him under. When his feet hit the bottom of the pool, he realized he was at the short end.

Sable chattered, trying to form the words. "I know where Auktelchnīk's going to be."

"Then we don't need the dogs." Chlawūch-tschāk offered his hand for assistance.

"Thanks." Even with this, Sable found himself barely able to crawl from the water. Jon and Chlawūch-tschāk had to prop him up almost all the way back to the lodge. They discussed their strategy as they clothed themselves in military battle-dress uniforms. In the Army tradition, they painted their with faces black and green camouflage.

"I think we're ready, but I agree with Xhoots'een—once we've take care of Auktelchnīk, we must destroy the altar," Dan-e-wåk said.

"I have several sticks of dynamite in the back shed," Jon said as he handed each their share of ammunition.

Sable arched an eyebrow at his friend's comment. "Let me give Benson a call. I'm sure he can find something in the inventory that'll help. He can meet us on the way."

CHAPTER 35

As they crouched behind the bushes, Sable had a feeling of déjà vu. The amber sun was hot and bright in a blue cloudless sky. From a distance, the cabin appeared empty, but he could sense the closeness of Auktelchnīk. Though his friends and uncle knew what they were up against, he wasn't sure if they could kill Auktelchnīk. What chance did they have when the highly trained SWAT lasted but just a few seconds? He knew they had to try, even though they were only protected by ancient spells and the caduceus. After all he'd seen, he still found it hard to believe in the myth. He nervously checked the hands-free VOX communicator each of them had. It was similar to the ones the SWAT team carried, but with a greater range.

"Agán táchē (*the sun burns hot*) and we have a demtsakin ris-dīs (*new moon*). This is not good." Chlawūch-tschāk whispered. "Hāde-anagut (*He comes*)."

"I feel his kā-tschīchri (*shadow*)," Dan-e-wåk said.

Jon nodded. "A<u>x</u> lidé<u>x</u>'-x' awé tóo xwaanúk si.áat'ee át (*I felt something cold on my neck*)."

"Well, let's do it." Sable checked his pistol and slipped it back in the holster. They spread out about thirty feet apart as planned, then started low crawling. Though it seemed to take forever, Sable finally found himself within twenty feet of the altar. He unstrapped the light antitank weapon (LAW) and laid it next to him. Though he considered using the LAW, he knew it would be useless against Auktelchnīk's power. Sable pulled the .40 and waited. He didn't have to wait long before the shaman came out of the cabin carrying a struggling child. Auktelchnīk stopped and studied the forests and hills as if he knew he had company. The shaman almost glided to the stone, placed the young girl on it, and began chanting in a language Sable couldn't understand. He leveled his pistol at the shaman's heart and put tension on the trigger.

"I'm ready," Sable whispered into the mike.

"Wait. We need him entirely engrossed in his ritual. When we strike we'll have only a split second when he's defenseless." Dan-e-wåk said.

As the shaman ripped the girl's blouse open, Sable took a deep breath and bit his lip in anger, adding extra pressure to the trigger of his pistol. Suddenly, the color of the trees and grass fluoresced in a burnished amber light. Sable glanced up and saw the sun begin to merge with the moon. This was a first for him-- the moon being eclipsed. When he brought his gaze back to Auktelchnīk, the shaman had already drawn his knife and held it high in the air, poised to strike. In his earphone he heard the word "now" and automatically fired twice at Auktelchnīk's heart. The knife went flying as the man staggered back. Simultaneously, a barrage of silver bullets hit the shaman from three different directions. The explosive reports came over the radio almost deafening Sable. He turned off the radio. A confused look crossed Auktelchnīk's face, he wavered and then collapsed from view behind the altar. *This was too easy.* Sable was on his feet, weapon at the ready, rapidly moving forward. From the corner of his eye he saw the rest were doing much the same. They all stopped just feet from the ancient shaman.

Using the altar as a brace, Auktelchnīk pulled himself up, reached toward the sky, closed his fist and chanted in a dialect that sounded almost Arabic. The sun darkened even more.

"Again," Chlawūch-tschāk yelled.

Auktelchnīk weaved his hands in front of him as though he were forming a shield. This time each bullet vaporized into a ball of fire before it could reach its intended target.

"Dan-e-wåk, Klēd-jēlch, you've come back to haunt me," Auktelchnīk coughed, blood frothing from his mouth. "But you've forgotten the old ways and so you will die. This time I'm more powerful than you."

"We still have the weapons used by the ancients who killed you before." Chlawūch-tschāk lifted the staff of ages. A blue ball of electricity formed over the orb, sparks of energy lancing out and into the air.

"And I have your destiny. I am sending you back to the Tūtsch-schiā-nách." Jon drew the ax from his belt and raised it high above his head. Even after all the centuries, the golden-mirrored schenagóje reflected the sun's light, setting off an explosion of colors.

"You are wrong. I am your destiny and your destiny is death." Auktelchnīk raised his hands toward the sky and in a flurry of movements his hands began forming intricate patterns. From nowhere, lightening arched across the turquoise sky. It darkened as the clouds became a boiling mass, then the sky split into halves, forming a river, ever widening—an undulating darkness rivaling the depths of empty space.

Chlawūch-tschāk pointed the staff at Auktelchnīk and a bolt of lightening hit the shaman. For a second, the shaman teetered and as he was about to regain his balance another bolt hit him. Auktelchnīk went down on one knee, took a deep breath and stood again. Sable launched himself toward the shaman, using a technique he hadn't tried in years—a flying leap kick. The side of Sable's foot hit Auktelchnīk in the throat, and the force and momentum drove the shaman to the ground. Sable had dropped into a combat stance, prepared to take on the shaman, but knew that after crushing the man's throat, Auktelchnīk should be dead. But to his surprise, the shaman was back on his feet, taking a stance Sable had never seen before.

Auktelchnīk flicked his hand toward the ground and it began to rumble, shake and roll. Sable found it hard to maintain his balance and used every technique taught him by his karate senseis. From the corner of his eye he saw the others were equally off balance. Auktelchnīk lunged forward, throwing a series of strikes and kicks. Sable easily blocked each strike as he retreated. Finally, he slid forty-five degrees off the line of attack, threw a roundhouse kick to the shaman's solar plexus, following it with several punches to Auktelchnīk's face. Now it was Auktelchnīk's turn to retreat, but instead he flew forward, and drove an open palm strike to Sable's chest. Auktelchnīk screamed and pulled back a hand that burst into flame. Auktelchnīk had touched the tsāk-ssēt. Though Sable's chest felt as if it were on fire from the amulet, he pressed the attack, throwing lunge punches, front kicks, sidekicks and back spinning kicks. Jon nodded to Sable as he raised the schenagóje, its bright blade glowing in the sun. Chlawūch-tschāk raised the staff and pointed it at Auktelchnīk. Dan-e-wåk aimed a 30:06 at the shaman's heart. Sable wasn't sure what hit Auktelchnīk first--the bolt of lightning; the axe or the bullet—but the shaman, now headless, collapsed into a heap, arms and legs akimbo.

Jon picked the child up and took her aside. Sable walked over to her them. "She okay?"

"As well as can be expected." Jon shrugged. Sable looked down at her. He recognized Betsy from the photograph posted on office wall. She stared blankly into the sky. Sable shook his head. It could take years and the psychiatrists might not bring her around. He went to the altar and helped the others pack dynamite around it.

"How are we going to destroy this body, so he won't come back again?" Dan-e-wåk asked.

"I thought you guys had this all worked out," Sable said.

"First we had to solve the immediate problem and stop Auktelchnīk." Chlawūch-tschāk shrugged, then stuck another stick of dynamite under the stone.

"Just separating the body from the skull didn't work in the past." Sable said.

"Then I suggest that we put his body on the altar and blow him up," Dan-e-wåk offered.

"I don't know," Sable paused and sighed. "That would leave pieces of him scattered across the meadow. Couldn't someone come along and chant some spell over the pieces and bring him back?"

"We could cremate him and scatter his ashes over the state." Jon walked up behind them.

"I have a friend who runs a crematorium in Fairbanks. I might get him to do me a favor." Sable sighed.

"How are we going to get Auktelchnīk there?" Jon asked.

"That's where I have a back up plan—a chopper and a friend that won't talk." Sable unclipped a hand-held radio from his belt, raised its antenna and made the call.

Minutes later, they blew up the altar. It disintegrated, thundering into a plume of rock, dust and debris that nearly hit them in their hiding place. They did a thorough search of the cabin and found a number of artifacts archeologists would have given their eyeteeth for. These items they placed in a pile outside the cabin and burned.

Sable heard the chopper in the distance and breathed a sigh of relief. Everything seemed to be wrapped up with a nice ribbon. With a little sleight of hand, he could blame the children's deaths on Nicodemus. Then it hit him. He still had a killer—not a serial killer of serial killers, but a killer of perverts. When he reached the detachment, he gave Masters a call to see if he could help him find the killer, then explained the case with a considerable number of omissions.

CHAPTER 36

It had been an exhausting day. The troopers had taken the child, Betsy Jackson, to the hospital and called her parents. As he left the hospital, Sable reviewed the facts on Betsy's miraculous appearance. Since she hadn't been in Auktelchnīk's cabin when the SWAT team hit, where had she been for the last few months? That was the mystery. As he pondered the clues to the crime, he realized Nicodemus had been using the Auktelchnīk myth to kidnap children as well. Though Betsy and Adonica were safe, they remained in a trance or coma. When they came out of it, Sable guessed the girls would require years of psychological counseling to bring about some degree of normalcy.

When Sable finally stumbled through his front door, he collapsed in the Strato-lounger and found he could hardly move. With great effort, he pushed himself forward, grabbed the phone and called Lisa. After spending several hours talking with her, he asked her to move in with him when she wasn't at the dig. To his surprise, she agreed. As he hung up, his eyes fluttered closed. For the first time in a long time, Sable slept soundly.

The next morning, before Sable went to the detachment, he helped Lisa move. She set her suitcase on Sable's bed. "This is kind of sudden. Are you sure this is okay with you?"

"I'm certain." He folded her in his arms and kissed her deeply.

As they separated, she said. "All right, I'm convinced, but if you haven't really moved in to you're house . . ."

"Oh, you mean the unpacked boxes in the living room." Sable laughed, smiled sheepishly, and kissed her again. "Now, I have a reason to finish unpacking."

"Do you think you might sneak some time before you go to work?" Lisa gently caressed his face.

He shook his head. "Sorry, I still have a killer to catch."

Lisa pretended to pout.

****

It now had been two weeks since the confrontation with Auktelchnĭk. Life had pretty much gone back to normal. The troopers were issuing traffic tickets, resolving domestic disturbances, and tracking down lost husbands at local bars. Sable poured a cup of black coffee from the coffee maker he'd brought to the office, dropped in a couple sugars and returned to his desk. The evidence from the Albert Bosch and Mathew Farley murders was spread out over his desk. He knew the killer had to be Jackson. So far the surveillance he'd set up on the man had yielded nothing. Benjamin Jackson's routine rarely varied from work to store to home. As soon as he got through sorting it out, he would send the hair and fibers to the crime lab in Anchorage. With the DNA, he had his killer, Jackson.

"Got coffee?" Masters asked. Sable looked up, half wondering how his old partner had slipped into the room without him hearing.

"Just grab a cup." Sable nodded to the pot sitting on the half refrigerator in the corner.

"Why are you trying to catch this guy? I think that the governor should pin a medal on him."

"A murderer is a murderer. You just can't let someone get away with a killing even though the guys they're killing are scumbags."

"That's just it. He was just cleaning up the garbage--killing pedophiles, scum of the earth." Masters picked up the largest mug and poured the coffee. "Any witnesses?"

"Not yet. The maid found Bosch and we only found Farley because he went off the tracker." Sable held his pencil between his first and middle finger and tapped it on the desk.

The phone rang. Sable held up his hand to break the conversation and answered the phone. It was his friend Harold Wincoft from the Northern Lights Crematorium and Chapel. "Is the deed done?"

"Well, yes and no. I've got a problem."

Sable detected the worry in his friend's voice and sat straight up in his chair. His mind ran through a number of disagreeable possibilities, including one where their subterfuge had been discovered and he was looking at a prison sentence for covering up the destruction of a body. "Okay, hit me with it."

"Well, it's like this," Wincoft said. "I cremated the body, but my assistant somehow mixed up the ashes and sent the urn to a family in Grangeville, Idaho."

"Is there anything you can do about this . . . get the ashes back?"

Silence.

"Wincoft?"

"Sorry, but I can't afford to bring any attention to this special project you had me do."

"Okay. Thanks anyway." Sable felt a heaviness settle in his stomach. Could Auktelchnīk actually come back to life from the ashes? He wasn't sure, but after the Jackson case he'd look into it.

"Sabe, you with me?" Masters' voice was somewhere in the background of his thoughts.

"Huh. Oh sure." Sable placed the phone back in the cradle.

"Is this the evidence?" Masters picked up a plastic bag, then laid it back on the desk.

Sable nodded and picked up a bag. "We've got him--hair with the follicles still attached. Now all we have to do is get a court order for some of Jackson's DNA."

"Where's the hair sample?"

"This is from the Bosch crime scene." Sable tossed Masters a plastic bag he caught easily.

"Do you have any more hair, saliva, blood from the perp?"

Sable shook his head. "This guy was careful, extremely careful."

Masters opened the bag, took out the hairs and pulled out a lighter.

"What the hell do you think your doing?" Sable was out of his seat as if he'd hit the eject button on an Air Force fighter jet. But before he could get to Masters, the flame spiraled up the hairs and with a sharp pop, they were gone.

"I just saved a family from being destroyed."

There was a momentary silence. "Now I know you have lost it."

"What will his wife and children do without him—the cost of the trial, loss of their home, etc? His family didn't ask for this."

"We have lots of killers, robbers, and burglars who have families. Jackson should have thought about the consequences before he did this."

"It's too late now."

"I'm just going to have to put Jackson away some other way." Sable raised his hands in surrender. "You may have let Jackson off to continue killing."

"Well, follow my lead. We can scare the shit out of him so he'll never stray again."

****

"What's this all about? I heard you found the killer/kidnapper—a guy named Caleb Nicodemus." Jackson's grip was strong, confident and his demeanor was that of a Zen Buddhist. He took a seat opposite Masters and Sable at the interrogation table.

"But the question is--who killed him?" Sable asked.

Masters' eyes locked with Jackson's as he leaned partially across the table. "And we believe you killed Albert Bosch, Mathew Farley and Caleb Nicodemus."

Jackson folded his arms and arched an eyebrow. "I didn't kill anyone, but death was too good for that slime."

"All of them were tortured before they died." Sable pushed the morgue photographs of the trio across the table. He knew Bosch hadn't been tortured and suspected Auktelchnĩk killed Nicodemus, but he wanted to see Jackson's response.

"Good riddance to bad garbage." Jackson lips broadened into a wide smile. "But I didn't kill them."

"We're sure you did."

"I didn't." Jackson pushed himself from the table as if trying to keep Masters from his personal space.

Masters walked around the table and brought his face within inches of Jackson. "Well, we know you did. In fact, we found your hair at one of the crime scenes. You're going away for a long time."

"Then arrest me, if not, get out of my face and let me go." Jackson shrugged and put up a hand to block Masters' face.

"Then you're under arrest." Masters read Jackson the Miranda warning.

"I want a lawyer."

"We'll let you have a lawyer when we want to," Sable said. Nothing was going the way he had assumed it would. There was a hint that a chink was beginning to form in Jackson's armor, however.

"Look, I know my rights. When I ask for my lawyer, all your questions must cease."

"Did you hear him ask for a lawyer?" Sable pulled a pencil from his pocket and began tapping it on the table.

"Not a single word." Masters reached for Jackson's hand.

Jackson jerked his hand back. "Ouch, dammit. What the hell did you do to me?"

"Got a voluntary sample of your DNA." Master held a penknife up, blood covering the blade.

"Bullshit." Jackson jumped up from his chair. "Give me my lawyer."

"You're not going anywhere." Taking Jackson's arm, Masters eased him back into the chair.

Sable snapped the pencil he had been tapping in half and tossed the remnants into the trash. "It's my job is to search out evil and put an end to it. And you're just as evil as the guys you murdered."

"I don't have to say anything that would incriminate me. You can't get blood out of cabbage salad."

"It's a turnip." Masters laughed. "But I already have your blood."

"Whatever. You know what I mean—I'm not saying a damn thing."

"We have you dead to rights. But maybe we can come to some reasonable understanding—in other words, do something here that will benefit all of us," Sable said.

"What's that?"

"Some type of agreement." Masters sat on the edge of the table.

Silence.

"You know, you could go to prison for the rest of your life," Sable said. He turned toward Masters and winked so Jackson couldn't see him. "That means your family will be destitute or on welfare."

"What are you telling me?"

"We don't want to rob children of their father especially when their sister's in a coma." Masters again leaned toward Jackson to ensure he had Jackson's attention.

"If you promise us there'll be no more killings, the hairs found at the crime scenes could be misplaced permanently." Sable said. "And if murders start up again, the hairs could be easily found."

Masters raised the penknife, but it was an unspoken message that was no longer needed.

"I understand."

After Jackson and Masters left, Sable called Lisa and told her he'd be home soon. He liked the sound of that—he had love and a home again. Looking around his desk, Sable found the photograph of his wife and son. He reached out, picked it up and studied it. Fond memories of his family played on the screen of his mind. Though the pain wasn't completely gone, it had lessened. Smiling whimsically, he brushed the dust from the frame that had gathered over the last week. Then he opened his desk drawer and placed their photograph on top of a stack papers

Dark Shaman

and with a slight twinge of regret he closed it. Though he knew he'd never forget them, he had a new life—a new beginning. Sable spun his chair around to look out the window. The midnight sun was a golden orb of promise in the azure evening sky.

Dark Shaman

Epilog
Circa 450 B.C.

.

Sacred arrows, blessed by many of his peers, cut deeply into the shaman's back. He staggered from side to side, his moccasins thudding on the forest floor as his breathing became increasingly ragged. With each gulp of air, blood foamed from his mouth. The ícht'a *(shaman)* stopped, looked over his shoulder for his pursuers and listened. He must have lost them, leaving him time to heal. Bracing himself against the white-green bark of a tall tree, he twisted his arm behind his back and snatched at the arrows. He cursed the men he had called friends--the ones he had taught his knowledge and secrets to, for now they hunted him, using them against him. He laughed at them for they only held a fraction of his power. Only the staff of the ages could destroy him, but he had hidden it well within the chamber in his mountain. And even though they had found the staff, his tsāk-ssēt *(amulet)* still controlled it. He grasped the talisman for a fleeting moment of comfort and quickly pushed the thought from his mind. With his hands, he wove a fire spell in the air, causing the shafts to burst into flame and disintegrate. He then mumbled a healing chant that forced the arrowheads from his body, sealed the wounds and eased the pain. Raven hair and beads of cold sweat streamed into his eyes, stinging and almost blinding him. He looked up through the forest canopy where the summer sun, bright and yellow, burned in the pale, cloud-streaked, blue sky and pierced the branches of the trees with waves of its unrelenting heat. Wiping the sweat away with the sleeve of his buckskins, he felt relief momentarily wash over him. As he breathed deeply, he bent over and choked--his lungs, still tender from their healing, rebelled. Blood frothed from his mouth and left a metallic taste that he tried to spit away.

He patted the ta-chlēta *(knife)* that hung at his side—the one he used in ritual sacrifice. It was one of the many things that the villagers hated him for. They lacked his knowledge of forging metal, his understanding of the universe, and then, of course, there were the brutal deaths of the children—their lives forfeited to maintain his youth. At times he regretted taking the children's lives, thirteen lives every hundred summers before the solstice, but that regret had been softened by the centuries. He needed to drink their youth, to cut open their chest and rip out their beating hearts to drink the hot blood, then eat the throbbing muscle. Yet, . . . the regret still remained. He stood and began running again, his strength slowly returning, but not as fast as he hoped, for with each step the ground pulled at him.

"I found blood," a voice yelled, still too distant to be recognized.

"He can't be far," another voice chimed in.

"Death to Auktelchnīk! Death to Auktelchnīk! Death to Auktelchnīk!" The chant grew louder, spurring the shaman to run faster. Though he knew he could destroy the men who followed him, he was going to pick the time and place, not they. As he broke from the forest, in front of him lay an open field of tall, green, summer grass, waving in the breeze. The grass talked to him and lulled him, drew him, and the grasses told him to him to lie down and rest—to give up the fight. His head snapped up. He heard the muffled howl of a hunting gūtsch *(wolf)* in the distance. With the animal tracking him, it seemed useless to circle the field, for it would only slow him down. This time a pack of wolves howled and he ran again. Fatigue and exhaustion came as a veil, slipping darkness over his mind, but he fought it. He continued slogging through the waist-high grass that pulled at his legs, weighing down each step.

"Death! Death! Death!" Though his hearing had dulled, the excited, vengeful voices of the villagers coalesced and drifted on the wind.

At the end of the meadow, a tsüsk *(moose)* calf meandered from the trees directly in his path. Auktelchnīk stopped. The calf's chest had begun to broaden, foretelling of its great might and potential. Its rounded ears twitched with alertness and a short tail stood on end while wide brown eyes examined him over a muzzle that was wide and exaggerated.

"Where there's a calf, the cow can't be far away," he muttered to himself as he cautiously surveyed the tree line. He knew that getting any closer to the calf was suicide. So, he circled the young tsüsk, while giving it a wide berth. But then, without warning, the mother charged from the trees and covered half the distance between him and the baby, positioning herself between them. She snorted, her nostrils flaring, and stomped threateningly forward. Auktelchnīk froze for the tsüsk was one of the few animals he couldn't control—bear, wolf, and a few others. But his power was growing and soon he would. Slowly, cautiously, he uttered an incantation of invisibility, blinding men from seeing the cow and her calf, sealing it with an intricate web of hand moments. Though he couldn't control the mother, he could reinforce her spirit life with strength and power. He added the final subtleties when he heard shouts behind him. He turned--a group of thirty men raced out into the meadow. He smiled. Now that the trap was set, he moved toward the trees. With each step, the tsüsk snorted. But as the distance between them increased, she bent down and snatched a mouthful of grass, still keeping a wary eye on the departing intruder.

Moments later, Auktelchnīk heard the screams of the people he had once called friends, and smiled. In his mind's eye, he reached out and watched the carnage as the mother, invisible to the villagers, bore down on them like a wall of spring snow that roared down the mountain, ripping and destroying anything and anyone in its path. Arrows and lances flew from all directions, some driving deep into the tsüsk's chest while others missed or impaled the innocent. She staggered, shook her head, and continued her deadly onslaught. Auktelchnīk could only guess that the mother was almost dead, that the missiles had ripped her heart apart, but his spell kept her between life and death. The tsüsk slammed into the lead tracker's chest, throwing the man backward into the air. Auktelchnīk reached out and became one with the victim, feeling the man's lungs collapse. In the tracker's mind's eye, everything seemed disjointed as the invisible attacker trampled and stomped the men. The tracker's eyes became unfocused and the light dimmed while he watched and Auktelchnīk forced the man to see what was happening. With a last snort of rage, the mother collapsed in her final death throes on another man. Auktelchnīk pulled himself away from the dying man, for he knew he could easily be pulled into the whirlpool of darkness and death if he wasn't careful. He roared with laughter and coughed in pain.

Lifting his animal skin water bag, Auktelchnīk drank deeply, then forced himself to stagger forward. The wolves' baying was closer. He had wasted precious time removing the arrows and circling the tsüsk. He looked over his shoulder to discern the closeness of the remaining hunters, but as he turned, he stumbled and fell to his knees next to a precipice. Auktelchnīk pushed back his hair and looked over the edge. The veil of fatigue wanted to draw a curtain of night over him and lay the mantle of sleep on him from which he knew he'd never awaken. In front, lay death and release. It would be so easy if he died now. With his great powers, there was a chance to return one day. The shaman pushed the thoughts from his mind. Why was he thinking like this? His powers were greater than these insignificant insects. To the right and left lay the safety of the deep forest. There he'd confound his trackers with a spell or two.

How long had he lived? His birth name had been lost in the mists of time, but all knew him as Auktelchnīk. He had lived two hundred summers before he came to Alyeska. His tribe had crossed over a strip of land bordered by two large bodies of water. Since the crossing, the years had merged into one another.

Those first years had been harsh in the ice and snow, but game had been plentiful. His people had killed large four-legged, hairy animals with tusks. Those friends had died long ago and he would have died with them except for his secret. Through sacred rituals and sacrifices, he had maintained his youth. The baying of the wolves grew louder, driving fear deeper into his mind. The wolves were animals he couldn't control or destroy except in physical combat. The pungent smell of his drying blood was still thick. His breath came in painful gasps, as he sensed his enemies' closeness.

Auktelchnīk pushed himself to his feet and bolted for the foliage. He heard a shout. "I see him," an overzealous voice yelled.

"Fire the arrows!"

"Set the wolves on him!"

When he spun around, he saw an arrow in mid flight. Using the force of will, his mind reached out and deflected it. More arrows, seeming to come from all directions, flew towards him, but he easily deflected them. Simultaneously, the wolves hit him, their fangs flashing, ripping, rending his flesh and driving him to his knees. Auktelchnīk reached out, grabbed the neck of the lead wolf, snapped the animal's neck and tossed its lifeless body aside. He stood shakily with one wolf's jaws locked on his shoulder, another's fangs set deep in his thigh. Summoning a reservoir of strength, he pulled his hunting knife, lashed out at the animals, drove the blade to their hearts, and shook them off. More arrows came from all directions. He swatted them away as if they were insignificant gnats. A brilliant light hit him, dissipating his power and one arrow broke through. Clawing at it, he sank to his knees. He could feel the shaft in his beating heart. He pulled it from his body and made the sign of a healing spell, but before he could finish, another arrow thudded into his damaged heart. Auktelchnīk felt his life force slipping away as he slumped back to the ground. Slowly he began to rock and chant; a shield of burnished, red light swirled and formed around his body and the arrows disappeared. Auktelchnīk looked around, scanning for the shaman or man who had momentarily broken through his shield. For a moment he thought that he recognized a white-haired man, but like a shadow, he disappeared into the brilliance of the afternoon sun. Was it . . . no it couldn't be.

"We need more arrows," said a voice that Auktelchnīk recognized as the village chief, Klēd-jēlch *(White Raven).*

"What's the use? They're not working," another said. A large man approached, keeping his bow drawn. Klēd-jēlch frowned, creasing the scar that ran from his forehead to his chin. He was tall and heavily bronzed by the summer sun. "It is over."

"What's over?" Auktelchnīk looked at Klēd-jēlch and coughed the last vestiges of the blood that had been clogging his lungs.

"The killing of the children."

Auktelchnīk stood and laughed, flashing a set of perfectly white teeth. "You have no power over me. Nothing you can do will destroy me."

"Keep silent. We have the power of many shamans in our weapons." Klēd-jēlch dropped his bow, pulled an ax from his belt, and hefted it above his head. The sun's radiance reflected off the golden blade in a spectrum of shimmering colors. "This ax not only has been blessed, but has been forged with the merging of purest copper, silver and gold."

"Not even that can kill me. My power is greater than yours or any shaman's." Auktelchnīk stared at the axe with indifference as he felt a warm, burnished glow that still permeated and surround his body.

As the ax struck, Auktelchnīk smiled and he threw an extra mind shield around his neck. The force of the blow staggered him, but the blade glanced off. Several hunters charged, their knives drawn. With a flick of Auktelchnīk's hand, the men were thrown to the ground before they could cover even half the distance that separated them, as if an invisible hand had reached out and swatted them away. Another set tried to come from behind him but met the same fate. "Now you and your men will die."

"Not if I can help it. It's time for you to die."

"Dan-e-wåk." Auktelchnīk spoke the name as a curse as he turned toward the speaker. It was his favorite and most powerful student. Dan-e-wåk was a head taller than Auktelchnīk. His white hair crackled as it flowed in the wind, sparks of energy flying off the tips. In his hand he carried the Staff of the Ages. An orb, pulsating with a swirling rainbow of lights, topped the staff. "How did you . . ." Auktelchnīk found himself at a sudden loss of words.

"I followed you this solstice." Dan-e-wåk leaned the staff toward Auktelchnīk and the orb formed a beam of fiery brilliance and bolts of light that coursed toward Auktelchnīk.

"Traitor. Then death to you also." Auktelchnīk grasped the amulet that lay on his chest and felt its burning power radiate and sear into his flesh. He reached out with the palm of his other hand, deflecting the bolt back to Dan-e-wåk.

Dan-e-wåk moved aside, easily blocking the energy bolt. He then grasped something beneath his shirt Auktelchnīk couldn't see. "Two can do the same dance."

From behind him, Klēd-jēlch attacked and Auktelchnīk felt the sharp pain of the axe, though its blade barely cut his flesh. The bolt had absorbed most of his shield. Still, he laughed at the insignificant attempts of these men.

The chief raised his axe high in the air and Dan-e-wåk pointed the staff at him again. For some reason, his amulet lay lifeless on his chest. Auktelchnīk's puzzlement turned to panic and the blade cut through his neck. There was a momentary, excruciating pain then he found his head flying through the air. He watched as his body, spurting blood in long, red streams, folded to the ground in a series of rapid jerks. He blinked and his head bounced several times across the moss. The chief stood over him with the axe. Auktelchnīk focused a hateful stare at the chief and tried to mouth a curse, but his voice was no longer.

The chief stepped back from the head, apparently bewildered by the movement. "It is done."

"Finally, he's dead," a jubilant villager said with a sigh of relief.

Auktelchnīk, still listening to the mumbling of the villagers, reached out, and sent his consciousness into the mind of the chief. He had one last chance to live and that was to take over the Klēd-jēlch's body.

Within the chief's body, they circled each other on a battlefield of the mind, with knives drawn, lashing out at each other, parrying and reposting.

As he fought for control of the soul, he heard Klēd-jēlch say, "Leave the head for the ravens and seal Auktelchnîk's body in a cave."

"Don't touch the body," Auktelchnīk in Klēd-jēlch's body said, his voice was hollow and distorted.

Looking through the eyes of the chief, he saw the terror in the villager's eyes.

"Seal the body in the cave at the base of the mountains," Klēd-jēlch repeated.

"Leave the body alone." The chief's voice rapidly changed octaves then became the voice of Auktelchnīk.

The men remained motionless.

Dan-e-wåk placed the tip of the crystalline orb to Klēd-jēlch's shoulder and a white, all-encompassing light coursed through the man's body, driving Auktelchnīk out. Auktelchnīk fought with every spell he knew, felt his hold slip, and he found himself back on the ground, looking at the Klēd-jēlch. Auktelchnīk placed his mind and soul in a protective field as Klēd-jēlch picked up his bow and notched an arrow. Dying, Auktelchnīk knew a place of limbo set between the light and darkness, Tūtsch-schiā-nách, the black valley--called him. It was the void of blackness and he could not return unless he was called—and he knew there was no chance of that. He glanced up at Klēd-jēlch to see the shaft released. As it struck his head, Auktelchnīk felt no pain. He watched Klēd-jēlch turn, look one last time, then jogged away. Time passed, how long he couldn't say as he continued to stare unblinkingly as the man receded. Then, suddenly a cascade of colors and images merged into

pinpoints of light that flashed brightly in front of his eyes, letting
his consciousness coalesce with blackness that he now welcomed.

Auktelchnīk drifted in darkness, a void filled with
nothingness, just on the edge of light. At times, he could
remember everything—his life at the village, each year he had
lived. Then he drifted, remembering nothing, knowing nothing.
Time became meaningless. Within Tūtsch-schiā-nách, there were
no reference points. On occasion, he felt periods of extreme cold
and heat that he guessed were the seasons. Then he began to feel
strange—that he was being lifted and drawn to another place. He
couldn't analyze the feeling, but knew that his life force was in
the hands of someone with power. He felt the power flow through
him, caress him and surround him all at the same time. Rifts of
light seemed to appear on the horizon, pulling him closer and into
their bathing warmth. He heard the chant of the sacred words.
The words resonated. A fire burst from deep within. He was a
being called back to life. But from where? Ah, yes, Tūtsch-schiā-
nách. In a swirling haze of smoke and fire, the shaman,
Auktelchnīk, breathed life once more. Coolness streamed over his
naked body and he shivered. He staggered and nearly fell in
confusion at the edge of a precipice that seemed so familiar.
Feeling the presence of someone watching him, he scanned the
surroundings. The chief--the warriors--where were they? No,
someone else--a young man with short, black hair and dark,
brooding eyes sat cross-legged, watched and chanted. The
shaman felt a weakness fall over him. Tendrils of many colored
lights reached out, trying to suffocate him. He began chanting,
but faltered. His voice was raspy and his mouth was caked with
dust. He felt the grasp on his body slipping and fading away. The
young man didn't know the proper words. Though confused, he
knew his power was greater than that of this intruder. He
continued chanting an ancient spell of power and healing. A
burnished red light swirled and formed around his body and he
drank of the young man's power and soul.

"Why have you brought me back?" Auktelchnīk asked as he sat across from the young man.

"To learn of your power," the man said in a language that sounded similar to his tongue with slight differences in pronunciation.

Auktelchnīk reached out and the man recoiled. Smiling, he laid his hand casually on the man's shoulder, then gripped it as he drove his mind and will into the abyss of the other's soul. Within minutes, he'd assimilated the knowledge of the day—a new world that was his for the taking.

ISBN 1553957787-3

9 781553 957874